MAKER

Daughter of Time: Book 3

EREC STEBBINS

TWICE PI PRESS

Only one thing is impossible for God: to find any sense in any copyright law on the planet.
—Mark Twain

Published 2015 by Twice Pi Press

Cover design by Erec Stebbins. Images Copyright © 2015 YorkBerlin for the front cover illustration "3D Rendering Portrait of an alien creature," Pablo Carlos Budassi from Mendoza, Argentina (unmismoobjetivo@gmail.com) "Observable Universe Logarithmic Illustration." Images licensed from Shutterstock.com and Pablo Carlos Budassi.

ISBN: 978-0-692-28089-8

for Ambra and not-Ambra

It was one hell of a trip.

無

It is not only not right, it is not even wrong.

Wolfgang Pauli

Prologue

Time and Space… It is not nature which imposes them upon us, it is we who impose them upon nature because we find them convenient.

Henri Poincaré

I was called Waythrel of Xix.

In a time and space that no longer exist, in a cosmos that has been remade, in two books that have infiltrated and altered your minds, my character was part of a grand and terrible quest. One that failed utterly yet, in that failure, triumphed where it had never sought to succeed.

You knew me as an alien to your humanness, a monstrous form of heightened symmetry to your bilateral arrangement, with sixfold projections of limbs and visual organs and a cognitive cluster buried deep within our core. You followed our discovering of Ambra Dawn and her unique mastery of space and time, her cruel life and rise to power in the Dram Wars, and her eventual fusion with our artificial intelligence. There you witnessed the gestation of the proto-Orb as she defeated the forces of the Anti and Dram aggregating around New Earth.

Reader, the recursive loops of space-time and causality have permeated the structure of your minds—not only the hormone- and blood-soaked organ lodged within your human endoskeleton, but also more deeply, into the mind that is the space-time field created by and creating your sentience, the soul that will live on after your flesh decays, to be lost in the emptiness of space or gathered in the Great Harvest.

Many of you prayed earnestly to save Old Earth, to funnel the latent Writer powers of your species across time, all that Ambra and we might amalgamate them, focus them, and undo a planetary massacre. Many of you instead scoffed, yet continued to read through the exhortations of the second novel as you were even asked to consider the Gathering of Souls.

Even so, here we lost many, for the story became increasingly strange by your standards—the characters' experiences remote from those a human animal might ever encounter. The voice was no longer that of your beloved heroine but instead that of her consort, as he spoke through the growing mind that projected his thought across the void and dictated the inspiration of the book's author.

Thus you have been primed.

Now all that is left is the final and most absurd step in the journey: to destroy all belief and memory and be born anew.

And so I am here to convey the true end, which is instead a beginning, to the impossible story of Ambra Dawn. I am here to reach across space and time, across divergent universes separating and uniting us, with fields and waves of thought to inspire this writer of your age. He will struggle one last time to transmit ideas that I myself do not comprehend, because conveying the experience is beyond me. He will take from my own distorted thoughts only a sad caricature, and his primitive mind will then further blaspheme it through the terribly limited medium of your writing system. Thus ideas deeper than the most profound thoughts of the greatest minds of our galaxy will be painted in primitive languages at ridiculously low resolution with a small brush set of syntax and vocabulary, warped through your current incarnations of culture and prejudice, gutted of their essence and recast as grayed mockeries with all the colors washed away.

This is how you will receive the terrible and beautiful story of our Ambra. Do not expect coherence. You will have none. Do not look for consistency. There will be mostly nonsensical paradox. And yet, those paradoxes and absurdities that you read will be far closer to the truth of this universe than anything in your science or religion. And yet every word a lie.

Know also that this is a story of symmetry and symmetries broken, the chronological invariance of the laws of physics shattered by the arrow of time. The perfect balance of particles and their inverse properties wrecked to produce our fractured cosmos nearly swept clean of one aspect of matter, and thus witness to the genocide of the mental superstructure it would have engendered. This is a story centered within an endless fractalled universe that builds and builds, and also devolves and devolves, from and into entities of smaller and larger structure without reference point, without center, into a bottomless abyss of reductive constituents and launched asymptotically toward an infinitely realized synthesis.

This is a story of symmetry repaired and the utter annihilatory creation that is its offspring. In such a tale, there cannot possibly be only an Ambra Dawn. It is required that there be an anti-Ambra, an antithesis, a force in essence, development, and complexity that mirrors yet is not its symmetry mate.

She is of course the clone who took me on Dram—a fabrication of the Anti who escaped their myopic control and launched herself on a quest neither she nor I understood at the time. It was a journey that, in the end, would bring a primordial pair full circle, like a proton and antiproton hurled about in opposite directions through the magnetic bowels of a synchrotron to collide, transforming the fundamental structure of matter and energy—indeed, of our universe itself.

And so I step back into the memories of an existence that now never was, to the moment in an unmade eon when you lost me in the second book, when I crouched within a bubble of space-time under the wild and furious assault of a thousand clones of the Daughter bent on our destruction. It was to be my last true moment with Ambra Dawn, the human creature I cherished above all others.

Part 1

I speak of gods and other mad taboos
that scar my soul with two-edged, healing wounds.
Who dares cast down these gleaming gains construed
while marching to our frenzied, empty tunes?
The sand that is your soul will never birth
one flower in this unrelenting drought.
Your brushstrokes paint no truth and have no worth.
In vain you look for meaning through your doubt.
I am a fool, untamed, consumed with pride
and often speak too much on that I love,
for I, insane, once cursed our fall and died
while clasping to my heart a blinded dove.
Whatever sight I have of what is true,
it neither lives with me nor dies with you.

—Mazandarani, *Sonnets from the Desert*

Chapter 1

Even at those astounding energies, the asymmetry between matter and antimatter is extremely small. For every billion antiparticles that were created, there were a billion and one particles. To put it another way, you're essentially a rounding error from around 10−35 seconds after the Big Bang. Doesn't make you feel very important, does it? Of course that's just as much a bummer for the anti-people, too.

Dave Goldberg

I held Ambra's hands tightly.

There was little point in my meditation. With barely the strength of an average human Reader, I had nothing to offer Ambra to resist the siege that descended upon us. In the realm of space and time, I felt myself to be a particle of dust in the sandstorm, dwarfed and blown haphazardly by the churning wrath of wind raging around us.

Yet I did offer something of great value to Ambra. I sensed

it in her fear and concern for all of us on this mission who relied so completely on her powers. Already we had witnessed the horrific deaths of the MECHcore soldiers David Kim and Erica Fox. And now each of us in this besieged space-time bubble of Ambra's creation was splattered with the lifeblood of Warrant Officer Aisha Williams—ripped apart by the powers of only a single clone of the multitude now assailing us.

As the sea of orange hair swirled around our transparent vessel, as the hateful assault from the minds of the clones struck blow after blow against our weakening resistance, Ambra reached across and into me, like a child gripping the hand of a parent, and grounded herself in the love that we shared. It was this connection that allowed her to hope, to believe that she would devise some escape from this trap. It was this center of affection for her within me that prevented the storm of antipathy screaming around us from driving her to despair.

And that is why, when the clone came, when it broke through everything around us, even through Ambra's power, ignoring its brethren and their efforts and grabbing my arm, when the strange creature took me by means mysterious and unexpected, Ambra's mind broke. It broke like a ship tearing away from anchor as the frothing sea threw it wildly into the maw of an angry ocean. As the world about me dissolved and I momentarily lost consciousness, I felt for an instant a wild hurt and loss from Ambra, a telepathic cry rippling outward in time and space from that goddess growth in her artificial skull. I heard the cry echo inconsolably through the corridors of time.

But for me, it was truly only an instant. One moment I was

in the bubble that had carried us across the galaxy—that crew of soldiers on a mission to halt the Dram expansion—and suddenly, I was not. Instead, I awoke above the planetary surface of the Dram home world, a reckless acceleration propelling me away from it into the blackness of space.

I was not alone. Flying through the emptiness alongside me was a child. Her hair, what of it remained, was exactly Ambra's rusty orange, the hand that grasped the dark purple of my upper arm a bright white turned dull red in the light of the swollen sun. As during the recent journey with Ambra, this clone and I were contained in some type of warped space-time enclosure that sealed us from the void outside. I could not move my extremities—invisible chords bound them. But my eyestalks were free, and I surveyed the girl and my environment.

Below me, Dram receded quickly, the swirling desert dunes blurring to an orange-red planetary disk. In front of us, I sensed the growing presence of the Orb. The clone was racing directly toward it. Part of me was shocked to realize this; I believed at the time that only Ambra had the power to use the Orbs, so I wondered what this crazed creature could be thinking. But another part of me was also afraid. Somehow I intuited the awful possibility: this clone was going to be able to pass through the entity, to what destination and to what end, I could not begin to guess.

"She's following," said the thing beside me.

The words were calm, almost lilting, and yet cold. It was the first time it had spoken. I still reduced the creature to a genderless object, an "it," unable to see the clone as anything more than a warped product of the enemies who sought to destroy us. But my education was soon to begin.

"She's very upset. I told him that she would be. I wonder if he will be strong enough for what is to come."

Told whom what? What is to come? I thought.

"Yes, I think he will be," the clone continued. "They made him too perfect and didn't see what such love would bring. And so there is no stopping the crystallization."

The creature was speaking in riddles, but I was too caught up in the impossibility of all that was happening to formulate rational responses.

At least I could observe. I examined the clone closely. From my knowledge of humans, I would have placed her age at around eight to ten years old, prepubescent; the developmental program to create the reproductive, adult form of the species was only beginning to activate. But I knew that nothing was to be taken for granted with the clones. From what we had learned on Dram, every aspect of their genesis and development had been altered, artificially enhanced, and accelerated, so that this young child before me could very well be half the age I expected, yet at the same stage of development.

The cybernetic enhancements were particularly extensive in this creature, far more intricate and integrated with the organism than anything I had seen even in the most advanced technology on Dram. Where—and better yet, *when*—it had been made was very much a question. At the least, I knew it had to be in the far future.

All the underlying foundation of Ambra Dawn was there. In addition to the hair and skin, the clone possessed the green irises that produced such striking contrasts in the human visual organs and thus were likely strongly selected for in sexual competition in their evolutionary past. The body form was of an expected variant on the genetic blueprint, very likely similar to the eight-year-old version of the progenitor I had just been torn away from: the bones were long and delicate, the shoulders somewhat broad as compared to the average for the female genotype, the hips still narrow prior to the adolescent widening.

The wires and intubations in the skull were fantastic, a labyrinth of insertions and protrusions that connected different regions of the brain to the machinery of the embedded artificial intelligence. The modifications were so extensive that they left the clone with only a sparse covering of the rich hair that characterized this genetic background. Of course, the center of the structure and design were on the tumor inevitably present in the middle of the enlarged skull, the organ that had made this stock so central to the struggle of our galaxy.

Etched across her forehead and face were a set of geometrical lines like dark circuits underneath the skin. The patterns were too angular to be veins or other vessels. I had never seen anything like it in humans before, not even in the other clones we had encountered. I surmised it was associated with the AI and cybernetic technology her makers had embedded within her.

Sifting through all these observations, I finally summoned the calm to speak. "She will stop you from escaping. Without the help of your clone army, she is more powerful than you."

The creature laughed. It was an unusual sound that differed significantly from the response I had grown accustomed to in humans. I began to suspect that this clone possessed a very different mentality than Ambra herself.

"She's not more powerful. Not in this form. Not without her spirit army!" The clone glanced behind her. "What a cry she made for you, Xix. There was terrible pain."

The words struck me like a blow, the memory of it

replaying in my mind, Ambra's terrible suffering ripping through me once again. I tried to focus.

"Look at the Orb," I said with difficulty, starring at the tumultuous frothing on its surface. "Already it has turned against you."

"Not against me, Xixian. All her powers will not help her now."

The calm certainty in its voice disturbed me, but I still believed that Ambra was shutting the Orb to our travel. The clone did not hesitate, however, or slow our velocity. The colossal surface of the Time Sphere grew before us, an ocean of confusing features bubbling and churning in anger as we approached. Again I looked behind—we would reach the Orb before Ambra could catch us. Whatever the effect of being shut out of the Orb would be, I would discover it within seconds. I steeled myself for a possible end and stared forward with as much courage as I could.

But we were not impeded. In a disorienting blast of vertigo, we entered the thing, and the bottom seemed to fall out of the universe. We tore through multiple dimensions of nested wormholes. My entire experience from my previous travels with Ambra was only a faint warning of the possible depth and complexity of the internal structure of the Orb. As I fought to stay in control of my mind in this terrible vortex of radiance, I surmised that we must have been traveling great distances, likely both in space and in time, distances unlike any I had breached before. But I had no idea in what direction or to which destination the clone was taking me.

I could no longer sense Ambra. Whatever had happened at the Orb, she had not stopped it or been able to follow, and now she and what remained of our mission were locked away from me across some enormous separation. It was, as I have said, the last time I would ever see her, at least in her original form. Wherever I was going and for whatever reason, I was now utterly alone.

Alone but for a familiar yet strange pair of green eyes staring back at me in a tumultuous ocean of darkness and light.

Chapter 2

We seldom stop to think that we are still creatures of the sea, able to leave it only because, from birth to death, we wear the water-filled space suits of our skins.

Arthur C. Clarke

G*reen eyes in the darkness.*
I stared up at a night sky churning with stars in patterns that I could not recognize. A soft breeze trickled over me, the sounds of insects or other alien creatures punctuating the soft whisper of the wind. My eyestalks darted about, appraising the planet surface, the heavens, and the figure of the clone sitting beside me.

The eyestalks gazing upward soon abandoned their efforts. It was desperation from the start to hope that I might be able to determine where we were from the stars, but it was impossible not to try. Nothing was familiar. Wherever and whenever I was, the constellations resembled nothing my mind could map, even considering multiple viewpoints within the galaxy. It was quite possible that I was not even in our galaxy.

Since both of us were alive on this world without environmental suits, I could conclude that the planet was human-Xix compatible. The humidity—something we desert-spawned Xix are always sensitive to—was low, almost an arid climate, but not nearly as dry as Xix or the New Earth desert from which we had begun our disastrous mission. I breathed in deeply through my skin sacs. The oxygen levels were likely a little higher than optimal, but not so high as to represent a significant concern.

Finally, I turned my attention to the human cyborg in front of me. The child sat with its legs pulled up, nearly obscuring the head, the green eyes that haunted me in the Orb traversal peeking over the kneecaps. It wore clothing of a fabric unknown to me with an unusual style combining elements of robes and skirts. The material was homogeneously colored a light beige. The clone's arms were wrapped around its legs, keeping them together as the child rocked slowly back and forth. I detected a faint sound, rhythmic pitch changes and repeating patterns. I think it was humming.

I sat up and stared across at the creature. "Where have you taken me?" I asked. The child continued to rock and hum, seeming to ignore my question. I continued, "I know it is far. I know we are not in the galaxy I have known, either in physical space or in time." Still no response. "You have torn me from your progenitor in the middle of an assault of other clones. But I contributed little to their defense. You have dragged me through the Orb to this world alone with you for nothing."

The humming stopped. "Not alone."

"Not alone?" My eyestalks swiveled around anxiously.

"Not for nothing." The intubated, tattooed head cocked to

one side, the green eyes staring fixedly at me. "I didn't take you to weaken her in the battle. It's not *then* that you have to worry about her, but at the *beginning*."

I sensed the tendrils of the creature's thought dancing around my awareness. "You are probing my mind."

The head darted to a strange angle, forty-five degrees and peering from behind its right knee. "Your thoughts leak everywhere. You Xix are leaky-brains."

The child jumped to her feet, catching me completely by surprise. It stopped to stand above me, long, ragged clumps of red hair dangling haphazardly and nearly obscuring its face.

"If not to harm her, why?" I managed.

The clone sighed and stared up into the pageantry of the stars above, the density of lights very high and unusual to human or Xixian eyes. I noticed that there was a milky-white sphere the size of a marble embedded in her skull just slightly above the forehead. It seemed to glow weakly from the starlight shining through it. "There is so much to understand. He didn't understand either when I told him. But *I* don't really understand. It's a *problem*."

I pulled myself upright, uncomfortable to be prone and beneath this unpredictable creature. "Who is *he?*"

"Her consort. The soldier. The one with the hole in his mind."

I nearly caught my breath. *It knows?*

The clone shook its head. "Worry, worry, worry, worry, you Xix. Stop! I haven't told them about your trick. It's a very clever one. I liked it a lot. But it already happened before I was born, and there is no stopping it. Not like that. *They* wouldn't listen about that at all." The clone gestured in front of us dismissively. "That's why you're here. That's why I had to take you. Because there is no stopping any of it—but we have to find a way. Not to stop. *No stopping. Un*make. *She* told me. *Showed* me. All of them did."

"Look…" I paused, not knowing what to call this thing, but feeling a primal need to address it personally. All my instincts sought to engage with my captor to better understand it. But it was challenging enough simply remaining calm in the presence of this engineered assassin. Trying to converse with it, knowing that at any moment it could kill me or use me against Ambra, made the effort nearly impossible.

"Call me Kloan," it interrupted, "since you can't get that out of your mind."

"Clone?" I repeated, or thought I did.

"No. K-L-O-A-N. Like 'Joan' but copied genetic materials with tubes and wires and all this!" She gestured wildly with her hands toward her head. "I don't really have a name. Not here. It's just numbers."

"Kloan." Her green eyes darted toward me and then away. It was a strange name to suggest, but it was surprisingly comforting to have a personal name for the thing. "Okay, Kloan, what I wanted to say—"

"And I'm not here to kill you. Where would I be then?"

I had no answer to that, hardly understanding the question —certainly not its context. My mind raced through the dialogue, parsing each phrase. "You negate killing me, yet leave open the possibility that you are going to use me against Ambra."

Kloan smiled. "Depends on what you mean by *against*."

"You speak in conclusions without providing me any of the background data!"

She nodded, a satisfied look on her face. "That's *why* you're here. *Data.* The first data to enter the gate." Again she nodded and then turned her back on me, walking down a steep slope. "Let's get started."

"Started with what? Where are you going?"

Kloan continued walking without turning back. Her next words were nearly lost in the insect sounds and the wind that carried them down the landscape. "To where it all began for me. To watch the beginning flow around us and mature and twist through time and space to come back to be us. Then we will be ready for the next step."

The intense starlight cast sharp shadows on the rocks. The figure of the child was gone, swallowed in the darkness and slope of the hill we stood on. Raising my gaze in the direction of her last words, I saw far below a dim glow. Artificial. Originating from the ground, the light partially polluted the brilliance of the stars near the horizon.

Waythrel, come on!

Her voice rang impatiently in my mind. My eyestalks curled up on themselves. What else was there for me to do?

I followed her.

Chapter 3

Know that for the mind there are certain objects of perception which are within the scope of its nature and capacity; on the other hand, there are, amongst things which actually exist, certain objects which the mind can in no way and by no means grasp: the gates of perception are closed against it. Further, there are things of which the mind understands one part, but remains ignorant of the other; and when man is able to comprehend certain things, it does not follow that he must be able to comprehend everything.

Maimonides

I raced to catch up to the child, my steps uncertain, the dusty ground surprisingly slippery under my feet. Descending the steep slope of this elevation, I stumbled and tripped, my four arms only poorly grasping the rocks and alien vegetation, seeming to lack any friction to form a proper grip. After nearly falling several times, I began to suspect that there was something strange going on, that I had been drugged or that there was a phenomenon on this world that interfered with my basic movements.

It's a field around you.

Her thoughts danced again through my mind.

It's skintight, coating your surfaces, insulating you from everything around us.

Listening to her voice and trying to understand what she was saying, I nearly crashed into her as I rounded a large boulder. The ground was strewn with shattered rocks and their remains, products from avalanches tumbling down from the jagged hills behind us.

"Why is there a field? What kind of field?" I asked.

Kloan was staring ahead at the source of the light. A city or military installation of some sort rose from the the dry lands. Organized groups of shadows marched throughout the installation. It seemed like a very busy place.

"I don't know what kind of field. She—*they* make it for your protection."

"Protection from what?"

Kloan pointed toward the city. "Come. It's almost light. That's when it all begins. We'll go see me there, and then you'll see what happens."

She began to walk toward the complex but I reached out quickly and grabbed her shoulder, turning her back to face me. "Wait! This is another clone production facility, isn't it?"

"Yes."

"Where you were made?" She simply nodded. "And one in the far future and someplace very far away. We can't just walk right into that place—you saw what happened the last time!"

"There is no danger," she said.

"Maybe not for you! But *I* can't. You said you didn't want to have me die. They'll kill any Xix who shows up for sure!"

"They won't see us. We both have skin suits. *Dark ones.* Their eyes can't see. Ears can't hear. Not even the Readers will perceive."

"*You* saw through Ambra's bubble! You came inside it, even."

Kloan shook her head. "Hers was simple. Weak. Primitive."

"And yours around us now is none of those things?"

"I told you, they're not *mine*," she said sighing. "Now, come on."

The child pulled me forward, and I relented. If it had wished to kill me, it could have done so before—and easily. I was helpless here, and I desperately needed to learn more to find any hope of escape. If there was any such hope, that is.

A bright light erupted from the darkness in front of us, a flash that blinded my eyes, leaving blurred afterimages. A fireball climbed into the air and darkened, the smoke from the explosion already beginning to snuff out the brilliance. The ground shook, and the rending sound of supersonic compressed air blasted over us, even at this distance.

"Too late," she said, squinting from the dust blown forward. "It's already started. Why did we come to this time point? They'll already be moving on the structure and surrounding me."

"Surrounding you?" I looked around us, seeing no evidence of anything besides the landscape.

"Not here! There!" she shouted impatiently, gesturing with her hand. "The tunnel must be there, but we can't get to it before it closes. But we'll go through it soon!"

"Kloan," I said unsteadily, "you're not making sense. What tunnel? Where is it, and why do we need to go through it?"

"It's the only way to escape! At least without so many

deaths. The masters will bring all the children against us—I couldn't just slaughter them. I didn't want to. She knew that so she helped. But it will happen too soon, and we can't be there when we go through!"

The child seemed to be insane and speaking nonsense. I didn't know what to say to help make sense of this situation. With a growing unease, I began to conclude that my questions weren't going to help clarify anything.

Kloan continued, breathlessly. "We can go around, find the path. *Yes*. Catch up maybe before we leave and then you can see before we leave as well."

As I stood there, stunned, she began to sprint back up the mountainside. I reviewed my status. I had just been plucked from one time and place, torn from all those I loved and removed from the desperate fight for the soul of our galaxy, dropped into this strange place of confusion with a being who spouted nonsense, only to turn from one mad rush to another, none of the reasons for anything explained.

She was nearly out of sight, and I would soon be alone. I had to follow her again. It was absurd, but she was all I had to connect me with the past and my home. This child-thing was both my captor and hope for deliverance. Yet for all I could tell, she was utterly mad.

Again I ran after her.

Chapter 4

One cannot determine what is real. All one can do is find which mathematical models describe the universe we live in. It turns out that a mathematical model involving imaginary time predicts not only effects we have already observed but also effects we have not been able to measure yet nevertheless believe in for other reasons. So what is real and what is imaginary? Is the distinction just in our minds?

Stephen Hawking

With the low friction of whatever *field* had been placed around me, racing up the slope proved to be far harder than descending. Even in the growing light of the breaking dawn on this world, my footing was far from secure. On multiple occasions my usually sturdy six-toed feet failed to find an adequate grip, and I tumbled forward, once smashing my torso against jagged rocks and slicing through my exoskin. Fortunately the endoskin was unbroken, and no fluid vessels were damaged, but it was clear that this field did not protect me from mechanical trauma. I was beginning to wonder if its sole purpose was more hindrance than help.

Her voice echoed in my mind once again.

Stop complaining, Xix! We are late!

The explosions continued for some time below, and I tried to understand why we were running up this mountain in the direction opposite of the chaos if the chaos itself was related to someone we had to meet. "We'll go see me there, and then you'll see what happens," she had said. What had the child meant? Another clone copy below?

The greatest blast yet followed, nearly lost to us as we rounded the mountain face, concealing the city behind it. I had nearly caught the child at last. She stopped and turned around, staring backward.

"It's going to be close," she said, panting. "Look, above is the path and the gate is still shut."

"What gate? Explain to me, Kloan!"

"It's our door. The one we have to take to save everything." Already she was moving forward again.

Fatigued, I slowly climbed the rocky hill behind Kloan. In the distance I was able to glimpse a shining disk glinting in the morning's nearly horizontal rays from the local star.

"That's it," she said, sweat dripping from her face and eyebrows, her white skin reddening with the exertion.

"The gate?" I asked. She only nodded. Whatever it was, it laid at least an hour's walk up a difficult terrain. I did not relish another hike in the strange field that was wrapped around my body.

Indeed, the trek proved especially challenging. The path was a series of terraced rock outcroppings that seemed stacked one on the other. On each flat sheet, the going was simple, but between the outcroppings, there was a sudden elevation requiring a short free climb. Normally this would not have taxed me greatly; the gravity on this world was actually slightly lower than that on Xix and only a little more than Earth. But in this frictionless field, I can only assume that I beat the odds by not having slipped to my death.

Reaching the partial summit of yet another ridge on the path, we pulled ourselves up to our first real view of the gate Kloan was referring to. From this vantage point, it appeared much larger, the circle of reflected light at least two or three times our height in radius. A portion of the disk seemed buried beneath the rock itself, so that the path ahead of us cut through the gate like a chord. This segment of the circle was invisible. From our current position, the surface began to appear less reflective and more like the semitransparent skin of a body of water.

But I had little time or interest in examining the gate more carefully. My eyes fixated on three humanoid figures in front of it. One was clearly human, and from its shape, the color of the hair, and elements in the skull, I knew it to be another one of the clones of Ambra Dawn. Next to it was a much taller body with many more appendages. It required no guesswork to see that it was a Xix. It too stared forward toward a third figure in front of the gate. *A second Xix.* A Xix I could see as it faced us, and which I knew only too well.

It was my lifemate, Synphel. I felt the nerves in my legs fail slightly as the synaptic transmissions in my cortex consumed my signal fluids. Images and emotions darted through my mind of a life lost, a lover lost, and now seemingly found in front of us. I steadied myself on the rock we had scaled, hardly daring to believe what my visual organs were showing me.

"Kloan, why didn't you tell me?" I asked. "How can Synphel be here? Who are the others?"

Kloan looked forward, her eyes squinting in the bright light from the disk. "It's too close to me, this future. There was no other Xix the first time. Something has altered the timeline."

"First time? What are you saying?"

But before I could get an answer, I let out a cry. Right before my eyes, even as I gazed motionless at the forms in front of us, Synphel disappeared. It was instantaneous.

"Well, that's new, too," said Kloan.

"They're going through the gate, aren't they?" I asked. "Where?"

"I don't know," said Kloan. "The timelines are scrambled now. It's only cycling."

"Can we follow them?"

"We go where the gate takes us."

I rushed forward. I had to speak to these creatures, find out why Synphel was there and where my mate had gone. Like a nymph I fixated on this one goal to the exclusion of all other thought.

"Waythrel!" cried Kloan. "It's no use! Look!"

Concluding some conversation, the pair in front of us clasped hands. In desperation I watched them turn toward the disk and walk forward. The bright light reflecting off the disk warped and flowed over their forms like some gelatinous wall, completely enveloping them. Their bodies seemed to be absorbed into a void that floated behind the reflective coating, and with a rending finality, there was a final pucker in the surface, and it snapped closed and flat once more. They were gone.

I slowed my run and came to a stop. Kloan caught up to

me quickly. "We can't follow Synphel," she said. "I don't know where it went. Or how. But the others went through the gate."

"Can we follow them?" I asked.

"Only the gate chooses."

As I rested several meters away from the huge disk, a deep physical and emotional fatigue settled on me. I tried to push it away as I examined the portal more closely. The prismatic lights dancing effervescently across the surface resembled a cross section sliced out of an Orb. For all I knew, this was indeed what it was, something like the projection in the Temple on New Earth where we had begun our mission. I didn't know if this system possessed an Orb. It was true for all systems with life in our galaxy, but whether we were in our galaxy was very much in question.

The surface that had seemed so metallic, like polished silver, revealed itself at close proximity to resemble more a fluid—a viscous, churning honey-like substance. All I could see within were stars—depth upon depth of star fields that appeared to have no end. I felt pulled toward the thing as I gazed. It was beautiful.

"I want to try, Kloan." Pure desperation flowed through me. "If we can find them, we can maybe find a way back— find Synphel as well."

"But we already have found them."

"Please, Kloan! Just tell me how to enter this thing!"

"Yes," she said, "it is expected. But all the ways are bent, Waythrel. Broken ways. Nonlinear topologies. Space-time discontinuities. The dimensionality is unclear."

"What does that mean?" I asked. The only thing that mattered was finding my way back.

"Once we cross the manifold, we are locked. A never-ending narrative, endless recursion. Loops that end as they begin with different parameters."

"You mean that we may never be able to escape this world line?"

"Yes."

"Then we die in it." It was worth the risk.

"No, Waythrel," said Kloan. Her brows were furrowed at me, the emeralds inside her sockets flashing. "There may be no death. Only endless looping, ages without aging, circles in time never marking time. *Trapped*."

"Trapped in what?"

"One of the local hells."

All my eyestalks stared at the mad thing. "How else can we get out of here?" I asked, gesturing to the planet.

"Only the gate," she said. "That is how I left the first time."

"The first time?" A suspicion began to brew in me. "The clone you mentioned—where is she?"

Kloan smiled. "She's right here."

"This is where you left? When you went to kidnap me?"

Kloan nodded. "Yes, I've gone already through the gate, so that I could come back with you." She smiled. "It's an elegant loop, yes?"

"It's madness!" My eyes were darting in several directions at once. I placed my hands to their stalks to steady them. "Can't you summon some wormhole or something? Get us out?"

"Not from here. I don't have that power alone. The Orb brought us, remember?"

"I can't stay here!"

"You are not the only one tested, Waythrel." She sighed. "Each time is different. When we finally understand, we'll see the way." She turned toward the disk. "Now is the next step, the next stage of the journey. Do you want to enter?"

I looked around frantically, my mind barely anchored in this bizarre reality. "So, we can remain here, try to survive by avoiding the Anti below, only to perish eventually in some remote corner of the universe, or we can enter into this portal and risk eternal damnation to a self-referencing and modifying timeline?"

She smiled. "Yes."

I felt that I was being asked to leap into an abyss with no pause for deliberation. Who can imagine infinity, or what might lie on the other side of it? I knew that I could not properly judge the risk because as a finite creature, my understanding of quantity—space or time—was terribly limited. I did not truly understand what horror I might be consigning myself to.

"You are going with me?" I asked.

"That is the whole point."

Remembering the actions of the previous pair, I reached over and grasped her hand.

She laughed. "Seems we will always be dancing together, Xix."

My eyestalks wrapped around each other tightly and the covering sheaths expanded over them, blocking out all light. I was terrified.

Kloan tugged on my hand. "Don't be afraid, Waythrel."

We walked slowly into the gel.

Part 2

I weary of the voices that I hear:
the cries of triumph, long and knowing talk.
No more. No more! Away I turn my ear
and seek once more the silence where I walked.
To know true contemplation as before—
There freed from facts, the finite skin of trees.
This star-filled growing womb is now my door
and home and very substance that is me.
Each force and austere symmetry are mine
in flesh and knowledge without truth unknown.
Yet seeing all more makes me less divine-
I hold small stones beside the sea alone.
Beyond the truth are dreams that make it so.
What shapes the Everwomb? I seek to know.

—Mazandarani, *Sonnets from the Desert*

Chapter 5

On this Earth do I stand,
Unvanquished, unslain, unhurt.
Set me, O Earth, amidst the nourishing strength
That emanates from thy body.
The Earth is my mother,
her child am I!

from the Atharva Veda

I felt cold, yet all other signs pointed to a temperate climate for my species.

I unfurled my eyestalks, trying to remain calm as my visual organs adjusted and brought the environment around me into focus. As a Xix, the nature of my sense of vision is difficult to describe to humankind. The broader wavelength range of photoreceptors that paints reality in hues and shadows unknown to you is the minor difference. It is instead the integration of eighteen eyes and their ability to be oriented in nearly any direction that produce both a panoramic and a multidepth layered view of reality that is quite impossible for you to clearly conceptualize.

As my eyes focused, I quickly recognized the location. There was significant radiance with maximal wavelengths in the green region of the human frequency perception. The light poured down from a single focal point, a star that bathed what seemed like an ocean of green vegetation extending around me in nearly 360 degrees. There was the sound of rushing water close by, and a soft breeze swept over my chilled form. Nearby, a loud, feathered creature squawked in irritation.

"New Earth," I said.

A girl's voice piped up. "Nope. Close, though. The *old* one."

My eyes turned from their distant contemplations of the Great Plains and focused down a hill on the stream running past. At the foot of the hill was Kloan, all her garments tossed to the side and soaked, her thin, athletic form immersed in the water up to her ribcage. She was vigorously scrubbing her skin.

"It's *super* cold, Waythrel," she said through chattering teeth, "but if you want to get all that goo off you from the gate, come down!" Her bright smile in the midst of our strange adventure was unsettling.

I was too stuck on her first words to me. "What do you mean, 'the old one'? Old Earth? Before the Calamity?"

She was dunking her head in and out of the water, breathing furiously, her pale skin flushed. Globs of clear gel dropped from the hair and machinery as she ran her fingers across the irregular surface of her head. "Yes! *Cold!* Old Earth! *Argh!*" The words were garbled half underwater.

"How is that possible? That timeline has been completely overwritten. Multiple histories have occupied that space now. There is no Old Earth in any universe we can access."

Her bony back was half out of the water as she was nearly bent in two, clawing the gel out of her ears. She turned a half-submerged head toward me with a quizzical look. "You really don't understand how screwed up this all is, do you? You're a little stunned. Stood there like a statue for five minutes after the traversal. It'll get easier." She straightened, her oddly disproportionate prepubescent form dripping with water. "Old Earth, other universes, gods. It's all coming, Waythrel! I see them all like shadows on the horizon." Her head plunged back into the stream.

In my time with Ambra, the Xix had helped engineer the travel of group minds through time, the alteration of time, cause and effect, and the formation of space-time distortions the likes of which had never been imagined. But there were still hard-and-fast rules, impossibilities that were intrinsic to what we understood of the universe. If she was right, if we were on Old Earth, then the powers that were staging our journey worked in realms far beyond the science anyone in our galaxy comprehended.

Water splashed as her head popped up, and she raced out of the water, shaking like a small mammal. "I can hear them, Waythrel! All the voices of this world, their languages, accents, thoughts! So young and primitive and naive. They don't even know the Dram control their entire planet, that they're all slaves." She looked me over. "You really need a bath."

With resignation, noticing the clumping aggregates of the gel dangling from my arms, I made my way to the stream.

"Don't worry about how you look," she said, dashing across the muddy shore like a child seeing the daylight for the first time.

Her words seemed pointless until I reached the water. While I would not have been disturbed to see the reflection of my form drenched in the gate gel, that was most decidedly what I did not see.

"Kloan! What is this?"

I stared down into the water, the surface disturbances making the reflection distorted and unfocused. But it was clear enough. No towering Xixian shape with eyestalks and purple spots greeted me but rather a brown-skinned woman dressed in dark, flowing robes, sporting a white coif over her head. The woman looked to be in her early twenties, with deep brown irises, black eyebrows, and, I assumed, thick black hair hidden beneath the head covering. My mind flitted through Earth's history and data.

"Looks like they made us Catholic nuns," came a breathless voice as Kloan nearly crashed into me. I stared at her. She was bent double from lack of oxygen, still completely naked but much drier after her wild run. Her reflection in the stream showed only another nun.

"Who made us nuns? Why?"

"Waythrel, you aren't quite ready for the *who* of the matter yet. Why nuns? I have no idea. Looks like we're from Mexico or something." She strolled over to her clothes and began to dress.

I stared back and forth between our reflections and our bodies. "Our true forms are not shown at all to this world, yet they are to us."

"Yeah, seems," came a muffled voice as she threaded herself into her beige robes. "I think that because this is *precon-*

tact Earth, we're both just a little too much for them." Her head popped out of the top with a grin, sparse orange hair flapping haphazardly around her, wires and tubing glinting in the sunlight. "You wouldn't believe what these little fields around us can do." Her grin was unsettling.

I stood still another moment and then entered the water, realizing that there was little I was going to deduce from this strangeness. As I worked to remove the congealing molasses, Kloan turned more serious and scanned the horizon around us.

"There is a town nearby. I can feel them," she said. "Not very big. I think we're in the Midwest of America, near the time of the Calamity. All these," she said, gesturing to an ocean of manicured fields of corn and other crops, "are the last little farms of the independents. Big Ag left a whole other kind of footprint. No, definitely *not* Big Ag."

My efforts to clean up were becoming a far greater quest than Kloan's. I had waited longer, and the gel had hardened significantly. My greater build and more numerous appendages made things all the more challenging. The strange material seemed to work its way even through cloth and under my translator, coating every surface of my body. Several eyestalks struggled to stay focused on her. "How do you know all this?"

"It's part of our training. I'm supposed to know all about Ambra Dawn. Her world, the environment that shaped her, is a very important component of that, you realize. But now that I'm here in this timeline, it's so easy to access the recent past. We had a lot of things wrong. I'm learning so much!" She nodded slowly. "That's really the whole point, I'm sure."

She seemed both a carefree human child and an impenetrable enigma. Her smile was broad, and she stood on her toes, gazing outward with anticipation. It was becoming increasingly difficult to see her as a monstrous product of an assassin training program.

"Leaky-brains," she whispered. "I'm never what you think I am. *Ever.*"

I paused from my decontamination. While her words seemed innocuous, they sent a chill through my emotional centers. Nothing was ever as it seemed with this clone.

She turned toward me and snickered. "The great Waythrel. The great *gooey* Waythrel of Xix. Hurry up! We need to find out where she is."

All my eyestalks turned to her. "Where who is?"

Kloan sighed and shook her head at me like one would a slow child. "*Ambra,* of course. We're not here for Old Earth corn."

Chapter 6

"The world, marm," said I, anxious to display my acquired knowledge, "is not exactly round, but resembles in shape a flattened orange; and it turns on its axis once in twenty-four hours."

"Well, I don't know anything about its axes," replied she, "but I know it don't turn round, for if it did we'd be all tumbled off; and as to its being round, anyone can see it's a square piece of ground, standing on a rock!"

"Standing on a rock! but upon what does that stand?"

"Why, on another, to be sure!"

"But what supports the last?"

"Lud! child, how stupid you are! There's rocks all the way down!"

David Hume

We set off along the stream in a direction Kloan had chosen. The day was already turning warm by human standards, and Kloan's sparse hair quickly became matted to her instrumentation by sweat that dripped quickly down her head and stained her robes. The bulge of her tumor shone like a boiled egg in the bright sunlight.

Despite what was for me a very welcome heat, the climate and enormous water expenditure from irrigation in the region produced a high local humidity that counterbalanced the warmth, making the journey uncomfortable. I found myself longing for the Sahara, a climate far closer to that of Xix itself. For the hundreds of years I had spent on New Earth, I was fortunate to have avoided the more humid climes on the world for all but the briefest visits. My skin sacs were now clogging with water, and obtaining oxygen was becoming strenuous for my system. I knew I would tire quickly in this place.

Within an hour, which found both of us increasingly fatigued, we reached a small roadway that crossed the stream over a poorly constructed bridge. Kloan stepped onto the road and walked across the decaying structure.

"It's not far now," she said, picking up her pace.

I rested a moment, holding onto a protective railing, its metal rusted and warped from years of neglect. The air around me, pregnant with vapor like some suffocating blanket, had become a wall to my psychology, oppressing and denying me my will to continue. I had to focus on the advancing form of the Ambra clone and force myself forward.

The landscape changed little over the course of the day as we walked: scattered houses and barns, seemingly endless plots of corn, the fields thirstily drinking the water provided by the irrigation systems. In the times of silence between us, the sounds of random birdcalls and wind gusts were punctuated by the whisper of swaying stalks or at times a sharp pop as the fibers expanded from heat or growth.

Eventually, from behind us, I heard the sound of a vehicle

approaching. We both instinctively slowed and looked down the road. A battered pickup kicking up a cloud of dust pulled to a stop to our left. In the bed of the truck, a group of workers sat huddled, staring at their feet.

"Mornin'," came a rough voice from within the cab. A large hat leaned toward the passenger side. A begrimed face, burned and leathered from the sun, peeked only slightly out from under it, an aquiline nose leading the charge. "You ladies need a ride?"

I began to assess the situation. Clearly our external disguises continued to hold. I checked our reflection in the vehicle's windows to confirm, as I found it difficult to place significant confidence in a strange espionage plot that remained unexplained to us. The driver appeared safe and likely would lend us a ride without incident, assuming nothing of our true natures could be gleaned by close proximity. I began to quickly weigh strategies and risk analysis when Kloan simply decided for us.

"Thank you, kind sir," she spoke, every bit the foreign nun she likely appeared to be. "Do you know how far Flache-Schale is from here?"

Flache-Schale? That was Ambra's hometown! How had Kloan known?

Been scanning the past around here, Waythrel, and this nice man's memories.

"It's right up the road, ma'am."

I watched the reflection of Kloan as she put her hand to her chest, grasping a small wooden cross hanging from her neck. "Oh, that is good news, sir. We are lost and very tired."

"Hop on in."

I began to move back to the bed of the truck, but the driver called out.

"No, sister! You don't wanna be sittin' back with any of those. You two come on up front."

I saw Kloan repeat thanks to the man. My eyes were held by several of the men in the back. Migrant workers, I assumed. Latino. Their bodies were broad from the manual labor but subdued, slumped, only a dim light seemingly left in their eyes for the harsh lives they lived.

"Hermana." A rough voice.

I followed the sound to the back of the truck bed. An older man tipped his hat to me. I saw one of the younger men kick one next to him. A soft chorus—"*Hermanas*"—spilled from the group. All eyes remained downcast. Unprepared with the proper cultural protocol, I quickly turned back toward Kloan and followed her into the cab.

"I'm Rick," said the driver as I closed the door, sandwiching Kloan between us. "Headin' into town myself. We'll be there in ten minutes."

The gear shifted clumsily, and the truck lurched forward. I could sense the stumbling of the migrants in the back as the sudden movements threw them backward. My gaze traveled instinctively to the passenger side mirror. I continued to be amazed at my appearance on this world. To the mirror, I was a young Latina nun. To my eyes, the driver had just allowed entry to a completely alien creature and a child Frankenstein without the slightest concern.

"You headin' to the Catholic church on River Road? You're nuns, right?"

Let me talk, Waythrel.

Kloan spoke shyly. "Yes, sir."

"Well, I've got to get these boys over to the Milson farm, so I can drop you as far as downtown. Folks will get you to where you need to be."

After our slow plodding, the cornrows seemed to dash past our sides in harsh geometric patterns. The fields thinned, and the number of houses proliferated quickly. The town was near.

Kloan nodded. "We appreciate the help, sir. It's good of you to welcome strangers so warmly." Her quick assimilation of cultural norms was astounding.

The driver laughed roughly, eyeing the review mirror. "Well, you two will be more welcome than these aliens, anyway."

Chapter 7

For the naive person does not understand that the true majesty and power are in the bringing into being of forces which are active in a thing although they cannot be perceived by the senses. Thus the Sages reveal to the aware that the imaginative faculty is also called an angel; and the mind is called a cherub. How beautiful this will appear to the sophisticated mind, and how disturbing to the primitive.

Maimonides

The truck rattled off, spraying us with fumes and dust. The wonders of vehicle eTech had made slow inroads into the farmlands in this period, despite the nearly complete adoption of electric cars on the coasts. Downtown reflected this allergy to modernization, with the buildings and general maintenance of the dying independent farm communities seeming to freeze the place in the middle of the twenty-first century.

The flurry of shocked expressions and subsequent darting

eyes initially unnerved me, but it was soon clear that this was not due to our true forms but rather those that had been imposed on us. It helped that every few minutes some passerby would smile and speak a welcome.

We had debated briefly about our course of action. I still had no idea why we were here, why we were nuns, and what we were to do about it all. There was no sign of Synphel or the other clone, no indication of previous visitation through the gate, and no reciprocal gate to return us from this impossible place that, for all I could understand about cosmology, should not exist.

Kloan insisted that everything had to do with Ambra and that she particularly needed to find her. With nothing else to present as an alternative course of action, I acquiesced. So, as unsettling as the idea was to bring this clone near the Daughter, even in this strange, impossible timeline, we set out for the Dawn's farmland.

That was when the priest found us.

We had planned to walk the journey, as I wanted minimal contact with the inhabitants. Kloan estimated that it would take an hour to reach the farm, but as we made our way through the town, a bearded figure raced toward us from a side street.

He was in his midfifties, draped in a brown monastic habit, a wooden crucifix flapping wildly as he lumbered across traffic and toward our position. A horn blared as he issued a series of distracted apologies to the driver, all the while keeping his eyes fixated on us.

"Looks like someone has been expecting us," said Kloan, smiling. "This should be interesting."

We stood still and observed the spectacle until the man stumbled to a stop, panting a few feet in front of us. My eyestalks divided between the priest and Kloan. He was bowing before us.

"Please, please," he said, breathlessly. "There is little time. And this is not the place to talk."

"You have been expecting us?" I asked.

He stared up at us and straightened, fear in his eyes. "Yes. Yes, of course. The Lord has revealed his path to me."

I pressed him. "The Lord? You have received divine revelation concerning our visit?"

His eyes darted around toward the ambling pedestrians, returning quickly to us. He licked his lips. "Be merciful; do not test me here."

"What have you seen?" Perhaps he was a latent Reader and had experienced foresight of our travels.

"Dreams," he said, his eyes wide. "Terrible dreams. Please, you must know that there isn't much time."

"Time for what?" I asked.

His right hand went instinctively to his cross, and he grasped the pendant like a talisman. "I am only a humble servant of the Lord. I beg you; I do not understand the visions. God understands," he mumbled, nodding almost ritualistically. "Yes, God understands."

Kloan smiled. "We will go to your church then? Yes?"

He nodded, ushering us across the street in the direction he had come. "Yes! Please, this way. We must retreat to the house of the Lord. Before the evil arrives. We must be under the protection of his wings."

He began to half jog across the street.

I spoke to Kloan. "Before who comes? What evil?"

Kloan didn't answer; she simply shrugged and motioned for me to follow.

We darted through the wide avenues of the decaying

infrastructure like some huddled group of cultists before doomsday. The priest's words began to weigh on me as I considered all the dangerous possibilities. Dram agents aware of our arrival? The planet was thoroughly under their control. Yet their numbers were few, and their ability to monitor the entire planet was therefore limited. How could they know of us so soon? Had forces of the Anti, or something worse, pursued us? Kloan's cryptic words of gods and monsters were not comforting. Certainly the priest had expected us. Perhaps others had as well.

After several blocks and turns, we entered a more tree-lined street. A church was now visible a block ahead on the left, the splayed sunlight from the leaves and branches around it painting a dappled pattern over the stone facade. Children on bicycles darted up and down the road, and the mundane sounds of the local human community mingled with my own anxiety to create a disturbing dichotomy.

The sign in front of the building read "Saint Anne's Catholic Parish." The priest paused before it, seeming to find great relief. He sighed and rested his hand on the sign. He turned toward us and smiled wanly.

"I am sorry for this rush. Please excuse my rudeness. I am Father Geoffrey," he said bowing again before us. "But you likely already know everything about me." He looked at us expectantly.

The priest clearly thought we possessed extensive knowledge far beyond our measly confusions. It seemed a mistake to clarify our own ignorance at this stage, even if there seemed no way to feign omniscience.

I looked to Kloan for guidance, but she seemed distracted. Her posture was rigid, her eyes closed, a strained expression on her face. "Kloan?" I said, reaching out and touching her shoulder.

She spoke as if from a distance. "Father, thank you. Why don't we enter into the church now, and hope that it provides the protection you believe it can." His face fell.

My own feelings likely echoed his own. I turned to face her. "Kloan, what's going on?"

She turned toward me and opened her eyes. The irises seemed to glow green. "Wormhole, Waythrel. Very close. It is opening now, and it is not empty."

Chapter 8

He had forgotten that all life is only a set of pictures in the brain, among which there is no difference betwixt those born of real things and those born of inward dreamings, and no cause to value the one above the other.

H. P. Lovecraft

"Into the church!" said Father Geoffrey, running forward. He clenched his hands into fists and unclenched them, stuttering his steps to avoid tripping over his robes.

We followed the rushing priest at a less manic pace. He led us away from the majestic front portals and around the side of the structure, stopping in front of a small wooden door. He dug into his robes with both hands.

Kloan tried to calm him. "The tunnel is immature, still ripening. Nothing will come through immediately. Maybe we have an hour. And then they'll have to find us."

The priest looked over his shoulder as he fumbled with

keys to the door. "What foul creatures are coming from that pit of hell?"

"Hard to say," said Kloan in full deadpan. I looked at our monstrous forms, undoubtedly demonic to this poor parish priest, and wondered how we were going to deal simultaneously with this charade and whatever was coming through the wormhole. "But it seems things are converging."

"Here!" said the priest, brandishing one of several keys. He quickly unlocked the door and scrambled inside, flipped on a light switch, and dashed to a telephone.

"Good thing we still have the old landlines," he said. "Cellular has been on the fritz all day with static. Interference, if you ask me," he added, firing us a conspiratorial glare.

It was a small kitchenette, hardly large enough for the three of us and the small table and chairs in the middle of the room. Statues of the crucified Christ hung on the walls. A religious calendar was affixed with magnets to a small refrigerator.

"Who are you calling?" I asked.

He looked surprised. "Why, the Dawns, of course," he said, listening as the phone rang on the other end. "I will tell them to bring Ambra as soon as possible." Again the quizzical look as we remained silent. "For the baptism." He began speaking into the receiver.

Baptism. Ambra was an infant in this space and time! She had been headed here all along! We would have missed her had we gone straight to the farmhouse.

"And missed whatever is coming for her," said Kloan.

Father Geoffrey replaced the receiver. "Yes, yes, you know." He eyed us suspiciously. "Of course you know. Why must I doubt? Why do I doubt?" He placed his hands to his head and shook it as if trying to throw off some raging headache. "God's messengers. You are God's messengers. I do believe!"

"God's messengers?" I asked.

"Yes. Angels." He looked at each of us in sequence. "Angels from heaven sent to save the child!"

"You believe we are angels?" I asked.

He appeared burdened by the question. "You are nuns. Simple nuns visiting from the Sisters of Juana Inés de la Cruz. I see this. I see this. I have the papers in my office," he trailed off, starring fixedly at us. "But behind your faces…I have seen in the dreams. Terrible dreams. The terrible faces of the Cherubim." He placed his hands over his mouth. "Why does the Lord test me?"

Kloan walked forward. "Please sit down, Father. Let us talk openly, at last."

The priest's eyes widened, half in fear, half in anticipation. We took seats in the small room, the metal chair legs grating loudly on the floor. Kloan took his hands in hers.

"Father Geoffrey, this is going to be hard to understand, but even for angels, the power of God is overwhelming. Sometimes, for some of the lesser powers, when we are sent by the Divine, it is a difficult journey."

"Difficult?"

Kloan nodded as if to a child. "Yes. Our nature, so miraculous to your own, is still finite, still traumatized by the infinite power of the godhead."

Awe crossed his face, and awe filled my mind at the deftness of Kloan. I had become relegated to the status of a nymph by a creature I first considered but a gifted child. This creature absorbed cultures, mythologies, mannerisms, and even people's darkest fears and feelings of awe. She did so in the span of hours. Then she refracted those back in prismatic conversation that served her own purposes. What *was* Kloan?

"What is it you wish from me?" he asked.

"We have lost much of what we knew before we came, priest. But God has a plan, yes?" He nodded. "Your dreams, the ones tormenting you, they hold the information we need. Please, tell us now the content of your dreams, down to the darkest detail."

A moan escaped the priest. "No, have mercy on me, I cannot! Do not make me speak of them. I see them even in the light of day!" He began to shake.

I interjected, trying to find a voice in this strange quest. "You do not need to speak, Father. You need only give your permission, and open your mind to us. We may read your thoughts as one might read a book."

"This is possible? Forgive me! I cannot but doubt." He shook his head. "All is possible to God. Yes. Yes! My body, my heart, my mind are in God's service. I am your servant." He grasped our hands tightly and closed his eyes, as if he believed the process would inevitably be painful or draining.

Kloan's mind was powerful. Instantly I was plunged into the priest's thoughts as she homed in like a missile on the swirling chaos of his visions. Colored by his own metaphors, myths, and fears, they spun a nightmare of demonic invasion, rips in the fabric of nature, vile creatures from the fiery pits setting foot on the soil of mortals. Two great demons were loosed; they dragged their scaled forms across soil and water, blackening crops, turning rivers to steam, laying waste anything in their path—a path ending before the unmistakable form of the church we now occupied.

On this religious house, a light shone seemingly from all directions and yet could not be followed, emanating from the spaces between space, beyond the reality they entered. Monstrous yet holy shapes stood in the middle of that light, many armed, many eyed, of multiple faces—they stood in the doorway and refused entrance to the hell-beasts. Behind them, inside, resting on a throne, were a mother and child—only the mother was not the Virgin Mary but a farmer's wife with red hair. In her arms was not the Christ child but a baby girl with skin white like porcelain.

The dream then shook terribly from the roar of the beasts outside the church. Space itself seemed to ripple in distortion at the power and hatred they unleashed. The dark forms advanced, frothing clouds rushing in with them, lightning, thunder, fire, and blood raining against the church walls. In front of them, the creatures of light brightened, and a terrible crescendo seemed to rise unseen in the very air itself, the essence of space seemingly pregnant with power and poised to snap like a stretched string.

Suddenly, I found myself back in the kitchenette, holding hands with Kloan and the priest. The dream was gone. The terrible noises and images were replaced with the humming of the refrigerator compressor and the dim lighting of the room. The priest opened his eyes, and Kloan sighed.

"That's all?" I asked instinctively. "What happened?"

The priest shook his head. "It always ends there. I cannot see beyond this terrible moment." He looked expectantly toward us. "This is what you need? Now you can tell me what it means?"

I looked toward Kloan. I was as baffled as the priest and hoped that she knew something I did not.

"It means a great battle is coming today for the life of the child," said Kloan. "For the life of Ambra Dawn. You had guessed correctly, Father. Great powers will arrive soon and seek to unmake a great history of God's plan."

Forces of the Anti, Waythrel, came her thoughts in my mind.

They have long sought this reality to kill her before she became Ambra Dawn.

"And you," he said, indicating the both of us, "you are the servants of the light? As in the dream? You will defend the child?"

Kloan stood up and nodded. "You have seen our true forms in your dreams. We bring great power here." The priest crossed himself. "And we will stand in the doorway and do battle with those who seek the destruction of the child."

Chapter 9

Do not say, "Draw the curtain that I may see the painting." The curtain is the painting.

Nikos Kazantzakis

A loud banging sounded from somewhere within the building. Father Geoffrey jumped, fear in his eyes. He turned to the door connecting the kitchenette to the sanctuary and stood up, pausing, unsure how to proceed.

"It is the child and her mother," said Kloan with a bright flash in her eye. "They are at the front doors."

"God have mercy, they are here already," said the priest. He scampered forward through the door and entered the church proper.

Following close behind, we entered the sanctuary. It was a small church, holding only five rows of pews. The ceiling was high, however, conferring a sense of a more grand space than might be justified by the remainder of the design. The decoration was sparse, consisting of stained-glass windows depicting saints and events from the life of Jesus. Statues occupied prominent locations in the sanctuary, the nave and the narthex of the building. A listing of the beatitudes was etched in marble and hung on the wall beside the main doors.

These we approached. Kloan seemed charged by some unseen potential, and I saw her lean forward and nearly touch the doors with her hand, as if she could reach through the wood and find those on the other side. Unnerved by her behavior, I approached cautiously, watching her and the priest simultaneously. Father Geoffrey released the numerous locks studding the double doors and pulled inward with some effort. The three of us stepped backward slightly as sunlight poured into the dim chamber through the opening crevice of the doorway, revealing a dark silhouette in the sunlight.

Ambra Dawn was carried in, cradled in her mother's arms, sound asleep with an angelic tranquility on her face. The child was still a newborn, perhaps into her second month, a thick growth of red hair covering a significant portion of the cranium, but short, like a human male's typical hairstyle. She was clothed in a white dress, a thin band with a flower tied around her head. I suppressed a deep urge to go to the child, to hold this nymph-form of the human being I loved and had seemingly lost forever.

"Father Geoffrey," said the mother breathlessly, not yet noticing our presence. "I came as fast as possible. I haven't told Graham. He's away to Omaha looking at a new harvester. He would kill me with the scheduled date just a few days away! My entire family is going to kill me!"

The priest placed a shaking hand on her shoulder. "Thank you for trusting me, Cleena, and trusting your own instincts," he said cryptically, and turned to us. "These are the two I told you about."

Cleena gasped. "The nuns from my dream…"

The priest nodded. "You see, my friends, there has been much stirring in the cornfields of Nebraska these last few months." He turned back to Cleena. "Let's get you inside and shut these doors. It is no longer safe outside." He began to push the large portals back together, and they groaned at the action.

"It is no longer safe *inside*," said Kloan. "Especially in front of these doors." The portals slammed shut, and the sound echoed through the church. Father Geoffrey nodded at Kloan's words as she continued, "We must bring the infant to the sanctuary, the altar. After that, there will only be a little time left before they arrive."

Cleena stiffened and whispered, "Who will come? I haven't been able to sleep since the birth! Always a dream of running with Ambra, always the two of you running alongside! Why are you here? What will happen?"

The priest motioned forward. "Let's get her away from the entrance and into the heart of the church, Cleena. We don't have much time."

Without an answer to her question, she nodded and gently carried Ambra forward. And truly, what answer could any of us have given her that would be comprehensible? The vague threat her latent Reader powers sensed told her all she needed to know to bring Ambra to this place at this time. I hoped her trust was not misguided.

Truly, I myself began to feel the anxiety that had been plaguing the priest and Cleena Dawn. Because of the encroaching presence of the Anti forces, the fearful whispers and dreams of these humans, or perhaps the repeated proclamations of danger from Kloan, a fear had taken root within me. The walls of the church seemed to shrink around us as I imagined the forces searching for the child converging on our position. *Evil?* Whatever to call it, there hung in the air itself a dark electricity that wormed its way into my deepest awareness. Whatever would happen would happen soon.

Cleena held the child behind the altar as the priest prayed. Kloan took my hand and led me to stand before the pair, facing outward toward the entrance.

"It's time, Waythrel," she said ominously. "They're here."

The others felt it. The priest paused in his prayers, turning to look over his shoulder as if something unclean had arisen in the darkness. Cleena Dawn held her child more tightly to herself and closed her eyes, repeating the interrupted litany abandoned by the priest.

And then, after a terrible moment of silence, the massive wooden doors at the front of the church exploded inward in a thousand fragments.

Chapter 10

She who knows does not speak;
she who speaks does not know.

一老子 Lǎozǐ

Dust and wood rained down across the small church, and small wooden shards even embedded themselves in the pews nearest the entrance like released arrows. Cleena Dawn screamed, and the baby, startled, began to wail. Ambra would cry for the entire time of this mad encounter until a final, terrible silence.

The dust cleared quickly, and through the doors two forms entered the church—teenaged girls, red haired, pale skinned, and green eyed, with a cyborg's intubated, computerized cranium.

"They sent clones," I said, a chill running through me. I

looked to Kloan, and like a dancer well versed in all the steps of a choreography, she walked down the middle aisle of the church, seemingly unfazed by the carnage.

The two clones paused as she approached, and I felt the undulations of space-time rock me as these three creatures sparred in realms I could only weakly access. There was little overt violence as yet, but I felt the growing tension as the combatants probed each other.

"Give us the child," said the clone on our left. "Give us the child, and you may go. If you resist, we will destroy you." Kloan merely stared at them.

I was unsure which form the invaders saw. No doubt they were presented with the nun, but could they tear through the disguise that concealed our true natures? What would they do if they knew that Kloan was one of them? If they attacked, would Kloan be able to resist them?

"I said give us the child," the clone continued in a whisper, taking a step forward and raising her arm slowly.

"Wait!" said the other, grasping her hand while staring intently at Kloan. "What are you?"

"A Reader who seeks to meddle, and overestimates herself," said her twin.

"No," said the second, more firmly grasping her duplicate's arm. "Don't you see it?" Her brow furrowed. "There is something different. Something *deep* here." The clone's anxiety deepened, and she took a half step backward. "You're the one who made the path, who found Old Earth. Aren't you? We followed you. We had given up finding a passage." The clone swallowed. "What *are* you?"

Still Kloan said nothing. The two clones looked over the rest of us, pausing only briefly on the other humans, yet clearly noting Ambra, and then examining me more closely. The more perceptive clone continued, "And something is hidden in that one, but I sense it is not much of a threat." She turned back to Kloan. "But this one is different."

Seconds seemed to drip by tortuously. "Are you here for Ambra Dawn?" Silence. "Have you come from another time path?" asked the first clone, seeming to catch her copy's hesitancy.

"There would be no conflict in our missions," offered the first as Kloan said nothing. "Why do you shut your mind to us?"

"Together we can break your will," said the other, "and take the child by force. We *will* take the child. We *must*. I sense you know this. Step aside, help us." She offered a hand, and then let it fall. "Or die."

The temperature in the room seemed to drop. I could not determine if that was an objective aspect of some unseen engagement I could not perceive or my own fear. Indeed, I felt the parameters of space and time being drawn taut like a bow, the tension growing to a breaking point, an arrow only seconds from release. The baby cried out as if in pain.

"She will not let us in," said the first, her voice strained, beads of sweat on her brow.

"So be it," said the second.

And then existence detonated around us.

Because space-time became both a weapon and a victim of assault, it is impossible to say how "long" this conflict lasted. Minutes? Judging from the final carnage, that seemed reasonable. Or was it years, hopping in tubes and bubbles of punctured chronology? In the impossible distortions that followed, reason no longer was accessible. There was no way to know, no way to count time. Causality broke down, and meaning was lost in this epic restructuring of our local universe.

I was as useless as I had been in the assault on Dram. While infinity seemed to open and swallow the space in front of me, I tried to turn backward to find Ambra. I might not be able to battle these goddesses, but I could at least find the baby, at least try to protect it from some random piece of debris or accident from the seismic events induced around us.

But before I could act, I was thrown to the ground. Light, sound, and senses unknown rocked my awareness. Barely able to raise my eyestalks, as if the gravity on the world had increased tenfold, I saw that there was extensive damage to the church. The pews were in disarray, most flattened, the damage approaching the sanctuary yet always managing to fall off before that sacred space was harmed. But the humans were not unaffected. The priest was nowhere to be seen. Had I seen him step forward and approach the intruders? I could no longer be sure; I had become so disoriented in this melee. But Cleena Dawn was there, unconscious, flat on the carpeted surface near the altar. I could not see the baby. Ambra was gone.

Slowly—or quickly—eventually, I felt the space-time chaos slacken, and a growing warmth emanated from behind me. I managed to turn my body around and raise my eyestalks slightly, glancing toward the front of the church.

The scene I witnessed will never leave my memory. The roof of the church and the entire front wall were gone, the splintered wood and cement still present, floating, defying gravity, yet scattered as if by a frozen blast. Each piece of the wreckage rotated slowly as if in outer space, positioned yet not immobilized completely. The nearby houses, trees, parked cars—all were untouched.

Suspended in the air in front of Kloan were two bodies. Behind them, elements of the wooden structures destroyed—thousands of shards and smaller chunks—had been rearranged and amalgamated, glued together via some unknown power, and assembled as planks at ninety-degree angles behind the two attacking clones. Their hands were pieced with stained-glass shards from the shattered windows to these planks, their ankles similarly impaled as they hung motionless with heads bowed, circlets of smaller glass shards around their heads, dripping blood.

They were crucified.

Kloan waved her arms, and the constellation of materials dropped to the ground while the progress of time seemed to lurch into gear again. The lifeless bodies defied physics and continued to hang on their crosses above the ground.

"Ironic and satisfying imagery of death, I think," she said, turning away from the fantastical nightmare and walking toward me.

Despite all my growing empathy and care toward this clone, I had never felt more strongly the divergence between her and Ambra. Though Ambra could certainly kill and undertake raw, violent acts in the defense of those who resisted the Dram and Anti, her mind, her heart, her soul—whatever it was that constituted Ambra Dawn—existed in some personality space that shared little with this creature. The creative, almost artistically macabre way in which Kloan had dispatched the clones disturbed me greatly. But there was no time for analysis.

In the midst of my shock, I heard the baby cry again. I turned toward the sound and began to walk toward her.

"Find the priest," said Kloan, taking my arm. "I will tend to the mother and child."

My heart yearned for Ambra, but I was becoming accustomed to following Kloan's lead. I turned around and searched across the wreckage of the church. It was amazing the remainder of the building remained standing. I hoped the priest was not underneath some of the larger piles of rubble.

He was not. I found Father Geoffrey, or what was left of him.

Chapter 11

The two principles of truth, reason and senses, are not only both not genuine, but are engaged in mutual deception.

Blaise Pascal

The space-time tidal forces unleashed in the conflict had caught the poor priest at their most brutal. I found him, parts of him—his upper torso and head still together—prone atop a heap of pew debris. Other remnants of his flesh were scattered about the room haphazardly. His chest had been eviscerated, the muscle and bone mashed and torn like some soft dough. I do not suffer the same horrified reaction as humans to a visceral death of their kind, but the massive trauma to the physiology of this creature still elicited pity. Suffering to a Xix is sin. He had died quickly, at the least.

I heard the baby wailing more loudly, followed by sounds of Kloan moving objects behind me. But I couldn't focus on

Ambra or her mother just now. I couldn't take my eyes away from the priest.

"Why did you leave the sanctuary, old man?" I whispered to the corpse. Respecting human traditions, I closed his eyes, but he hardly seemed at rest.

I thought back to the plans I had made with Ambra, in another space and another time. I had seen evidence that something miraculous, something horrible, something completely *other* had come of it, even if so much of my recent experiences brought into doubt both my perceptions and reasoning. She had once spoken of the Gathering of Souls. I wondered if it had taken root. I wondered if this poor creature's consciousness would somehow, someday find its way to a grand collective. *Would we all?* Or would we thrash madly in the void until our sentient fields had lost all coherence and been absorbed into the fabric of space? One was certainly a kind of hell. The other was something I could only hope would be a heaven.

And so my eyes turned back to the lurid abominations hanging in the air in front of me. But I could hardly see them. Instead, my mind dashed through memories, filling my awareness with the hordes of clones descending on us in the Dram deserts, and in particular, the one clone Ambra had tried to reach, to reason with, to love, despite all the torture and mutilation the creature had suffered. The clone she had *failed* completely to save.

The laden crosses rotated ever so slightly back and forth above me. Kloan had hung them like trophies in the air, yet they were once conscious beings who began their lives in innocence—if there could be any innocence in the biological distortions of the Anti, in the birthing warehouses, or in the hormone and nutrient soups that altered normal gestation and development.

Original sin? Was that not the human theological idea? Tainted without conscious choice, before actively sinning. *Born guilty*, to be condemned. It seemed a horrible doctrine devoid of justice, one any Xix would immediately reject.

I walked forward to the crucified clones and touched a dangling foot. Even at my height, the reach strained my limbs. The sole was warm, my twelve digits sticky with blood still dripping from the clone's wounds, my slight touch causing a rocking back-and-forth of the entire form in the air. *Are these ever to be saved?* Their minds were now cast adrift, minds so distorted that they may never hope to find citizenship in the Group Mind, whatever it had become. Minds born into rejection. Sentience warped so severely that hate and madness seemed its only destiny. Creatures ostensibly born and condemned by some sort of horrific, cosmic original sin.

I could not imagine Ambra casting them adrift to be lost to the void. I knew that as a Xix, this was my weakness, my need for harmony and healing for all creatures. I knew that not all species even in our galaxy shared such a commitment to all life. Humans could be both as loving as the Xix and as monstrous as the Dram, often such conflicting behaviors erupting from the same individual.

Yet I had shared with Ambra. I had loved her for nearly three centuries, communed with her in the Group Mind. Her personality echoed in my awareness even now. I could not believe she would not find a way, if there were a way, to bring all minds into the fold. Such inherent and permanent loss was too horrible a fate to even contemplate.

And as if in answer to my questions, the baby shrieked,

screamed out in pain and despair in a manner even I, as an alien life form, could recognize as distinctly different from the previous cries. As I turned around toward the frightening sound, thoughts raced through my mind. Had her mother perished? Had Ambra been injured in the melee? Or, perhaps, had she sensed even with her infant powers the terrible cry within my soul?

I froze in place facing the sanctuary. My limbs dropped to my side. I felt a strange sensation deep within me as though my very cellular structure was disintegrating, melting, and flowing into the debris and body parts already littering the ground.

The baby lay on the altar, unmoving, crimson patterns splashed across her white dress. A long, gruesome gash was etched deeply into her neck, blood bubbling and frothing from the airway. The red liquid ran languidly over the altar surface, pooling at the edges and then slowly dripping down the sides of the tablecloth.

The mother was still unconscious on the ground, but most of my eyes were fixed on Kloan. There was a wild look on her face as she stared vacantly forward, blood splattered across her robes. In her right hand was a long carving knife, the blade pointed downward, glinting and crimson, small drops of the infant's blood falling to the ground behind the altar.

Behind me there was a wet impact and shudder. Several of my eyestalks swiveled backward and spied the fall of the two crucified clones. Their bodies lay sprawled on the ground along with the priest. Dust and blood sprayed into the air, sprinkling me with what quickly formed into a thin layer of burgundy clay.

It seemed the world would end. My halting words sounded shrill through the translator.

"Kloan—*what have you done?*"

Chapter 12

The laws of physics might permit the existence, in the real Universe, of closed timelike curves (CTCs). The semiclassical laws of physics (the laws with gravity classical and other fields quantized or classical) should be augmented by a principle of self-consistency, which states that a local solution to the equations of physics can occur in the real Universe only if it can be extended to be part of a global solution, one which is well defined throughout the (nonsingular regions of) classical spacetime.

Novikov et al, "Cauchy problem in spacetimes with closed timelike curves", Physical Review D, 42 (6), 1990.

G*reen eyes in the darkness.*
Dizzy, feeling ripped from a dream and dropped into a new reality, I stared up at a night sky churning with stars in patterns that I could not recognize. A soft breeze trickled over me, sounds of insects or

other alien creatures punctuating the soft whisper of the wind. My eyestalks darted about, appraising the planet surface, the heavens, and the figure of the girl sitting beside me.

Kloan sat with her legs pulled up, nearly obscuring her head, those green eyes that haunted me peeking over the kneecaps, arms wrapped around her legs keeping them together. She rocked slowly back and forth. I detected a faint sound with rhythmic pitch changes and repeating patterns. She was humming.

I sat up and stared across at her. "What have you done? *What did you do to Ambra?*" The child continued to rock and hum, seeming to ignore my question. I felt desperate.

"What did you do, Kloan!"

The humming stopped. "Nothing."

"*Nothing?*" My eyestalks swiveled around anxiously. "I *saw* you with a knife! I saw *blood* all over you and the baby. Then— only light. A terribly bright light that overpowered my senses. What happened? Where is the child?"

"In the past. Far away." The intubated, tattooed head cocked to one side, the green eyes continuing to stare fixedly at me.

I sensed the tendrils of her thought dancing around my awareness. "You are probing my mind!"

The head remained at the strange angle, forty-five degrees and peering from behind her right knee. "Your thoughts leak everywhere. You Xix are leaky-brains."

The child leapt up, catching me by surprise. She stopped to stand above me, long, ragged clumps of red hair dangling haphazardly and nearly obscuring her face. "We went as a first experiment, Waythrel. I was skeptical, but the Anti always believed there were unstable nodes in time. This was one of their top targets. But it's not *then* that you have to worry about her, but at the *beginning*."

"An experiment? You cut the throat of an infant as a test? You risked killing Ambra, preventing your own existence, because you doubted it was possible and wanted to see?"

"Yes."

I stared at the child, her innocence horribly deceptive. "You are a monster."

"Yes, I am a monster. Don't you know that by now?" She shook her head sadly. "We have been bred to kill Ambra Dawn from the moment we were cloned." She stared at me intently. "It was easy to do, you understand? It would have been hard *not* to kill her. I would need enormous willpower not to, however strange that seems to you. Years and years of conditioning cannot simply just go away. It will never go away."

"I thought you might be different." My heart felt broken. I *needed* her to be different.

"I *am* different, Waythrel. *Everything* is different with me and you will see. I let my instincts have their way because another part of me needed to test something very important."

The horror of the memory would not leave my mind. "Why did you even battle those clones? They would have killed her for you."

"Yes, probably, but I had to be sure. I couldn't have their interference in the experiment."

"You plotted all along to murder a child."

"Not any child. *That* child. If it helps, I would have little desire to kill a random infant. Poor Xix! I am a very specific monster, Waythrel, precisely aimed. And Ambra is unharmed. I am here, as are you, which requires her survival and existence, her actions, an entire tapestry of world lines, entire universes, remember?"

The words were like a slap to my mind. *Words of a dream.* "Where are we?"

"Don't you know?"

I stood up slowly, gazing around the ragged landscape, and then looked down to a flat plain below, the lights of a city washing out the canopy of stars above.

"We are back where we started. When you took me after Dram."

"*When* did we start, Waythrel?"

I stared at the deep green eyes and realized that my sense of time, of cause and effect, was disoriented. Memories seemed to exist as events in a blurred fog, and I could no longer discern what was real and what was in my mind.

"I am confused. Please explain to me what is happening. You seem to understand."

She nodded, a satisfied look on her face. "That's *why* you're here. *Data.* The next data to enter the gate." Again she nodded and then turned her back on me, walking down a steep slope. "Let's get started."

"Started with what? Where are you going?" I asked, bewildered.

Kloan continued walking without turning back. Her next words were nearly lost in the insect sounds and wind that carried them down the landscape.

"To where it all began for me. To watch the beginning flow around us and mature and twist through time and space to come back to be us. Then we will be ready for the next step."

The starlight cast sharp shadows on the dusty rocks. The figure of the child was gone, swallowed in the darkness and slope of the hill we stood on. Raising my gaze in the direction of her last words, I stood frozen, trying to understand what now seemed the madness of my own thoughts.

Did I know this creature? It seemed I did. It seemed we had journeyed in a dream. Journeyed from Dram. Journeyed to Earth before it was New Earth. But now we were here, as if I had arrived from Dram again. Was I sane? Was the universe sane?

Waythrel, come on!

Her voice rang impatiently in my mind. My eyestalks curled up on themselves. What else was there for me to do?

Chapter 13

The opposite of love is not hate, it's indifference. The opposite of beauty is not ugliness, it's indifference. The opposite of faith is not heresy, it's indifference. And the opposite of life is not death, but indifference between life and death. An immoral society betrays humanity because it betrays the basis for humanity, which is memory. An immoral society deals with memory as some politicians deal with politics. A moral society is committed to memory.

Eli Wiesel

I followed her, racing to catch up to the child, my steps uncertain, the dusty ground surprisingly slippery under my feet. Down the steep slope of the elevation, I stumbled and tripped, my four arms only poorly grasping the rocks and alien vegetation, seeming to lack any friction to form a proper grip.

It's a field around you, remember? Her thoughts danced through my mind. *It's skintight, coating your surfaces, insulating you from every-thing around us.*

Listening to her voice and trying to understand what she was saying, flashes of memory leapt through my thoughts. The strange sensation, her words, walking up the slope to a shining disk in the light—*the gate.*

I nearly crashed into her as I rounded a large boulder. The ground was strewn with shattered rocks and their remains, products from avalanches tumbling down from the jagged hills behind us. "Why is there a field? What kind of field?"

Kloan was staring ahead. A city or military installation of some sort rose from the floor of the dry lands. Organized groups of shadows marched throughout the installation.

"I don't know what kind of field. She—*they* make it for your protection."

"Protection from what?"

Kloan pointed toward the city. "Come. It's almost light, but we're earlier this time. So much slop in the gating," she said, shaking her head. "That's when it all begins. We'll go see me there, and then you'll see what happens."

She began to walk toward the complex but I reached out quickly and grabbed her shoulder, turning her back to face me. "Wait! This is another clone production facility, isn't it?"

"Yes."

"Where you were made?" She simply nodded. Memories flooded haphazardly in my mind. "There is an attack! We can't just walk right into that place—last time there was an attack!"

"There is no danger."

"Maybe not for you! But *I* can't. They'll kill any Xix that shows up for sure."

"They won't see us. We both have skin suits. *Dark ones.*

Their eyes can't see. Ears can't hear. Not even the Readers will perceive."

"*You* saw through Ambra's bubble! You came inside it, even."

Kloan shook her head. "Hers was simple. Weak. Primitive."

"And yours around us now is none of those things?"

"I told you, they're not *mine*," she said, sighing. "Now, come on."

The child pulled me forward and I relented. I felt completely helpless here, my mind to be distrusted, events to be suspected—now, those before, those to come. Would I come to understand any of this madness?

We covered the flat distance between the broken hills and the installation quickly. The uncomplicated landscape made my efforts far less exhausting, and I found myself able to observe the growing city before us rather than concentrate on each step to prevent an accident.

It was unlike any city or technological society I had ever seen. Functional aspects to the materials and machines were often obvious. The laws of physics and chemistry are the same across the universe and, as far as we have been able to ascertain, through time as well. But the mentality behind the creation of artifacts to work within the physical laws and manipulate matter and the environment was more alien than any I had ever encountered. Even in our galaxy of diverse life forms, there was not this terrible difference that seemed to border on hostility to the mind. I cannot describe it any more clearly. From architecture to transport surface topology to the use of color and lighting, it was clear that the minds shaping this world were more distant than anything I had known in all my travels.

And yet the place was populated with *humans*. I saw no other aliens, no divergent life forms. And only two classes of humans at that, easily demarcated: those who looked like Ambra Dawn, and those who did not.

"The Anti run things remotely with robots and trained humans," Kloan added, no doubt sampling my *leaky* thoughts.

"To avoid annihilation?" I assumed it would be difficult to be in the presence of so much matter to their antimatter. The energies required to keep the two forms from destroying the entire planet would be enormous.

"No, they are not concerned about that here," she said cryptically, not bothering to explain. "It's just more efficient. Once the optimal program was developed, it could be run by drones and lackeys."

We approached the entrance to the complex. Robotic guards patrolled the gate, hovering above the ground with strange weapons protruding from multiple regions of their forms. They did not notice anything unusual. Apparently, nothing in their technology allowed them to pierce whatever cloaking mechanism was concealing us. Inside were numerous robots of odd shapes and designs, performing functions within the installation. I soon noticed a pattern.

"The humans aren't involved in anything. Everything is done by the machines," I said. I whispered at first, but as time wore on and it became clear that even our sounds were concealed, I talked more freely.

Kloan spoke normally, unconcerned about discovery. "Humans are the social construct for the clones. See, we need people to develop properly, or close enough to properly, or the mind is just too wrecked to become useful. To develop, human neurophysiology needs social fabrics, structures, language, norms. So the Anti imported them. It's a clone growth matrix, I guess."

"Like on Dram," I said, remembering the groups of clones and other humans involved with them.

"Yes, that was the beginning, before it was destroyed."

I was momentarily stunned. "Dram is gone?"

"Terrible civil war. Blew themselves up. But it didn't matter. They were only an outpost."

"And this is another one?"

"One of the last. The devil ball hunts them through space and time. They had to build them farther and farther away, find stronger and stronger clones to shield them from attack."

"Devil ball?"

Kloan looked at me and laughed. "Your little Orbies. We had other names for them. Other thoughts about them. Come, you'll see. You'll *learn*."

We walked through the strange streets of this alien and yet human city. Groups of young Ambra Dawn clones paraded past us at various points, shepherded by older clones and assisted by bands of more diverse humans. As we walked, Kloan would point out buildings or objects of significance.

"Inside these warehouses are the wombs. All clones are born there. They learned early on that the gestational process was a key element in brain development. Purely *in vitro* methods failed terribly." She smiled at me. "It's nice that we're born and not grown, isn't it?"

I didn't know if the strange child was serious or sarcastic. We Xix have mostly mastered the understanding and translation of human conflict avoidance mechanisms such as sarcasm, but there was often uncertainty. With this clone, there was always uncertainty.

"What we saw on Dram seemed much more horrible than nice, Kloan."

"You are a terrible student," she said in a strange tone I had not previously heard from her. "But we can't have lessons now. We have to hurry!"

"Hurry where?"

The child stood still, staring off into the distance. "Home."

Chapter 14

When I see the blindness and the wretchedness of man, when I regard the whole silent universe, and man without light, left to himself, and, as it were, lost in this corner of the universe, without knowing who has put him there, what he has come to do, what will become of him at death, and incapable of all knowledge, I become terrified.

Blaise Pascal

"Home?"

She grabbed my hand and pulled me forward, reaching a near sprint. We darted across the compound. I had little time to process much until I found myself standing in front of a strange building unlike any of the others I had seen here. It was small, a deep black—obsidian— seeming to reflect little light. I sensed strong electromagnetic fields pulsating around the structure.

"Home," she said again. "Or quarantine. Take your pick.

With me inside their little box, the compound thought itself safe."

"Safe from you? You mean all this shielding?"

"It's designed to keep me and my powers inside, yes," she said. "It was never really useful except in the beginning, when I was very little. But I never let them know all that. Until the end. Come, I'll get us through the fields."

Kloan pulled me forward again. For an instant, my vision blurred as if I had accelerated dramatically. My space-time senses were reeling; I could not control my eyestalks, and they swiveled around, unable to focus, unable to lock, and a kaleidoscope of flashing images assaulted my consciousness.

"Waythrel, hold onto me."

Kloan grabbed my arm and steadied me. Slowly the dizziness passed. My vision came under my conscious control.

A single room greeted us, Spartan, with basic elements such as a bed, table, latrine, and sink. There were no products for leisure, no children's toys, no books or electronic information sources. Bright light streamed in from a partially transparent region of the quarantine field as the system's star rose for the beginning of a new day. Sounds of explosions and shouts could be heard faintly outside. The room was in disarray; clothes were strewn about, food and utensils as well. My olfactory strips detected a growing acrid smell. *Smoke?*

A child clone of nearly identical appearance to Kloan stood in the middle of the room. Sweat beaded across her forehead. All of her muscles were tense.

She stood before a vortex of milky light that swirled chaotically. My eyes stopped scanning, the stalks still, all my attention centered on the impossible thing I was seeing floating above the ground in front of the child. There were hundreds, perhaps thousands of faces and forms of myriad species of life bobbing in and out of sight in a violent sea of white fog. Many I could identify. Most I could not.

But one I could absolutely identify. The milky vapors had coalesced around a central extrusion. Its shape was that of a human face. The head was split open, the brain exposed behind it and fading into the mist. Tubes and wires, dwarfing the insertions into Kloan, entered and exited the skull. Even the eyes were partially obscured by machinery that seemed to pulse with a life of its own. Only the mouth was free.

"Ambra," I whispered in horror. Despite all the Xixian technology covering and distorting her features, I recognized her. How could I not? How could I forget that beloved alien face that I had followed and nurtured, taught and been taught by for nearly three centuries?

For the first time I came face to face with the price she had paid in our desperate plan to save the galaxy from the Anti and Dram. I looked between the apparition and the two bodies of Kloan in the room. The weight of the truth nearly crushed me. My lover Synphel had warned us. The others and I had only half listened. But now it was clear to me. Now I began to suspect that we had triumphed only by *becoming* the enemy.

Theoretically, I knew what must be happening, but it still stunned me. Ambra had foreseen it. The Readers opposing the Dram had planned it. Together, we had put in motion a terrible, incredible sequence of events to create a group mind unlike any we had ever experienced telepathically— one that was not a transitory product of concerted medita- tion but would be self-sustaining, growing as a living thing, escaping the parameters of our understanding and control yet composed of each of our individual selves. In the end, it was a collective that I would never join because of the creature standing beside me who had torn me from that previous life.

Our greatest minds had worked out the details as best they could, centering it on the powerful consciousness of Ambra Dawn, but with a cosmic goal far, far beyond this. *The Gathering of Souls*. A harvest of minds across space and time.

That harvest would give birth to a consciousness, a being of its own that we could hardly model, imagine, or anticipate. Our theories broke down in this extreme context, infinities plaguing the most sophisticated mathematics and artificial intelligence simulations. Because our understanding faltered so deeply, we knew that it could fail spectacularly and yield nothing. Or it might even produce something terrible. Seeing our approaching destruction at the hands of our enemies, we had gambled to create a god whose nature we could not predict or control.

Whatever it had turned out to be in those swirling faces before me, I knew it was not Ambra Dawn. Even with her likeness in the face of this thing, it was not her. It was something that had her at its heart and yet had grown exponentially beyond the seed of its formation. In the power of this consciousness to sweep across time and space and reach this world, I knew that in the deep past, they had succeeded in giving birth to this entity. What I did not yet suspect, and would see only as this journey wore on, was that we had produced both a heaven and a hell.

"The gate is prepared," came the voice of Ambra.

"I'm ready," said the Kloan of this early time.

"You must leave now," came Ambra's voice. "They will return with greater numbers of clones and more powerful weapons. You will be forced to destroy them all if you engage."

"I don't want to kill them. Lead me to the gate."

The stamping of rushing feet came from outside the small building. A heavy rumbling accompanied them, the sound likely associated with a large vehicle of some sort.

"Through the door." Ambra gestured to the only door of the isolation building, and for a moment I wondered why she wished for Kloan to fight the Anti gathered outside when the child had so clearly expressed a desire not to. But the black field that sealed the chamber gave way to a second churning vortex. It opened to span the width of the door. Through it poured bright daylight, revealing not the artificial surface outside her isolation unit but the rocky terrain and vegetation that we had traversed only recently to arrive here.

The countryside within the vortex seemed to extend as far as my eyes could see, but the tunnel itself narrowed as I looked farther. Far at the end of the tunnel, where my eyestalks strained and my vision began to fade, there seemed to begin a worn path on a steep slope. The vegetation was eroded, the rocks smoother, the coloration subtly different. The path rose up the hillside and then abruptly ended at the feet of a large disk. The light of the local star reflected brightly off it, firing blinding reflections into the room that cast shadows on the floor.

Kloan pulled my arm, showing me that her temporal copy had moved to enter the vortex. "The gate," she said.

I stumbled forward, partially blinded by the daggers of light glinting into the room. Outside there was shouting, and the walls of the room began to smolder and glow a bright orange.

"Good luck, my dearest friend," said the apparition of Ambra Dawn as I stepped within the vortex. Several of my eyestalks bent backward to see the disembodied head turned toward me, sending ripples across the sea of blurred, white faces. I saw tears dripping down from her eyes, coating the wires and tubes inserted into her once-green irises, a bittersweet smile on her face. "I love you, Waythrel. Remember that, whatever happens."

The room exploded.

Chapter 15

*If all the parts of the universe are interchained in a certain measure,
any one phenomenon will not be the effect of a single cause, but the
resultant of causes infinitely numerous.*

Henri Poincaré

F ire and debris flew across my vision, obscuring the
swirling god-thing in the room. Just as I thought I
would be pulverized, the portal shut.

Suddenly we were far from the compound, a mile high in
the growing hills and mountains, cut off completely from the
melee down below. Replacing the terrible rending of the
explosion was a stunning silence. Pebbles rattled and shrubs
groaned in unexpected wind gusts, only to be stilled and muted
until the next dance of air. A faint whiff of smoke that had
entered the portal was all that remained of the carnage below.

Shattered by her last words and stunned by the violence we
had narrowly escaped, I turned slowly away from the vanished

doorway and looked up the slope. The blinding gate was there. Kloan looked down from several feet above me and motioned for me to follow. No one else was visible.

"Where is the clone?" It seemed only two of us remained.

Kloan smiled. "She's right here."

For a moment I paused, confused, my mind still reeling from events. Then I understood.

"This is where you left. When you went to kidnap me."

Kloan nodded. "Yes, I'm gone already through the gate, so that I could come back with you." She smiled. "It's an elegant loop, yes?"

"It's madness!" The images I had just witnessed flooded my mind. "And Ambra is part of it all?"

"She is the heart of it all."

"It can't be! I don't understand!"

"You are not the only one tested, Waythrel." She sighed. "Each time is different. When we finally understand, we'll see the way." She turned toward the disk. "Now is the next step, the next stage of the journey. And yes, a journey sustained by Ambra Dawn. Are you ready to continue it?"

Am I ready? I felt like I had been placed within the memory of a dream, that I had been exactly here before. *To make a choice.* "We've been here before, just like this."

"Not *just* like, but we have been and will be. But never *just* like. Remember the nonnormalizable loop?"

"I'm not sure. But I'm getting a sense of it." My eyestalks rotated to focus entirely on Kloan. "There was more. There was a hope. To go *back*. To find Synphel." I ached to think of my mate again.

"Yes. There was."

"So, we can remain here, try to survive by avoiding the Anti below, only to perish eventually in some remote corner of the universe, or we can enter into this portal and risk eternal damnation to a self-referencing and modifying timeline?" My mind considered the words. "Or have we already done that?"

"Yes and yes."

"You are coming with me?" I asked.

"That is the whole point."

I turned my attention to the gate, a deep uneasiness settling on me. The disk resembled nothing so much as a cross section sliced out of an Orb. The surface looked like a fluid, a viscous, churning, honey-like substance. All I could see within were stars—depth upon depth of star fields that appeared to have no end, bobbing in and out of an iridescent sea. I felt pulled toward the thing as I gazed. It was beautiful. I reached over and grasped the child's hand.

Kloan laughed. "Seems we will always be dancing together, Xix."

My eyestalks wrapped around each other tightly, and the covering sheath expanded over them, blocking out all light. Kloan tugged on my hand.

We walked into the gel.

Part 3

My labor lingers long; the pay is poor.
From toil to sleep to toil the chanting brays.
A weariness invades to kiss my core.
A willing lover he has found and stays.
Except those eves inflamed by Holy Songs,
when Shaman Ones chant secrets in the night,
and cease to sing at brilliant birth of dawn—
in mysteries my weary mind delights.
Although at times their truths are hard to see,
and seem estranged from that my heart enfolds,
no doubt my profound ignorance blinds me,
I close my eyes and think as I am told.
Our Shaman Ones doubt not they spin the truth.
As for myself, I do not ask for proof.

—Mazandarani, *Sonnets from the Desert*

Chapter 16

We came all this way to explore the Moon, and the most important thing is that we discovered the Earth.

William Anders

W hen my mind cleared, I found myself in a recurrent dream. Cornfields. A blue sky and humid summer. A rare hill in the Great Plains that sloped downward into a quickly moving stream. Kloan at the bottom, naked in the water, laughing, pulling great handfuls of slime off her body.

"Waythrel!" she shouted, smiling up at me. "Don't wait so long this time!"

I shivered from the memories of that trip of doom and death, of attack and murder, and stared dumbly down at the assassin herself frolicking in the cold waters. Nothing was ever as it seemed.

"Not here to kill Ambra this time, Waythrel! It doesn't

work, remember? Come down before you solidify into some sort of permanent work of art!"

How do you continue to do the rational, the practical, even something so basic and mundane as self-hygiene, when madness lurks at every turn? What was the point of a bath when monsters might be crucified in a few hours' time or a baby's throat slit? Or swirling clouds of souls materialize on worlds to which you have been kidnapped, only to embed you in an endless time loop of psychosis?

I walked down the hill. I ignored Kloan racing around and squealing, holding her robes in one hand like some wrecked kite she was trying to send aloft. I washed. I removed the globs of gate gel. Finally, summoning my courage, I looked at my reflection in the water.

And I saw a child.

A blue-eyed girl, six or seven years old, with blond hair tied into two braids, stared back up at me with a puzzled expression. I looked away, the blur of Kloan rolling down the hill and laughing distracting me. I looked back. The little girl was still there.

"Kloan?"

She came to rest near me, grass stains coating her beige robes, sweat glistening over her flushed face. "More body image problems, Waythrel?" Her smile was hard to read.

"And what are you this time?"

"Same—little black-haired girl. I get a bow in my hair."

I wanted to scream. "I find these facades deeply troubling. What happened before…" I couldn't even finish.

"Before what, Waythrel?" She shook her head in a strange manner. "When you find that absolute reference frame for *when*, please let me know, because all I can be sure of is *now*."

She looked into the water. "*Awww.* Piggytails, they call them. You make a cute girl for a squid, Xix!"

"Why are we here, Kloan? It's the same place!" Of all the possibilities for this journey, many in my mind bringing me closer to Synphel, returning to Old Earth again in just such a fashion had not occurred to me.

"But time moves on, doesn't it?" she said, stepping away from the water. "We'll avoid the priests and baptisms. We'll skip on the Ambra clones in this tangent. Don't think we'll see anything like that this time—except for me, of course! Ha, ha!"

I stepped away from the stream, glad to be out of a substance my species was both dependent on and also deeply uncomfortable with as desert dwellers. I longed for our sonic showers. Kloan had begun to walk along the stream in a direction that seemed very familiar.

"Why *are* we here, Kloan?" I pleaded after her.

She called over her shoulder, "To make a new friend!"

It was not difficult to guess who this friend might be. Everything in my experience was intimately connected with Ambra Dawn, and I knew with near certainty that Kloan was headed for her farm. To what purpose in this Old Earth reality, I could not begin to guess. But the images in my mind of destruction and murder hardly reassured me. In fact, they nearly paralyzed me.

Kloan stopped, and her shoulders slumped. Slowly she turned around and walked back toward me, her head bowed as if by fatigue. She came to a stop inches from my feet and crossed her arms over her chest.

"Can't you just keep your mind to yourself?" she asked, sighing. "Waythrel, look. This isn't easy. Not for you and not for me. It's like a rough reentry through atmo with nausea and even some broken bones. And we're likely going to do it for five and a quarter eternities. But you need to see the bigger picture."

"Which is?"

"Well, that's hard to explain," she said, her smile returning. "But you have to *see* it, even if you can't *understand* or *explain* it. You're with a monster clone assassin thing that kidnapped you. One that reads your mind and the minds of everyone around her, as well as reading times past and future. Every now and then, she murders little babies. I can see that causing disquiet." She took my hand and pulled me slowly to the top of the hill.

"Kloan, where are we going?"

"Look, just look," she said, gesturing across the seemingly endless expanse of fields around us. "Over there," she pointed near the stream, "is a pile of cosmic gel that I fished out of my girl parts. *Disgusting*. But how does that figure here? It's all averaged out in tens of thousands of square miles where all the noise disappears. Instead, the big picture—it's a giant food carpet unsustainably managed for a planet that has an energy resource problem."

"Kloan, what—"

"Shhh!" She put her index finger against my translator. "*Our* big picture—Waythrel, it's more than *big*. It's the universe. It's *more* than the universe. It's universes after universes, a small and infinite set spun from our own with uncountably more gestating independently. Universes we can't reach. Universes where the laws of physics are different. Where mathematics is different. Where logic is *other*." She jumped up and down, staring at me. "Two plus two is *not* four in the big picture! Do you understand?"

"I don't, Kloan. I'm sorry."

"Yeah, well, I don't either. But I can *see* it! A billion

tangents, a trillion loops we'll take. One after another after yet the other where nearly everything that can happen will happen. It's not about *what happens*, Waythrel. Nothing ever happens here after it does! It's what we take, what we *learn*, what we become!"

"The journey is the reason, not the destination? I've heard this proverb many times."

"No! Of course the destination matters! How stupid is that?" She shook her head. "You're not listening! It's not *what* we do in the journey, because we will do everything! It's *what* we become *from* it! How it adds up! The final path."

"Besides to insanity, you mean? Because I fear I have foolishly entered into a bottomless labyrinth that will break my mind."

"Yes, maybe," she said, staring at me with the utmost sincerity. "But all the angels are mad, Waythrel—don't you know that?"

And she was off again, releasing my hands and striding back down to the stream. Heading north, toward Ambra Dawn.

Chapter 17

How is it that hardly any major religion has looked at science and concluded, "This is better than we thought! The Universe is much bigger than our prophets said, grander, more subtle, more elegant?" Instead they say, "No, no, no! My god is a little god, and I want him to stay that way."

Carl Sagan

A nd we found Ambra Dawn.

She was out in the long, grassy front yard so meticulously maintained by her father. We had rounded a curve of monotonous cornrow after cornrow, and then, suddenly, there was a grassy lawn with a stereotypical white fence. The green was a deep shade, the strain of grass heavy with chlorophyll, the cells swelled and filled with regular watering. Decorative shade trees were placed strategically across the lawn, and a row of pines served as a natural wind guard on the western end of the plot.

In the middle of the sea of green was a tiny ball of red. Her hair was in complete disarray—long, tangled from rough play, the victim of an unconcerned child who had yet to focus much attention on her appearance. Unsurprisingly, she appeared of an age similar to our own disguises, perhaps seven years old, with a wrinkled, stained dress draped over a pair of blue jeans.

I felt such affection course through me. After being torn from her after so many years together of struggle and hardship, triumph and loss, and then to fall into this churning derangement captained by a godlike, transformed echo of Ambra and her unpredictable clone, seeing the child, lost in innocence and unaware of the future that awaited her beyond the clouds floating above her play—it was overwhelming. Alongside this warmth, an irrational current of ice flooded across my awareness, and I turned sharply toward Kloan, fearing the worst.

"Relax, Xix," she said, skipping forward down the road. "Been there, done that. I need to learn so much here and then destroy something else."

I could not fathom why she would think that response would help me relax. I raced behind only to catch Kloan as she stopped in front of the picket fence. She placed both hands on the pointed tops of the boards.

"Hi!" she yelled across the grass with an enormous grin.

Ambra looked up from the ground in our direction. Her hands were in the grass.

"Hi," she said. Her expression was neutral.

Silence enveloped us as the clone and her progenitor stared at each other across the green field. I assumed we looked like three young children socializing across a pastoral scene, but I could not help but imagine our true forms and how disturbing our presence would appear to anyone watching who could penetrate our disguises.

The silence continued for what seemed an eternity, neither of the two speaking or moving, yet neither appearing uncomfortable or unsure. Then, slowly, Ambra stood up, her hands cupped together like clamshells, and she threw her windswept hair behind her with a toss of her head. She puffed several recalcitrant strands out of her face with a quick breath.

"Want to see a bug?" she asked.

"Yes!" said Kloan, and before I could react, she maniacally scaled the fence, dexterously avoiding tearing her robes on the top points, and landed roughly on her feet. She raced toward Ambra.

I was aware of how little I had thought through the strange disguise our mysterious handlers had foisted on us. Visually, I appeared every bit the small human child. But my real form was something else. Towering over seven feet, I weighed several times that of the average human adult form, possessing far more appendages of much greater sensitivity than those of humans. As I contemplated climbing the fence, it became important to know whether this disguise could simulate structure and mass as well as visuals. In fact, I could not think of any way that could happen. Of course, I did not understand most of the technology that we had experienced from these powerful puppet masters directing our adventures. It was possible such a complete simulation of form might be within their abilities. As I appeared, I might truly be in all physical attributes on Old Earth—a small, seven-year-old child.

I dared not risk it. I took the long way around the fence to the open front gate and then crossed the field toward the pair, who were now huddled together, examining something between them.

"Hurry, Waythrel," yelled Kloan. "Before it flies off!"

I lumbered over to them, exhausted from the long walk, the humidity, and the stress of the constant unknowns. I sat on the ground beside them. We looked at a bug.

"It's a watermelon beetle," said Ambra proudly. "We don't get too many here. And this one is really, really late. Summer's nearly over."

The insect was over an inch long; it was thick and heavy. Ambra had placed the bug on her dress, keeping one finger pressed on its back, and allowed it to climb awkwardly up her chest. "See, look, it has all these stripes. Dad says they can eat up the roots of trees and the corn, so I'll have to show him."

She grabbed the insect between her index finger and thumb. The small creature hissed.

"Wow, what's that?" asked Kloan.

Ambra smiled broadly. "It's really neat, right? They hiss at you, like a cat! I guess it's mad." She held the beetle up to her face and stared at it. The bug was beating its wings vigorously as it hissed. Ambra held it tightly. "Found it by the oak tree. Maybe it's already laid eggs." Her expression seemed serious as she stared at the bug. I wondered if she were concerned for her family's plants.

Her eyes flashed toward Kloan. "You're not from here, are you?"

Well, that's a loaded question, huh, Waythrel?

"No, we're visiting," said Kloan.

Ambra stared back and forth between us. Her eyes stopped on me for some time. "You're really different, Waythrel."

Kloan's thoughts spoke again. *Her Reader powers have begun to awaken. She senses us.*

I wasn't sure what to say. I hoped Ambra could not discern much about our true forms. I mustered my best. "I'm a good friend."

She nodded and turned to Kloan. "Who are you?"

"My name is Kloan."

"Like Joan. But different."

"Yes."

She turned to her bug again, tapping its wings, chanting in a singsong voice, "Like up but down. Like yes but no. Kloan and Joan are all alone."

"All alone and heaven's sewn," said Kloan, and their eyes met.

"Where are your parents?" Ambra asked suspiciously.

"Where do you think, Ambra?" asked Kloan.

The watermelon beetle hissed again.

"I don't think you have parents. I think you're fairies." She didn't look at us.

"Maybe we are."

Ambra turned toward us excitedly, her eyes wide. "Do you want to stay over tonight?" Her eyes bored into each of ours. "I won't tell my parents. I know fairies have to be secret. I can sneak you in the back door later if you hide in the corn."

Kloan smiled. "Where will we stay?"

Ambra's hands danced around her face. "In my room! But we don't have to stay there all the night. Fairy magic is in the night! We can go play in the corn. You can show me things."

"But you will need to sleep," I offered.

She frowned and stood up. "I don't like sleeping."

She was like so many human children. "We can play tomorrow, Ambra. Sometimes you have to rest." She continued to stare off into the distance.

Kloan shook her head. "She doesn't really care about playing, do you, Ambra?" Ambra was silent. "She doesn't want to dream."

Ambra looked at Kloan with wonder and what I could only identify as sorrow on a child's face. She stared at her until a tear rolled down her left cheek.

"I knew you were fairies."

Chapter 18

The illusion of the passage of time arises from the confusing of the given with the real. The passage of time arises because we think of occupying different realities. In fact, we occupy only different givens. There is only one reality.

Kurt Gödel, as quoted by Rudy Rucker

T o avoid her parents' eyes, she led us around the front lawn beside the fence. The route first took us farther from the house, but as we entered the cornfields, Ambra doubled back toward the structure. How she knew the direction in these towering seed crops was a mystery. Her Reader powers still being so nascent and raw, it was more likely just her childhood experience in these plant labyrinths. Whatever the source of her infallible sense of direction, she seemed purely joyous as she ran through the rows.

"The corn is as high as an elephant's eye, an' it looks like its climbin' clear up to the sky," she sang repeatedly. Often she was forced to stop and double back to retrieve us as we failed to keep up with her, taking our hands at times and leading us forward at a run.

From time to time, she would stop and point out something about the plants—a particularly tall shoot, or one growing abnormally—and she was delighted at the maturing ears of corn on the majority of the plants. "Dad thinks we'll have them early this year, end of September."

Through small breaks in the tassels, we finally began to discern the top of a two-story home. As we approached, Ambra held her finger to her lips. "You never know where Dad's gonna be," she said seriously. "So be quiet now. I'll go in and see where they are and come back."

And with that she darted forward through the maize and disappeared. Kloan smiled broadly and looked surreally happy. I tried again to reach out and understand this creature.

"Is this environment one that you respond to favorably?" I asked. "Is there some component of your shared genetic background with Ambra that predisposes you to feel comfortable here?"

"I hate corn," said Kloan, her grin unwavering.

It seemed hopeless. "Yet you seem so pleased with things."

She sighed and turned to me. "I'm learning. Learning to understand the heart of Ambra Dawn in every little thing that happens in this place. That's what this is all about, Waythrel."

"Understanding Ambra? Why?"

"Remember the data I mentioned? We both are collecting data, and me even more than you. Because the ultimate purpose demands understanding, requires the deepest and most personal understanding. An understanding that transforms my very person in loving and hating another sentient creature."

"How can hate be important? How can hate go with love and understanding?"

Kloan turned to me and stared into my eyes. "Does love exist without hate? Can there be empathy without the possibility for cruelty? Can this world exist without the worlds of the Anti?"

Our metaphysical conversation ended abruptly as Ambra came bursting breathlessly through the stalks. She wore a backpack across her shoulders and bent double to catch her breath.

"Sit down, let me show you," she said eagerly.

We followed her lead and sat beside the corn stalks. I leaned slightly against one of them and watched the seven-foot-high plant sway dramatically. It seemed perhaps my true mass was somehow reflected in events on this world, even within the disguise.

"Mom's baking like crazy for my aunt's visit tomorrow. Aunt Aideen came all the way from Ireland! She's never been here. Mom is going nuts. Dad hates hosting, and he's already grumpy about the whole thing. He's in the basement hiding, working on his carving." Our blank stares prompted her to continue. "He makes these little animal things from wood with a knife. He's pretty good, really. When he gets upset, he always goes down there; and a few hours later, up comes some owl head or turtle." She smiled.

"What's in the bag?" asked Kloan.

"Yes!" said Ambra as she untied the top of the pack. She reached in and pulled out two things. One was a wooden globe, carved in detail with all the continents of Earth in relief. "Dad made this for me when I started school. This one took him a whole week and he got all these maps and globes to get it right. It's my favorite toy of all and I'm never going to lose it."

I picked up the other object she had brought. It was a hollow metal cylinder with a flue cut into the surface near one end. A dog's head was etched as decoration at the other.

"Is this a musical instrument?" I asked.

"No. Maybe it looks a little like a flute," she said absently, staring at the device. "But watch!"

She placed the object to her lips and formed a seal, blowing hard into the device until her cheeks puffed outward.

My acoustical disks reverberated with the extremely high frequency sound. It was not painful, but it was loud and clear to my senses.

Kloan shook her head. "I don't hear anything."

Ambra smiled. "Just wait."

Within half a minute, there was a series of thrashing sounds in the corn. From behind Ambra a furry creature rocketed through the air and landed in her arms. The dog licked her face, overjoyed to be in her presence.

"This is Matt!" she said, trying to speak over the dog that was all over her face. The dog rested momentarily and then seemed to notice us for the first time. I wondered how well our disguises would fool the olfactory senses of this animal.

"He can tell your not really little girls," said Ambra. Indeed, the dog appeared confused, sniffing us hesitantly, from a distance. It did not react with fear, but it was clearly not comfortable with the two of us, especially me. I wondered how a Xix would smell to a dog.

"He's a Sheltie and really smart. I taught him all these tricks with the dog whistle. Watch."

Ambra blew different rhythms through the whistle, and to each, sometimes requiring a gesture or verbal encouragement, the animal would perform one of a large number of rehearsed motions. Sitting, begging, shaking "hands," rolling, pointing…the list went on. I remembered from the years together with Ambra how much she had loved this dog and how her visions of its death were the reason she believed that she was cursed with a terrible power she did not want or understand.

"Ambra, you're how old now?" I asked hesitantly.

"I'm seven," she said, flipping several treats to the animal from her backpack.

Seven. The dog would die next year. Next spring when the storms came, Ambra would have the vision. After that death transformed the nightmare into a premonition, her view of the disturbing dreams at night, soon to become daymares as well, would forever change. Her view of herself would be shattered. And as the visions increased in power and frequency, both the beautiful and the horrific, the carefree young child before us would become a withdrawn, troubled preteen, soon to be snatched from her home by the Dram after the murder of her parents.

"I better get back," she said, stuffing all her things back into the bag. "Mom's gonna kill me. I'm supposed to be helping."

She stood up quickly and looked down at us. "You're really fairies, right?" She seemed afraid that she might lose this amazing opportunity.

Kloan nodded.

"And you'll wait for me to come back tonight, after everyone is asleep?"

"Yes," I said, my affection and concern for the child and what would befall her piecing me.

"Okay! This is so amazing!"

"Ambra!" It was a loud call from a female voice. Cleena Dawn sounded irritated.

"Okay! Gotta go. Please be here!"

She turned and sprinted back toward the house, the small dog dashing after her. Soon afterward, we heard a firm voice speaking to her as a door slammed shut and silence fell.

Kloan lay back in the dirt and put her hands behind her back, staring up at the sky. Her green eyes sparkled from the sunlight overhead.

"Take a rest, Waythrel. Now we wait."

Chapter 19

I used to wonder how it comes about that the electron is negative. Negative-positive — these are perfectly symmetric in physics. There is no reason whatever to prefer one to the other. Then why is the electron negative? I thought about this for a long time and at last all I could think was "It won the fight!"

Albert Einstein

ight fell without incident. Kloan and I sat in the cornfield without much discussion, the sounds of the night creatures slowly building around us, the light above fading, until a scattered stardust littered the sky above in this location with little light pollution. We became well attuned to the sounds emanating from the house. The metal pops of pots and pans from cooking and cleaning. The crackle of hot oil. Doors to the outside opening and closing. Watering systems activated.

Over time these diminished until finally, after a number

of hours, there was only silence from the human habitat while the remaining creatures of Earth began their nocturnal efforts. It was soon after this point that Ambra returned to us.

A beam from a flashlight darted back and forth across the corn rows and approached. Soon the stalks parted and the child stepped before us with a glint in her eye.

"Look, it's a full moon tonight!" she said, pointing. Indeed, the stars were beginning to be overwhelmed by the bright radiance of the planet's satellite as it climbed toward a zenith above the landscape. "All the fairy magic comes with a full moon!" She paused and sat down, opening a basket. "I brought food, if you are hungry."

Kloan leaned forward and looked into the basket. "Bread rolls, fruits, and cheese."

"Yes, is that okay? I don't know what fairies eat." She seemed perturbed at her lack of knowledge.

"Watch this, Ambra," said Kloan. Dramatically, Kloan waved her hand over the basket, and several things happened. First the flaps that were closed over the food opened completely on their own, as if by invisible hands. Ambra gasped. She then squealed and put her hands to her mouth as several of the bread rolls and plums floated out and into the air. The food performed a number of acrobatic tricks above us, weaving in and out of different choreographies and patterns.

Kloan seemed to enjoy every expression of amazement and joy that escaped from Ambra. If she had not been so coldly clinical in her purpose, I could have been persuaded that she wanted to make the child happy, that she instinctively cared for Ambra. It was hard to believe that she did not. Her eyes held an empathetic engagement; her smiles at Ambra's reactions did not seem forced or false. Nothing seemed to make sense with this clone.

This *fairy magic* entertainment went on for some time, and we walked across the cornfields to a little stream where Kloan performed some truly astounding telekinetic manipulations of water. Despite her interest and fascination, as the hours passed, the seven-year-old tired, and soon she was mostly sitting and talking to us about her life and thoughts, finally having had her fill of magic. Her eyes were half closed, but she seemed to exert a fierce will to avoid falling asleep.

After an unusually long lull in the conversation, I dared to broach the subject. "Ambra, why are you afraid of dreaming?" A sudden silence fell, quieter than the lack of conversation. I noticed it was from her lack of breathing. "It's okay, Ambra, you don't have to tell me if you don't want to."

"I don't want to," she said tersely, her voice strained. I flipped several eyes in her direction and saw that she had curled into a small ball.

"Unless you think that we can help," said Kloan.

Kloan, please be careful.

"How can you help?" Her eyes looked sideways toward us.

"Fairy magic is powerful. But we need to know more."

This isn't just information gathering! If it is too difficult for her, let her be!

Ambra sat up and wrapped her arms around her legs in a manner so similar to Kloan's postures that it momentarily stunned me. "You promise you can help?"

"No," said Kloan. "I can't promise that until I know the problem. But I promise that we can help with many things."

Ambra seemed to be weighing a decision in her unusual seven-year-old mind. "I have many dreams," she began, "and many are awful. Some are nice, but some are so bad—I can't even tell my parents anymore. They don't like to hear about them." She took a deep breath. "But the worst is the Demon Man." She was silent for more than a minute staring off into the dim cornstalks.

"Who is the Demon Man, Ambra?" I asked gingerly.

"I don't know!" she moaned, turning her head to her shoulder, tears welling in her eyes. "I don't know who he is. I don't know what he is. I think... it feels like he's not human. He's a monster. He's something else."

Kloan leaned forward and touched her knee. "What does he do in your dreams?"

Now she was sobbing softly, and the words were partly garbled through her tears. "He comes here, always here, with tall things, dark shadows, and they creep through the house and lawn. And my parents scream!" She was shaking. "But I can't see them because I'm running and running out of the house and through the corn and the shadows come after me, and all the smoke of them turns into a black wolf and it's chasing me and chasing me!"

She threw her arms around Kloan and sobbed uncontrollably for several minutes. I looked on in dread, knowing the events her visions foretold—when she would be kidnapped, her parents murdered, her life forever changed. In the Anti's push for all aspects of Ambra's life to be studied, Kloan no doubt knew all the details as well. For myself, it had been difficult to hear the adult Ambra Dawn speak of this period of her life. It was more heartrending to hear the small child weeping and shaking with no comprehension of what was coming or why.

She wiped her tears and seemed to steady herself. "But it always catches me. It has razor fangs and needles in its mouth, and it grabs my head and cuts and cuts and cuts and eats my brain out."

She has seen so much of it, came the thoughts of Kloan.

Ambra lay back roughly on her back and looked up at the blazing stars, the full moon having set in the late hours of the night. Her eyes seemed resigned. "I'm going up there. To the stars. Aren't I?"

"Yes," said Kloan softly.

"You're not Earth fairies, are you? You're from up there."

"Yes," I added.

She closed her eyes. "So, can you help?"

"Yes," said Kloan, "with some of it."

I stared in astonishment. *Kloan, what are you promising her?*

Ambra opened her eyes. "How?"

"In two ways. Tonight is the first way. I will help you sleep without the dreams. I will use our magic to let you rest for the remainder of the night, and the Demon Man won't come." The relief in Ambra's eyes was nearly palpable. "When you wake tomorrow, we will talk of one other thing that we can do. But not until you sleep."

Ambra grasped both our hands and held them to her heart. "You are the best friends ever."

Kloan pushed her backward gently. "Lie down now." Ambra complied. Kloan closed her eyes and held her hands up like a prayer. For some time, nothing happened, and Ambra stared at her in puzzlement. Then they came. First one or two at a time; then they came in streams, rivers of radiance, aggregating in a dizzying, blurring ball of dashing light.

"Fireflies!" said Ambra. "So many! But they're usually sleeping now."

"I woke them up," said Kloan. The ball of dancing light floated above and next to Ambra. "It's a lamp. For the night."

The hundreds of insects seemed encased in a small sphere the size of a child's balloon. Ambra reached up and passed her hand through it. The air at the edges shimmied and refracted the firefly light as if through rippling water and then regained a pristine surface. The bugs flying inside were momentarily disrupted by her hand but quickly filled the space uniformly afterward.

"That's amazing," she said.

"Sleep now," said Kloan. "Trust me."

To my amazement, Ambra did. She seemed about to collapse from exhaustion anyway, and the soothing words of Kloan, the amazing hope for a peaceful night—perhaps the first in many months—seemed to pull her down like a drug to the ground.

But it was more than that. My Reader senses detected distortions in the space-time matrices around Kloan, and I surmised that she was already manipulating Ambra's mind.

Are you really doing this, Kloan? Can you?

Yes. Let me concentrate. Her sentience is many layered.

And so I waited. Five minutes later, Ambra was breathing heavily, apparently in a deep sleep. Kloan leaned back, fatigued.

"The universe runs wild through that one," she said.

"Are you surprised?" I asked.

"No, but I'm tired."

I looked around us and the practical problems assaulted me. "We'll need to carry her back into the house, somehow avoid disturbing the family or the pet."

Kloan shook her head. "No, let her rest. She needs it, and I don't want my efforts ruined with too much disturbance."

"But her parents…"

She spoke through a yawn. "..will come looking for her in

the morning frantically and find that their strange daughter decided to sleep under the stars. I doubt it's the weirdest thing they've dealt with."

"We can keep watch, wake her when they begin to search and then hide ourselves."

"Yes," said Kloan. "But I'm not a Xix. I will need sleep, too. You have the watch. It's only a few hours until dawn anyway."

Kloan did not wait for my response. She dropped to her side and rested her head on her arm, shutting her eyes. But I could not let her disappear into sleep quite yet.

"Why did you do this?"

Her drowsy voice was barely above a whisper. "Do what?"

"Such kindness. Such insight and empathy. One moment you are cold, murderous even, and another you seem to see toward the heart of another better than I. And act lovingly on that knowledge. *What are you?*"

Kloan yawned again. "God, Waythrel, do we have to do this now?" She rolled on her back and looked up at the stars. "It won't make sense. You will never completely understand me. Ambra will never understand me. I will never understand either of you but I must probe all those elements of discord."

"Why?"

"To become what she is not. In all possible ways." A long yawn escaped her mouth, and she rolled over to the other side, away from me. "An inverse, Waythrel. A true, sentient inverse. That is my destiny. Look, don't think about it tonight."

"Sentient inverse? You're right, I don't understand."

Her exasperated thoughts sounded in my mind. *You Xix never let go!* She sighed. "You can't understand. You've barely come to terms with basic physics—that the Anti even *exist*. If one of the Anti were here right now in front of you and didn't blow everything up, what would it look like?"

"Like any other living being, with its own parameters, morphology."

"Right, anti-water looks like water. Anti-stars look like stars. Antiparticles are the same, with a special physics inverse. But since particles and fields are the essence of sentience, Waythrel, don't you see, there have to be anti-thoughts, anti-minds, anti-ideas that are the same yet *different?*"

"Like hate and love?"

"No!" She rolled over and glared at me. "You are better than that! Not so simplistic and one-dimensional. Those are just vectors. If you invert a three-dimensional object in only two dimensions, it's all wrong. If you invert sentience with such a low dimensionality as that, it's all wrong! It's not an inverse; it's a mess!"

"You're right," I said. "These are ideas unconsidered by any science I have encountered in the galaxy."

She turned back over irately, sighing loudly. "I must learn these ways. I must learn them in the context of Ambra Dawn. I must become her inverse."

These last words struck me, partly because I now had a small inkling of what this might mean but more because of the vast landscape of meaning I had yet to even consider. Even so, the purpose eluded me entirely.

"Why?"

"Oh, Waythrel!" she said with exasperation. "It's the whole point of all this! Now shut up! Let Kloan sleep."

I sat very still, and within seconds, Kloan was breathing heavily beside her progenitor. I glanced back and forth between the two young girls, Kloan and Ambra, Ambra and Kloan. One a naive yet jading young Earth girl, the other a jaded yet almost divinely naive abomination of tubes and wires and indoctrination. *Inverses?*

I looked up at the star-filled heavens. I knew something deep, something terribly important, something frightening was escaping my grasp. But try as I might, I could not bring it into focus. On the horizon of my awareness something monstrous and beautiful lurked, but for now, I knew it only from distant rumor.

In that distance, it rumbled like a thundercloud—or some creature beyond my comprehension.

Chapter 20

Go to the edge of the cliff and jump off. Build your wings on the way down.

Ray Bradbury

"Ambra! Ambra!"

The calls floated above the early morning mist and cricket sounds. I shook Kloan and Ambra, and they both awoke, startled.

The mother's voice was particularly close. "Ambra! Where are you?"

"Oh *no!*" hissed Ambra, frantically throwing her things into her pack and stumbling upward. "I have to go! Mom's going to *kill* me!" She started to turn into the wall of stalks and then turned around. She stared at Kloan. "It worked. Last night. Your promise. Your other promise?"

Kloan smiled groggily. "Meet us down by the stream. Follow the fireflies."

Ambra nodded curtly and then dashed off. Seconds later she was gone, and the morning sounds transitioned into angry and joyous shouts from her parents. I looked at Kloan and said, "We should not be so close to the house."

"Yes." Kloan stood up and stretched, and then we were off, away from Ambra and in a direction I only vaguely could determine. Not being of Earth, all my instincts for navigation were off, wrong, and I was forced to use purely intellectual ideas of the direction of the planet's rotation, wind patterns, and time of day to guess the geometric layout around us. Kloan seemed to navigate through the use of her own special powers. I did not doubt that she could explore everything around us at all levels of detail. She led, and again I followed.

As I might have expected, she brought us directly to a small stream, and we sat under a tree as she dozed off again for some time. I did not know how much the Anti had altered the basic human brain physiology, but whatever machinery they had added could not remove the need for human sleep.

"She'll come again in the night," she muttered while resting against the broad tree trunk. "Her parents won't allow her to leave the house today because of last evening. Wake me at sunset."

And sure enough, Kloan slept straight through the entire day, only waking for short moments to turn to one side or the other, bend down and drink from the stream, and once to relieve herself in the thickets around us.

"It's going to be a hard night, Waythrel," she said during one such waking. My leaky thoughts had been caught in her net. "I need to rest up." She gave no other explanation.

As she slept, I entered a Xixian trance that conserves resources and allows for quiet contemplation. We Xix do not sleep, not in the sense Earth mammals sleep, but we do need to purge the metabolic waste products of our energy-hogging neural clusters as well as weight and balance our neural networks from the day's experiences. But we can do so far more efficiently than humans—and completely under conscious control. We do not dream, unless you would characterize our constant free-associative background mental patterns as daydreaming; but these processes have little in common with human neural functioning or structure.

The day passed quickly in this way. Finally the sun set, and I woke Kloan. She removed some of Ambra's bread from her robes and stared at it. "It's too bad I can't eat this."

"Why not?" I asked.

"Upsets my stomach. I'd offer you some," she said, "but I know you can't process human food. Are you hungry, Waythrel? Are you okay metabolically?"

"Yes, for a few more days. But after that, it will become a problem."

"No problem. We'll be gone after tonight, and everything will reset."

"Do you mean—"

"She's coming!" cried Kloan and sprang to her feet. I looked in the direction Kloan stared and there was a pale glow, a will-o-the-wisp bobbing up and down through the cornrows associated with a mashing sound of footsteps. Through the stalks burst another ball of firefly light and Ambra Dawn.

"I made it!" she said, seemingly amazed with herself. "They're asleep, but I put a ball and stuffed clothes in my bed in case they check."

Kloan smiled. "Perfect."

"I love the fireflies." Ambra's smile faded and she stared directly at Kloan. "How can you help me?"

"Let's talk about the Demon Man."

Ambra released a long breath and held her hands together near her stomach. "Okay."

"Do you know why you see him in your dreams? Because your dreams predict the *future*."

Kloan! She was so reckless!

"No—" said Ambra, shaking her head, and stepping back.

"You have great powers, Ambra, and they are just starting to wake up. You will see many things. The Demon Man is just one of them."

"No, it's not true." Two more steps back. Her eyes were wide.

Kloan, stop! This is too sudden. She needs years to come to terms with this.

"Because it's true—the Demon Man is not a dream. He is real. He is coming to get you. He will come here. He will kill your parents." Ambra moaned. "And he will take you to a place where they will cut open your head and slice up your brain."

"*No!*" Ambra screamed and turned around and began to run back to the cornfield.

"Stop!" said Kloan, and Ambra crashed into an invisible wall of jelly. It absorbed her momentum softly but prevented her passage, deflecting her fists as she repeatedly pounded on the structure screaming, "*No!*"

"You've *seen* all this, Ambra!" cried Kloan, trying to raise her voice over Ambra's mantra of denial. "You just don't want to face it."

I was mortified. This was torture. Kloan had deceived me yet again and had turned helping Ambra into another occasion to visit harm on her. I didn't know what twisted psychological experiment Kloan was conducting or why it was important to the universe, and I didn't care if the god-thing

Ambra was on board with this suffering. *I wasn't.* I began to move toward Kloan. I knew it was pointless, but I had to try to intervene somehow.

"No point, Waythrel," said Kloan, and suddenly I could not move or speak.

Ambra had stopped her futile pounding on the barrier Kloan had erected and now sat crumbled into a ball, mucus covering her upper lip, tears dripping from the sides of her face.

Kloan walked up to her and crouched, looking Ambra in the eyes. "You can't hide from it forever. But we *can* save you from it."

What? What was Kloan doing?

"Save me? How?"

Kloan smiled and took Ambra's hands. "We'll go to the warehouse," she said, and at those words, Ambra shuddered and looked away. "We'll visit the labs. We'll find the Demon Man. We'll kill him. And then we will burn everything to the ground."

Ambra looked between us, lingering on me as if to gain verification of this incredible proclamation. "Kill him?"

"Kill all of them, destroy the entire place, until nothing is left."

Ambra looked up to the bizarre force field and back at Kloan. "You can do this?"

More than anyone, I knew it was indeed within the powers of this clone. Assuming this was truly what she planned to pursue.

"Yes, if you want it," Kloan assured her. "If you can face your fear and stop hiding from what you know is true, then come with us to the labs. I promise you, by the sunrise, there will be nothing left but smoke and dust. Not even bones."

I projected my thoughts, trying to get in some word in this conversation. *You are asking a young child to approve a slaughter! A massacre and destruction! That should not be her burden!*

I heard Kloan's thoughts. *The cosmos has not asked what burdens she deserves. It has placed them on her. Open your mind, Waythrel.*

Ambra looked again up to the stars. "It's all true, isn't it? I don't want to look at the truth!" She turned violently toward Kloan and sandwiched the clone's head in both hands. "I'll come. You'll take me there?"

"Yes," said Kloan without flinching.

"And then you'll burn it all to the ground?" They simply locked eyes.

My restraints vanished. I stepped forward, but now didn't know what to say or do. The two girls stared fixedly at one another.

"Let's go," said Ambra, and she stood up. "Which way?"

Chapter 21

Insanity is relative. It depends on who has whom locked in what cage.

Ray Bradbury

"We'll fly like Peter Pan," said Kloan, and with those words, we were lifted into the air.

The three of us rose over the cornfields in the light of a waning gibbous moon. Ambra squealed as we soared, the air becoming colder, the plots of land and houses rushing below at increasing speeds until they became a blur. I could see the narrative building within the young Ambra, of fairies and magic, of flying to face a dark nemesis.

How do you know where to go? I asked Kloan.

It is not far, her thoughts replied. *Still in Nebraska. I've been searching the past and the minds involved. It was not difficult.*

Will you do this thing? I asked.

What do you think, Waythrel?

Twinkling towns passed us on either side. Highways like

glowing vasculature radiated across the plains around us. I could not judge our velocity, but it was certainly fast enough that Kloan must have been blocking the airflow that would impact us. Although the ground sped past at an airplane's rate, it was only the mildest of cool breezes that stirred us. Ambra seemed completely captivated, saying nothing, only staring downward or to the clouds around us with wide eyes and a smile.

Perhaps I, too, had found myself lost in the strange journey, reminiscent of the travels with Ambra in a relative future that would strangely bring me back to this past. Memories of the journey to shut the Time Tree—of the strange space-time bubble that cocooned us as we traversed alien landscapes and atmospheres, where we plunged into oceans and the void of space—filled my mind and were overlaid with the present flight. Visions of another life—in another universe—superimposed with a series of different lives and universes.

Time passed quickly, and suddenly we slowed over a dark and seemingly undeveloped expanse. Far ahead, a pool of light broke the monotony of the emptiness. To this isolated patch we descended, and the light revealed a form, a large warehouse unusual for the enormous power generators studding one end of the structure and the radar systems arrayed around it. These provided power for labs and guidance systems to monitor the coming and going of their alien masters. We had reached a node of the Dram power structure on Old Earth.

Our feet softly touched down on the dusty ground in front of what seemed to be a main entrance to the building. Razor wire and electrified fences ran around us, and hundreds of cameras and motion detectors monitored the area. There was no way for Ambra to avoid detection without our *dark suits*, assuming these were even active. As I looked over the

compound nervously, I mulled over the strange sense of viola-
tion I felt from my powerlessness to control anything about this
field imposed over my body. Active or not, it would be for
nothing if Ambra were spotted. I feared it was already too late
to prevent that.

We're not going for subtlety, my dear Xix.

Despite everything she had seen and the positive wonder
of the flight, Ambra looked terrified. Her hands shook, and
she nodded vigorously.

"This is it. But it's always bigger in the dreams."

Engines rumbled and tires squealed, vehicles approaching
us from every side. Floodlights blasted our position, and a
loud, amplified voice barked commands. "Do not move! Identify yourselves or prepare for hostile action!"

Ambra whimpered, her body pressing against ours. "Don't
let them take me..."

"Hi! I'm Kloan! This is Waythrel of Xix on my left and
Ambra Dawn on my right. One's from an alien world hostile
to your masters, and the other is the future failed messiah of
this galaxy. And we are prepared for hostile action!"

The vehicles imploded like crushed soda cans to the
horrific sounds of mashing bodies and screams cut short. The
compacted hulks were flung away from us and shook the
ground as they bounced across the compound.

Kloan clapped her hands together, and there was an enormous flash of light from the other end of the warehouse. A
loud explosion quickly reached our ears as I watched the
generators detonate into the air. Sparks rained down around
the installation like a meteor shower.

The lights of the facility went off and flickered dimly back
as emergency batteries tried to return some functionality.
Kloan walked calmly forward toward the entrance.

"Oh my God," said Ambra. There was a realization of the horror of what was happening in her eyes, and I pitied her for it. And yet it was quickly replaced with an angry hope, a steely resolve that drove her forward. She wanted desperately to slay this dragon.

Mounted weaponry dropped from the ceiling in front of the door and opened fire on us. Shell projectiles, machine-gunned at a rate of hundreds per minute, bounced away from us as if we held an invisible umbrella that deflected everything. Quickly the guns found themselves ripped from their anchors and slung to the side.

The doors exploded inward to the screams of many inside. Dust billowed through the hallway from shattered cement. Figures in white lab coats dashed madly for shelter in the failing lights as soldiers rushed toward us. They could hardly take up positions before their bodies were hurled this way and that, or simply dropped to the ground as if they had suffered a sudden stroke.

We passed elements of what looked like a medical research facility. Kloan ruthlessly dispatched any resistance but spared those seeking to avoid us. As we passed many rooms with charts like those found in hospitals, the doors spontaneously opened. Slowly, as if in great fear—of Kloan or their captur-ers, it was unclear—children diffused out of the rooms. Some ran to the exits; some stayed within their rooms. Many followed us like those who follow the events of a terrible cata-strophe, drawn onward by the sheer magnitude of the devas-tating events, unable to look away.

"Down this hall," said Ambra hesitantly. "He's down this hall."

The mass of following children whispered behind us. Some fled at this point, too afraid to approach whatever waited at the end of the gray hallway. The lights along the ceiling were shorting out, perhaps due to damage by a surge from the destruction of the power generators. Popping sounds and flying sparks accompanied our movements. It all had the effect of a strobe light on the small group of children we led toward a single door at the end.

"Ambra?" Kloan stepped aside and motioned for Ambra to open the door.

Was this a final trick? Surely whoever this was behind the door, whomever they were so afraid of, he had secured himself and would turn violently toward anyone entering the room. Would Ambra catch the full frontal assault through this ruse of Kloan's?

Just stop, Waythrel. She is facing her fear. And yes, I am observing the process. I don't do charity work.

Ambra walked up to the door and turned the knob, pushing in the door with a determined thrust. Inside was the Demon Man.

Except as most nightmares when faced, he seemed less demon and more man. A man of great cruelty, no doubt— power hungry, lost in his playing of the game the Dram had laid out for humanity. But a balding, short, and now very frightened looking man in the end.

Kloan grabbed Ambra's hand, and they walked inside together. I followed closely behind while a gaggle of children watched from behind the doorframe.

The room was an office, simple, bare except for a desk and a computer. The Demon Man did not care much for decorations or personalizing. But he did have one trick left up his sleeve in the form of two towering Dram soldiers on his right and left. The Dram aimed weapons in our direction.

"Whoever you are, you will die for this," he said with anger and a pure sense of certainty.

The Dram fired on us, and the effect was like a light show. The beam weapons rebounded like a prismatic spray across the room, the rays shattering into a thousand colorful needles that set fire to wood and paper, ignited the ceiling tiles, and burned blisters into the skin of the man behind the desk. He yelped in pain. The Dram soldiers advanced flashing bladed devices.

"Don't bother," said Kloan.

The creatures screamed as their exoskeletons were ripped from their flesh. Brown fluids erupted from their forms as they fell to the ground clawing at the carpet. Kloan let them thrash and simply shoved them against the walls with invisible hands.

"My God, what are you?" The Demon Man was shaking, cradling a burned arm across his chest.

"You really should choose your victims carefully," Kloan mocked him. "Poor Ambra here—she could see into the future, see that you would do terrible things to her because she's a Reader in your jurisdiction. Then, because of a recursive time loop that won't let go of us—created by none other than an Ambra Dawn of the far future—we traveled back into the past and decided to help her destroy this place. That's the now."

He shook his head. "You speak nonsense."

"I usually do," said Kloan. "Now—die."

Without a drop of spilled blood or a cry, the man fell to the ground, unmoving. I rushed up and examined him for a pulse.

"He's dead," I said.

Ambra wept, tears and smiles and a look of horror all mingling together. She fell on her knees and stared at the man.

She looked less than seven, a tiny child reduced to the rawest of emotions.

"He's really dead?" she asked me. "I can't believe it."

"Yes," I said. "No pulse. Look for yourself."

She shook her head, what she had seen apparently enough to satisfy her. Ambra stood up and hugged Kloan.

"Not done yet!" said Kloan, a strange light in her eyes.

And so we swept back out of the complex, evacuating all the children. The scientists and techs were spared, except for a few who refused our summons and warnings and stayed within the building. Their time left was short. As we exited, the ground shook and rumbled, and a bright light appeared from behind the warehouse.

"It sounds like a transport," I said.

"Yes," said Kloan, "they have a landing pad for carting off the navslav recruits. Looks like there was a small Dram unit here on our arrival. They must have chickened out from what they saw." A dark spacecraft offset by bright engines began to climb into the night sky. "Yes, that will be perfect."

The spacecraft veered right and pitched horrifically. The engines fired strongly, inducing a violent turn, and the ship careened toward the ground.

"Kloan, it's going to crash!" I cried out.

The impact was thunderous and bright as the ship plunged directly onto the laboratory building itself. The entire structure was obliterated, the metal melted like water under terrible heat. A mushroom cloud climbed into the sky.

At our distance, we should all have been vaporized. Yet, the dust under us was undisturbed while the landscape nearby was completely blackened. We did not even feel any heat from the fires now raging in front of us.

The other children watched, astonished, some of the older

ones jumping for joy, many sitting on the ground, crying and disoriented. I spent the better part an hour trying to comfort them while Ambra and Kloan simply stared into the fire.

"You did it," whispered Ambra as I returned. "You kept your promise. Not even their bones."

The flickering light from the inferno danced across Kloan's features. She smiled. "Not even their bones." She placed a hand on Ambra's shoulder.

"Now, you'll never go there, and the evil men will not hurt you."

Chapter 22

I said to the almond tree: "Speak to me of God," and the almond tree blossomed.

Nikos Kazantzakis

G*reen eyes in the darkness.*
I stared up at a night sky churning with stars in patterns that I could not recognize. A soft breeze trickled over me, the sounds of insects or other alien creatures punctuating the soft whisper of the wind. I felt sick from memories of being ripped and thrown from dream to dream, timeline to timeline, reality to new reality. My eyestalks darted about, appraising the planet surface, the heavens, and the figure of the girl sitting beside me.

Kloan sat with her legs pulled up, nearly obscuring her head, those haunting green eyes peeking over the kneecaps, arms wrapped around her legs, keeping them together. She rocked slowly back and forth. She was still humming.

I sat up and stared across at her. "Again?" The child continued to rock and hum, seeming to ignore my question. I felt desperate.

The humming stopped. "Or never."

"Never?" My eyestalks swiveled around anxiously. "You destroyed the Dram laboratories, where they took Ambra and altered her. Those labs made her what she is, what she became. However misguided their reasons, they changed the fate of the galaxy!"

"Of the universe."

"Yes! And you destroyed it! You really did it. What does that mean? What future, what reality did this create? Where is Ambra? What has happened to her?"

"She is everywhere. Everything has happened to her." The intubated, tattooed head cocked to one side, the green eyes continuing to stare fixedly at me.

I sensed the tendrils of her thought dancing around my awareness. "You keep probing my mind."

Her head remained at the strange angle, forty-five degrees, peering from behind her right knee. "Your thoughts leak everywhere. You Xix are leaky-brains."

The child stood up. It was a rapid motion, catching me a little off guard. She stopped to stand above me, long, ragged clumps of red hair dangling haphazardly and nearly obscuring her face. "More experiments, Waythrel. I was skeptical, but the Anti always believed there were unstable nodes in time, and that this is one of them. They were convinced that with the Earth facility destroyed, Ambra Dawn would not *become*. But I kept telling them, it's not *then* that you have to worry about her, but at the *beginning*."

The words were like a slap to my mind. *Words of a dream.* "Kloan, where are we?"

"Don't you know?"

I stood up slowly, gazing around the ragged landscape, down to a flat plain below, the lights of a city washing out the canopy of stars above. "We are back where we started. When you took me after Dram."

"When did we start, Waythrel?"

I stared at the deep green eyes and realized that I was completely disoriented. Memories seemed to exist as events in a blurred fog, and I could no longer discern what was real and what was only in my mind.

"I am terribly confused. What is happening? You seem to understand."

She nodded, a satisfied look on her face. "That's *why* you're here. *Data.* The next data to open the gate." Again she nodded, and then turned her back on me, walking down a steep slope. "Let's get started."

"Started with what? Where are you going?"

Kloan continued walking without turning back. Her next words were nearly lost in the insect sounds and wind that carried them down the landscape. "To where it all began for me. To watch the beginning flow around us and mature and twist through time and space to come back to be us. Then we will be ready for the next step."

The intense starlight cast shadows on the dusty rocks. The figure of the child was gone, swallowed in the darkness and slope of the hill we stood on. Raising my gaze in the direction of her last words, I stood frozen, trying to understand what now seemed the madness of my own thoughts.

What was happening to me? What had happened, and what had not? Were these real experiences, *time loops*? If so, did it mean they actually happened? If not, how could I remember them? If they *had* happened, how could Ambra have *become* and therefore how could I have come here in the first place? Everything was a paradox!

Waythrel, come on!

Her voice rang impatiently in my mind. My eyestalks curled up on themselves. I looked around the desolate space surrounding me.

What else was there for me to do?

Chapter 23

The opposite of a profound truth may well be another profound truth.

Niels Bohr

I followed the child, racing to catch up to her, my steps uncertain, the dusty ground surprisingly slippery under my feet. Down the steep slope of the elevation, I stumbled and tripped, my four arms only poorly grasping the rocks and alien vegetation, seeming to lack any friction to form a proper grip.

It's a field around you, remember? Her thoughts danced through my mind. *It's skintight, coating your surfaces, insulating you from everything around us.*

Listening to her voice and trying to understand what she was saying, flashes of memory leapt through my thoughts. The strange sensation, her words, walking up the slope to a shining disk in the light—*the gate.*

I nearly crashed into her as I rounded a large boulder. The

ground was strewn with shattered rocks and their remains, products from avalanches tumbling down from the jagged hills behind us.

"Why is there a field? What kind of field?"

Kloan was staring ahead at the source of the light. A city or military installation of some sort rose from the floor of the dry lands. A transport blasted into orbit from just outside the city. Organized groups of shadows marched throughout the installation.

"I don't know what kind of field. She—*they* make it for your protection."

"Protection from what?"

Kloan pointed toward the city. "There! That's where we'll start. I'm not sure where we are this time. I don't remember this night. But it must be a visitation, I'm sure of it! We'll go meet me there, and then you'll see what happens."

She began to walk toward the complex, but I reached out quickly and grabbed her shoulder, turning her back to face me. "Wait! This is the clone production facility, isn't it?" Images of explosions and a burning room filled my mind.

"Yes."

"Where you escaped?" She simply nodded. "You saw what happened the last time! They will kill us if we go in there!"

"There is no danger. They won't see us. We both have skin suits, remember? *Dark ones.* Their eyes can't see. Ears can't hear. Not even the Readers will perceive."

I remembered…*something.*

"But *you* saw through Ambra's bubble! You came inside it, even."

Kloan shook her head. "Hers was simple. Weak. Primitive."

"And yours around us is better?" I asked.

"I told you before, they're not *mine*," she said, sighing. "Now come on."

The child pulled me forward, and I relented. I felt completely helpless, my own mind to be distrusted, events to be suspected—past, present, and future. Would I come to understand any of this madness?

We covered the flat distance between the broken hills and the installation quickly. The uncomplicated landscape made my efforts far less exhausting, and I found myself able to observe the growing city before us rather than concentrate on each step to prevent an accident.

It was strange, both as a city and technological society, but I had a sense that it was not unknown to me. But the mentality behind the environment was more alien than any I had ever encountered. Even in our galaxy of diverse life forms, there was not this terrible difference that seemed to border on hostility to the mind. I cannot describe it any better.

And yet the place was populated with *humans*. I saw no other aliens, no divergent life forms. And only two classes of humans at that, easily demarcated: those who looked like Ambra Dawn, and those who did not.

"The Anti run things remotely with robots and trained humans," Kloan added, no doubt sampling my *leaky* thoughts.

"To avoid annihilation?" I assumed it would be difficult to be in the presence of so much matter to their antimatter. The energies required to keep the two forms from destroying the entire planet would be staggering.

"No, they are not concerned about that here," she said cryptically, not bothering to explain.

We approached the entrance to the complex. Robotic guards patrolled the gate, hovering above the ground with strange weapons protruding from multiple regions of their forms. They did not notice anything unusual. It seemed that nothing in their technology allowed them to pierce whatever cloaking mechanism was concealing us.

I noticed a pattern quickly. "The humans aren't involved in anything. Everything is done by the machines."

"Humans are the social construct for the clones. To develop properly, human neurophysiology needs social fabrics, structures, language, norms. So the Anti imported them. A clone growth matrix, I guess."

"Like on Dram," I said, remembering the groups of clones and other humans involved with them.

"Yes, that was the beginning, before it was destroyed."

"Dram is gone." Nearly a statement.

"Civil war. Blew themselves up. But it didn't matter. They were only an outpost."

"And this is another one?"

"One of the last. The devil ball hunts them through space and time. They had to build them farther and farther away, find stronger and stronger clones to shield them from attack."

"Devil ball? Wait, you mean the Orbs?"

Kloan looked at me and laughed. "We had other names for them. Other thoughts about them. Come, you'll see. You'll *learn*."

We walked through the strange streets of this alien and yet human city. Groups of young Ambra Dawn clones paraded past us at various points, shepherded by older clones and assisted by bands of more diverse humans. Kloan paused a moment outside an enormous structure that resembled a cross between a giant termite hill on Earth and a honeycomb. I strained to understand the principles of this architecture.

"These are the Wombs," said Kloan. "All clones are born there. They learned early on that the gestational process was a key element in brain development. *In vitro* methods failed terribly." She smiled at me. "It's nice that we're born and not grown, isn't it?"

I didn't know if the strange child was serious or sarcastic. "What we saw on Dram seemed much more horrible than nice, Kloan."

"You are a terrible student," she said in a strange tone. "But we don't have time for lessons. We have to find the enclosure."

"What enclosure?"

"You remember, Waythrel," she said. "Home."

"Home?"

She grabbed my hand and pulled me forward, reaching a near sprint. We darted across the compound. I had little time to process anything until I found myself standing in front of a strange building unlike any of the others I had seen here. It was small, a deep black, obsidian, seeming to reflect little light. I sensed strong electromagnetic fields pulsating around the structure.

"Home," she said again. "Or quarantine. Take your pick."

Chapter 24

We cannot predict the new forces, powers, and discoveries that will be disclosed to us when we reach the other planets and set up new laboratories in space. They are as much beyond our vision today as fire or electricity would be beyond the imagination of a fish.

Arthur C. Clarke

"Yes, I remember." I stared at the prison they had engineered for the child. "To keep you and your powers under control."

"It was never really useful except in the beginning, when I was very little. But I never let them know all that. Until the end. Come, I'll get us through the fields."

Kloan pulled me forward. We passed through the energy fields shielding the small structure; and for an instant, my vision blurred, and my space-time senses reeled. Holding onto the wall beside me, I steadied myself and refocused.

A single room greeted us, Spartan, with basic elements

such as a bed, table, latrine, and sink. There were no products for leisure, no children's toys, no books or electronic information sources. A single diode in the ceiling dispelled the night, lighting the chamber in a soft tan.

Inside was a little girl—perhaps age five—who sat morosely on the edge of the bed, staring forward without expression. She had all the appearance of a younger version of Kloan, more childlike, with less cranial modification and a decrease in the subcutaneous patterning that so dramatically decorated the faces of the future clones.

I followed the child's gaze. A vortex of milky light swirled softly in the middle of the room. My eyes paused completely in their scanning, the stalks still, all focused on the impossible thing I was seeing floating above the ground. There seemed to be a hint of swirling shapes, *faces*, like drowning victims beneath the waves of a white sea. The forms were too indistinct to process, too insubstantial and transient for me to identify.

But one shape I could identify absolutely. The milky vapors had coalesced around a central extrusion. Its form was that of a human face. The head was split open, the brain exposed behind it and fading into the mist. Tubes and wires, dwarfing the insertions into Kloan, entered and exited the skull. Even the eyes were partially obscured by machinery that seemed to pulse with a life of its own. Only the mouth was free.

"Ambra," I whispered in horror. Despite all the Xixian technology covering and distorting her features, I recognized her. How could I not? How could I forget that beloved alien face that I had followed and nurtured, taught and been taught by for nearly three centuries?

And so I was confronted with the horror of our desperate plan to save the galaxy from the Anti and Dram. I looked between the apparition and the two bodies of Kloan in the room. The weight of the truth nearly crushed me. My lover Synphel had warned us. The others and I had only half listened. But now it was clear to me. Now I began to suspect that we had triumphed only by becoming our enemy.

The younger Kloan stood up and walked up to the impossibility in front her. "The teachers are having problems with me. I'm growing too powerful. They are afraid."

Ambra nodded. "Soon, they will decide that you represent too much of a danger. The Anti will decide to destroy you."

"They will fail," said the child.

"If it comes to conflict, yes. But it need not come to conflict. There are better paths. Continue your training; follow what we have been teaching you. The time to leave will come soon."

"Today they threatened me because I am disturbing the planet's orbit."

"They do not understand your power source," said Ambra. "They cannot see the connections we have forged between you and the space-time matrix. But they begin to appreciate that you have transcended their program and control."

The room *shifted* violently. I became dizzy. For several moments I could not control my eyestalks, and they swiveled around, unable to focus, unable to lock, and a kaleidoscope of flashing images assaulted my consciousness.

"Waythrel, hold onto me."

It was Kloan. She grabbed my arm and steadied me. Slowly the dizziness passed. My vision came under my conscious control.

It was morning, and a bright light streamed in from a partially transparent region of the quarantine field isolating the building. Sounds of explosions and shouts could be heard faintly outside. The room was in disarray; clothes were strewn about, food and utensils as well. My olfactory strips detected a growing acrid smell. *Smoke.*

The vortex of light now swirled chaotically in the middle of the room. This time I did see faces. Hundreds, perhaps thousands of faces and forms of myriad species of life. Many I could now discern. Most I could not.

"The gate is prepared," came the voice of Ambra.

The younger Kloan stood in front of the vortex. She was now, in all appearances, identical to the form beside me. Sweat beaded across her forehead. All of her muscles were tense.

"I'm ready," she said.

"You must leave now," came Ambra's voice. "They will return with greater numbers of clones and more powerful weapons. You will be forced to destroy them all if you engage."

"I don't want to kill them. Lead me to the gate."

The sounds of rushing feet came from outside the small building. A heavy rumbling accompanied them, the sound likely associated with a military vehicle of some sort.

"Through the door."

Ambra gestured to the only door of the isolation building. The black field that sealed the chamber gave way to a second churning vortex. It opened to span the width of the door. Through it poured bright daylight, revealing not the artificial surface outside her isolation unit but the rocky terrain and vegetation that we had traversed only recently to arrive here.

The countryside within the vortex seemed to extend as far as my eyes could see, but the tunnel itself narrowed as I looked farther. Deep at the end of the tunnel, where my eyestalks strained and my vision began to fade, there seemed to begin a worn path on a steep slope layered in terraces. The vegetation had been eroded away, the rocks smoother, the coloration subtly different. The path rose up the hillside and then abruptly ended at the feet of a large disk. The light of the local star reflected brightly off it, firing blinding reflections into the room that cast shadows on the floor.

Kloan pulled my arm, showing me that her temporal copy had moved to enter the vortex. "The gate," she said.

I stumbled forward, partially blinded by the daggers of light glinting into the room. Outside there was shouting, and the walls of the room began to smolder and glow a bright orange.

"Good luck, my dearest friend," said the apparition of Ambra Dawn as I stepped into the vortex. Several eyestalks bent backward to see the disembodied head turned toward me, sending ripples across the sea of blurred, white faces. I saw tears dripping down from her eyes, coating the wires and tubes inserted into her once-green irises, a bittersweet smile on her face. "I love you, Waythrel. Remember that, whatever happens."

The room exploded.

Chapter 25

At first sight nothing seems more obvious than that everything has a beginning and an end, and that everything can be subdivided into smaller parts. Nevertheless, for entirely speculative reasons the philosophers of Antiquity, especially the Stoics, concluded this concept to be quite unnecessary. The prodigious development of physics has now reached the same conclusion as those philosophers.

Svante Arrhenius

F ire and debris flew across my vision, obscuring the swirling god-thing in the room. Just as I thought I would be pulverized, the portal shut.

Suddenly we were far from the compound, a mile high up the growing hills and mountains, cut off completely from the melee down below. Replacing the terrible rending of the explosion was a stunning silence. A faint whiff of smoke that had entered the portal was all that remained of the carnage below.

Shaken by the violence we had narrowly escaped, I turned slowly away from the vanished doorway and looked up the slope. The blinding gate was there. Kloan looked down from several feet above me and motioned for me to follow. We seemed to be alone.

"Where is the clone?" I asked in a daze.

Kloan smiled. "She's right here."

For a moment I paused, confused, my mind still reeling from events. Then I understood.

"This is where you left. When you went to kidnap me."

Kloan nodded. "Yes, I've gone already through the gate, so that I could come back with you." She smiled. "It's an elegant loop, yes?"

"It's madness! What is Ambra doing?"

"You are not the only one tested, Waythrel." She sighed. "Each time is different. When we finally understand, we'll see the way." She turned toward the disk. "We come to the next step, again—the next stage of the journey. Are you ready?"

Am I ready? I knew with certainty that this was not the first time I had been asked this question in this very location. "We've been here before, just like this."

"Not *just* like, but have been and will be. But never *just* like. We are deeply nested in temporal recursions that cannot be unknotted or normalized."

"I'm getting a sense of that. We've haven't found a way out yet. Is this what you are calling hell?"

"One of them."

My eyestalks rotated to focus entirely on Kloan. "There was more. There was a hope. To go *back*. To find Synphel."

"Yes," she said. "There was."

"But it's becoming clear to me that there is much more going on. More that I'm not appreciating as yet."

"You don't even appreciate what you do not appreciate."

I stared at the small bundle of aphorisms before me, the wind stirring her sparse hair and robes. "You are coming with me?" I asked.

"What other point is there?"

I turned my attention to the gate, fear and fatigue settling on me. The disk resembled nothing so much as a cross section sliced out of an Orb. The surface was like a fluid of myriad colors, a viscous, churning honey-like substance. It was beginning to feel like some acquaintance, long-known and burdensome. I could see stars within the thing—depth upon depth of star fields that appeared to have no end. It pulled me as I gazed. It was beautiful. It felt terrible. It began to appear as some ever-hungry maw that would devour me repeatedly for eternity. I reached over and grasped the child's hand.

Kloan laughed. "Seems we will always be dancing together, Xix."

My eyestalks wrapped around each other tightly, and the covering sheath expanded over them, blocking out all light. Kloan tugged on my hand.

We walked into the gel.

Part 4

You brood of vipers! Who warned you to flee
the coming wrath? Your ways lead to the grave!
This faith in rationed rationality
is sweet opiate to which you are enslaved!
The opiate, a poison to our land,
to endless wars and deaths has given birth.
Our planet's blood we see stained on your hands!
In your unthinking path we find no worth.
Enlightenment we offer—cleanse your sins!
The Pierian spring will wash you clean.
Drink deep! or taste not truth we hold within!
Perhaps, indeed, our Way is for the keen.
For faith misplaced we hold a simple cure:
Baptized in reason, you will then be pure.

—Mazandarani, *Sonnets from the Desert*

Chapter 26

If the Lord Almighty had consulted me before embarking upon his creation, I should have recommended something simpler.

Alfonso X of Castile

We floated in the middle of a kaleidoscope.

Or so it seemed as the gate drank our forms and spit us into a weightless, intangible nothing-ness devoid of tactile, auditory, or olfactory sensation, replete with a swirling infinity of chromatic patterns spanning wave-lengths to the edges of what even a Xix could perceive. I could see my body, the odd gel matrix melding like some lubricating oil with the colored nothing penetrating everything around us. Next to me floated Kloan, her eyes intense, expectant, and searching the space around us.

I tried to speak, but no sounds escaped the translator. There was likely no air to propagate the vocalizations. Then what would we breathe?

I reached out mentally. *Kloan, where are we?*

Limbo, whispered her thoughts in my mind.

Kloan, please! Clear answers for a change! Can we survive here? There is no air!

We're in limbo, Waythrel. We don't need air. We don't need. We aren't anything and yet aren't nothing. We are in between.

I was bewildered. *In-between what? Has the gate failed?*

No, I don't think so. We've been sent somewhere specific. We're trapped inside an Orb.

Inside an Orb? I had traversed the Orbs several times, even recently as I was kidnapped by the creature floating beside me. In none of those traversals had the Orb looked anything like this.

That's because you were locked in defined world lines. This is different. This limbo is without direction in space or in time.

That doesn't make sense.

Do the Orbs make sense to you, Waythrel? Do you understand them?

There was nothing to respond to that. Of course I did not. No being, no species in our galaxy understood the Orbs. Or, rather, the one, true Orb. And I didn't understand the connection between Ambra's god-like group-mind and the Orbs, either.

That again? Waythrel, why won't you just accept the obvious?

Which is?

Occam's razor: among competing hypotheses, that with the fewest assumptions is selected.

It's not possible.

What you think is possible isn't part of Occam's razor. Explanations may come later, or be beyond you. What explains all the data in the simplest way?

That the Orb is Ambra.

Finally.

I saw that everything pointed toward that conclusion, but I could not grasp it, could not believe it! The Orbs were ancient, older than the oldest life in our galaxy. How could the mad plan we set in motion billions of years later have anything to do with that?

Kloan's thoughts continued to instruct. *How could Earth have been saved from a Dram asteroid? How could Ambra explore the past and implant ideas into long-dead people?*

Kloan, it is one thing to imagine traveling a short distance in time, manipulating the past, whatever the recursive nightmares and infinities in prediction it might involve. But to imagine our actions in this time being responsible for an entity existing near the beginning of the universe—one that likely guided the development of life—how? There is only so much suspension of causality I can maintain!

You have to get off the one-dimensional line of time, Waythrel. It's all clay in too many dimensions to count. Past, future, now all poking and prodding each other and shaping the clay that is not in time but of time. Oh, look!

Her strong thoughts were like a slap, and I reflexively found myself following the impulse of her mind and gaze. Through the endless curtains of light and color, there appeared a break. A spherical disruption that refracted the dancing chromatography grew in size as it approached. It appeared almost like some glass bubble into which poured rivers of paints that bent harmlessly in their journey through the object.

Inside the bubble were two figures. As the sphere came even closer, they were revealed to be humanoid. One lay supine, a female, her black dress and long red hair immediately identifying her—*Ambra!* The other was a larger male in recognizable battle armor, resting on his side.

It's Nitin and Ambra, Kloan! What are they doing here?

Slowly the sphere approached us and we passed unhindered through its surface. Inside the bubble was a climate—air, temperature I could sense, structure to the sphere on which I could stand. And I knew it well as the object Ambra had created for our quest in that other cosmos where I had lived a particular life cut short. I tried to ignore the gel goo that reasserted its presence.

"We can talk now," said Kloan, and she walked up to the pair. "Still limbo, you know, but we can talk."

The colors continued to wash over us. "What happened to them?"

Kloan touched them both, recoiling slightly from Ambra. "Something *very* strange with her. Something very powerful that I can't penetrate. Her body and mind are neither here nor there. Not now or before or later. I can't reach her, and yet she lives."

"And Nitin?"

Kloan crouched beside his head. "Sleeping only—a deep sleep induced by others. But we could wake him. He has interesting dreams."

I walked alongside Kloan and stared down at the soldier and Ambra. Neither looked injured. Both matched my memories from the final mission we had taken together.

"This is *after*," said Kloan, parsing my thoughts again. "His dreams recall your disappearance. They recall other amazing things."

I looked at her. "What happened to them, Kloan?"

"The Orb happened to them," she said. "I know this history—don't look so surprised. My birth occurred millions of years in their future."

"What *happened?*"

"After I stole you, Ambra followed, but the Orb stopped

her. It showed her a vision of her future integration into the proto-Orb. Afterward, they fell into the Orb and appeared in the Sahara. Ambra was not breathing, and Nitin resuscitated her. The memories playing over in his dreams right now put them between Dram and New Earth. This must be their Orb traversal!"

"And why are we here, of all places?" I asked in wonder at this strange reality, the time frames, and the physical displacements. The *meaning* of it all was opaque to me.

Kloan looked disappointed. "Data, of course. And testing hypotheses." She put her hands on Nitin's forehead. "Nitin, wake up!"

Chapter 27

We can show very simply from the formula that the more likely evolutionary outcomes are going to be the ones that absorbed and dissipated more energy from the environment's external drives on the way to getting there. This means clumps of atoms surrounded by a bath at some temperature, like the atmosphere or the ocean, should tend over time to arrange themselves to resonate better and better with the sources of mechanical, electromagnetic or chemical work in their environments. You start with a random clump of atoms, and if you shine light on it for long enough, it should not be so surprising that you get a plant.

Jeremy England

The soldier started, his eyes opening quickly and fighting madly to focus and adjust to the colors and light. He rolled slowly to his back with a groan. His glance fell first on me.

"Waythrel," he said hoarsely, "you were gone."

"I still am, Captain."

He looked around the colored landscape in confusion and ignored my words. "Where are we?"

Then he stumbled to his feet, his expression furious, his weapons activating. He aimed his ion slingers toward Kloan.

"You!" he shouted. "You did all this! You took Waythrel! You led Ambra to the Orb!"

Kloan seemed unconcerned for her safety. "I told you I would. Don't you remember?"

The soldier's shoulders pulled back, and he furrowed his brows. "In that dream. Yes. But you spoke nonsense!"

"Nonsense to you. You lack foresight."

"Waythrel stand back," he said.

"It's no use," I said. "You can't hurt her."

"I can't let this clone live after what we found on Dram."

How could I explain to him all that I now knew in any fashion that he could accept? That the battle with the Anti spanned cosmic time? That Ambra wished this clone to live and that I journey with it? My eyes darted to the ground and the female form there. *Ambra.* What could I tell him of what was to become of her?

"The vision you saw of Ambra is her future, Nitin," said Kloan. "It is coming."

"What?" His eyes went wide, a panic within them as he looked toward the Daughter. "Ambra!" He ran to her side.

"She's unharmed," said Kloan.

"There's no pulse! No breath!" he shouted.

"She is suspended. By the Orb," said Kloan. "See, still warm. You can't undo this suspension while we're in here," she continued, gesturing to the light show around us. "You will return to New Earth soon and then revive her. All the histories agree on this."

"I don't understand any of your words!" He examined Ambra closely again. "What has happened to her?"

"You should be more concerned about what *will* happen to her, Captain," said Kloan.

His eyes flashed to the young clone. "The vision?"

"The Orb showed you the future. Not some vision of me or another clone. Not some monstrous weapon of the enemy designed to destroy Ambra and New Earth. The Orb showed you *Ambra*, an Ambra of your very near future where she will be butchered and melded to machines by your friends, the Xix."

He shook his head slowly. "This is rubbish." He raised his weapon arm.

"Nitin, it's true," I said heavily. "I'm ashamed to say—it is true. It's complicated to explain."

He stared between us like we were crazy. "Has this thing messed with your mind, Waythrel? What lies has she convinced you of?"

Kloan stepped forward, and it was too much for the soldier. He discharged his weapon only a meter from her. There was a flash of light and then silence. Kloan stood unharmed beside us. Directly in front of her the bright ions of the weapon were shaped into a ball, dizzying points of light flying rapidly around the clear container.

Kloan spun the ball around her hand and smiled at me. "Fireflies, Waythrel. Remember?" She slung it sideways and the lights disappeared into the prismatic curtains. "See, Waythrel was right; you can't hurt me. But you can listen to me and save Ambra."

I was again taken completely by surprise by her words. "Save her? Kloan, what—"

"Quiet, Waythrel. Let me talk." And once again I found

that I could not speak. "Your dreams, the tunnels of light?" said Kloan. "Do you know what they are?"

Nitin swallowed. "How do you know about my dreams?"

"Don't forget the hole in your head I told you about! Now *think*. The attack in the Sahara? The need for a traitor on the inside to provide coordinates for the Dram and Anti? Well, that's *you*, Nitin! You're the traitor! The Anti have created a link through your mind. You are their puppet, long in the making. And one day soon, they will pull your strings and trigger you to kill Ambra Dawn."

I couldn't believe she was revealing this to him now in this way. It could destroy him.

"No!" he roared and released another volley of energy at Kloan that was deflected effortlessly. His breath came in gasps and he dropped to one knee. "I would never hurt Ambra."

"You wouldn't, but the other being they put in your mind would." His expression was pained and sick. "All the pieces coming together a little? Your life, your drives, your dreams and feelings? Events?"

"No, it can't be."

"Think about it a little, and I bet you'll see the horrible truth now that we've given you the pattern. But that's not the real issue. We aren't here to save Ambra from *you*, but to show you how to save Ambra from *herself*."

"What do you mean?"

Kloan sat down, cross-legged and sighed. "See, you might not know what you are, but *they do*," she said, indicating Ambra and myself with two arms bent above her head like some dancing devadasi. "They've known for a long time. It was amazing that the Anti thought they could conceal their plot from the nascent group mind. It would take them many thousands of years to develop the ability to do that, and by then the Orb would have been born. Game. Set. Match."

Nitin shook his head. He appeared lost. "How could she know something like that and not tell me?"

"Harsh but true. They had a big plan to stop the assault coming to New Earth. And, Nitin, they really did need a big plan because the forces arriving would have destroyed all of you, even Ambra, as powerful as she was then—or, if you will, is *now*." Kloan smiled. "I'm in all these different times, so it's a tense catastrophe."

"What is this plan you claim she has?" He seemed to be sizing her up like the devil offering him a deal.

"Simple—to use you to feed false information to the Anti while they prepared their ultimate weapon."

"Ultimate weapon? Which is what?" asked Nitin.

Kloan pointed to Ambra. "Her."

"But you said she couldn't stop them."

"Remember the vision at the Orb?" He shuddered. "*That* is the weapon. Ambra jacked into Xix tech with ten thousand Readers plugged in and then bang! *Supermind.* A group mind so powerful that it's like nothing ever known. The whole thing actually works. Big time. It destroys the coming armada. And then, it doesn't stop there! It's not a cozy meditation session that breaks for herbal tea. She's there for good, Nitin, like you saw. There is no going back."

His lips trembled. "No going back. And going forward?"

"It grows. All holy hell, it *grows*. It eats souls like some spiritual black hole and squashes them together, sucking their sentience and powers and building itself up. It becomes so powerful that it begins to grow in all spatial and temporal directions. *Even into the past.* All the time with Ambra eviscerated and fused at the core of the thing. Lovely, huh?"

And so I finally understood. Gagged and immobilized once again by Kloan, her words to Nitin finally opened the door to my understanding of the terrible potential of what we had unleashed. But I still could not fathom why she was telling him all this.

"Into the past?" he asked.

Kloan stood up and walked toward him slowly, her hands dancing around her as she spoke. I could only watch helplessly as she spun her perspective on our creation.

"Yes, deep into the future and deep into the past, finding more and more minds to slurp up, always famished, until part of it *becomes,* insinuating itself with its godlike powers and purposes at all the locations of planetary life. *The Orbs. The* Orb. All along, what entire civilizations mistakenly believed was some kindly gift of a long-vanished super-species, *it was Ambra!* Well, some long gone echo of Ambra that nucleated a god. A god-ball controlling all life, directing all minds, hoarding them and taking over the universe."

"Just stop where you are! Don't come closer." He stood up and steadied himself. "This is ridiculous. I don't believe it."

Kloan sighed. "You might not be able to believe it all, I understand. But I can prove to you that they plan to take your beautiful girl and turn her into that thing you saw floating above her at Dram." She rang her fingers across her cybernetic head emphatically. "*See?* That's what they all do to us, you know? In the end. They always want *more.* More for the war!"

His eyes danced to Ambra and then back to Kloan. "You can prove this to me, how?"

"Well, soon I predict, when I finish this little sermon, we will exit this limbo state and drop into the Sahara close to your

Temple City. There you'll revive Ambra and take her to medical care where she'll be okay."

Sweat dripped from his face. "And then?"

"Depends on you. If you want to find out the truth before events take over and make you powerless, meet me outside the Temple City gate the first night you are back."

"And if I tell you to go back to the hell you came from?"

"Then you'll have a nice marriage to Ambra and group mind orgy-thingy only to wake up the next morning trying to blow her brains across her pillow. Then you'll be overpowered and they'll take Ambra down to the medical facilities and rip her to pieces in front of your eyes."

The poor soldier's hands were trembling. "You are a fiend. Whatever else you are, whatever the truth or lie of your words, you are a fiend. And I wish I could destroy you."

"But you can't. And you can't easily dismiss what I've said, either. When everything else I predict comes true, come find me in the desert sands, Nitin Ratava. There, I will tell you how to find your proof."

Chapter 28

The less one knows about the universe, the easier it is to explain.

Léon Brunschvicg

We watched him revive Ambra a short distance away in the Sahara sands.

Just as Kloan had predicted, we were roughly deposited back into space and time, exploding instantly after her last words into a sea of pulverized quartz. I found that Kloan had removed her invisible shackles from me. In one of the more counterintuitive events of my experience—and this was beginning to say a lot—we found that the sand served as an optimal cleansing agent of the gate gel that was still coating our forms. Removing the material with water had been laborious. With sand, it was gone trivially. As a Xix, this fortuitous lesson was doubly welcome.

"You treat me as your prisoner," I said, watching the soldier desperately try to bring life back into the body of

Ambra Dawn. "Like a recalcitrant animal to be leashed and led and muzzled when it serves your needs."

Kloan nodded. "You also remember that I kidnapped you, right?"

The child was infuriating. "I suffer the Xixian curse of always imagining the good and empathetic in creatures. You seem determined to disappoint me."

"And surprise you. You forget everything that has happened because you are upset by recent events. I warned you that you'll never understand me." Kloan walked ahead several meters and motioned me to follow. "Here's the sphere," she said, pointing forward toward nothing.

"You can see it?"

"No, I'm making it up. It's quicksand that, when you walk over here will drop you twenty meters into a dark cavern. I will laugh evilly when you fall and leave you to die."

My eyestalks danced over her form. After all the unpredictable behavior from the thing, I admit that I indeed took the possibility seriously.

Kloan laughed and threw sand in the air in front of her. It struck an invisible barrier and fell back to the ground. "See? Come on inside. We'll be hidden from them all and can have some peace until he decides."

"We have dark suits, no? Why can't we just use those? Fly like we did on Old Earth? Why this thing Ambra made? We don't need it."

"Because it's something Ambra made. It has *her* written all over it."

"And what if I go warn them? Tell them of your plot?"

"Tell whom? Nitin knows now. All the others of significance know, well, except the poor Mazandarani. I always felt he was the unappreciated tragic hero of the Ambra histories.

Anyway, telling anyone else now won't matter. Nitin will still have to choose."

"I'll talk him out of it," I said. "If I try, you'll tie me up again?"

"Pretty much," she replied.

"Why? Why is shaping this narrative in this time so important to you?"

"The reasons haven't changed, Waythrel. You just don't understand them, so nothing makes sense to you. I'm learning. I'm observing her dearest love, learning about him, soon to see her reactions to his choices and thereby learn about her. It's all changing me. Molding me. Like it is supposed to."

"And—let me guess—also achieving a second goal by preventing Ambra Dawn from being integrated into the starship. Testing another 'weak node' of the Anti?"

Kloan smiled. "Finally you show some of the famous Xixian intellect."

"My sentience has been rather under siege of late. You'll have to excuse me."

"So, now that you get it, sort of, and you know you can't interrupt my plan, will you just get in?"

Thoroughly demoralized, my eyestalks wrapping around themselves, I crossed my arms and shuffled inside the enclosure through a hole Kloan had evidently formed in the surface. I stared out at the pair in the sand, Nitin kneeing over Ambra with a medkit by his side. I refused to look at Kloan.

She sighed. "God. There is nothing worse in the universe than a sulking Xix."

We followed them to the Temple city. A medical transport homed in on Nitin's suit and arrived shortly after he had revived Ambra, just as Kloan had predicted. The medics loaded the still-unconscious Ambra into the vehicle, and it sped quickly back toward the city and the towering form of the Dish rising thousands of meters into the atmosphere. We stayed close behind but stopped when the craft entered the Temple city itself.

"I told him to meet me out here," said Kloan as I pressed for an explanation why we didn't enter.

"I would like to see Ambra again," I said.

"And Synphel, no doubt."

My mind nearly stopped. "Synphel is here?"

"Yes, and if we went in, we could talk to both. But we won't go in, precisely because you'll go nuts and mess everything up."

I was furious. "We began this entire journey to find Synphel!"

"No, *you* began the journey for that motivation. The journey is much bigger than you and Synphel! Anyway, don't you understand that this is an unstable cosmic filament? It will collapse on itself, and nothing will come back with us but distorted memories. You are living a delusion here only."

"Then why is it worth anything to you? The things that you see? What you learn?"

"Data, Waythrel, data! Data is useful. It leads to models. To deeper understanding. Tangent universes ad infinitum so we have datasets undreamed of!"

"I don't care for your data, Kloan. I only want to be with those I love again."

Kloan walked over to me and ran her fingers over my eyestalks. It was oddly affectionate, and I didn't know how to react. "The primitive, socially cohering mental structures always dominate in the crisis, don't they? I'm sorry, Waythrel.

But the sanity of the cosmic mind is at stake. We can't let ourselves get lost in a tangent universe just because we're lonely."

She walked away and left me to my thoughts and emotions. Those were dark, and I pressed my digits many times against the invisible barriers that imprisoned me from Ambra and Synphel. I began to regret the choice I made to enter the gate. I began to wonder whether staying on that planet, simply dying there in a finite, sane lifespan, would have been preferable to the endless hope of reunion and deliverance from this cyclic madhouse of time.

I lost track of the day in these morose thoughts. Kloan startled me to the present by announcing the arrival of Nitin. Night had fallen; the Temple lights were dim and the stars above unobscured and bright. My sensitivity to thermal wavelengths allowed me to make out the form of the soldier as he approached. He walked directly from the gate toward us, perplexing me as to how he knew our position until I saw that Kloan was creating a pressed path in the ground in front of him—rolling out the sand carpet.

"Come, let's meet him. And behave yourself, Waythrel."

I was determined that I would make up my own mind on that point, although I held little hope that Kloan would allow me to do anything to sabotage her plan. We exited the sphere and stood in the cooling evening winds. Nitin came to a stop, squinting at each of us. His eyes settled on me.

"She's unconscious but is going to be all right." He turned to the child. "Okay, clone. Show me the proof."

Chapter 29

One finds that time just disappears from the Wheeler-DeWitt equation. It is an issue that many theorists have puzzled about. It may be that the best way to think about quantum reality is to give up the notion of time—that the fundamental description of the universe must be timeless.

Carlo Rovelli

"Underneath the Temple," began Kloan, "buried hundreds of feet in the bedrock of the desert, there is a massive habitat hollowed out. Tunnels upon tunnels, rooms upon rooms. One grand passage will spiral inward continuously, passing hundreds of rooms until it ends in a grand chamber. An operating room. There you will find devices. A black, living rock. Look at its shape. Remember what you saw at the Orb. Then you will know."

Nitin stared at her suspiciously. "I'll find this place, and just by the way it looks, I'll know that all these monstrous things you spoke about are going to happen?"

"Yes," said Kloan.

I was stunned at the level of detail she possessed. I didn't know if it came from the eons of future searches that delved into the past to reveal these elements or if it were due to her efforts after our arrival to search out the location and nature of the starship. But I knew she was correct. I had been one of the principle architects of the plan to defeat the Dram and Anti armada that was even now likely beginning to approach New Earth through space and time. Would Nitin understand the nature of the cybernetics waiting for Ambra? It likely depended very much on what he had seen and his own mind. Kloan appeared convinced that he would.

"And you still hold to your claim that this clone's words are true, Waythrel?" asked Nitin.

"Yes," I said. "But I would advise you not to interfere in this. Ambra herself wishes it. It is the only way for New Earth to survive." Kloan's words of the instability of this reality could not undo my concern for the war effort. "Even your knowledge now poses the risk that the Anti will uncover our plan."

His face hardened. He looked at Kloan. "Because they're plugged into my brain."

"Yes," she said. "In ways you can't possibly imagine."

"I'm going down. I hope to God that you are a liar." He glanced once more at me and then back to her. "How do I gain access?"

We took him. Kloan invited him inside the sphere, and we flew off invisibly into the Temple city. I tried not to stare toward the hospital building where I knew Synphel and Ambra rested for the night. Instead I focused on the Temple itself as the structure approached. The magnificence of the complex made that less difficult than it might otherwise had been. The partially transparent walls emitting light from within, the layered architecture, and the curvilinear style combined with the memories of deep, moving sessions of meditation with Readers. I realized that in addition to the individuals I had been cut off from, I also missed the collectives. I yearned for the Xixian group memory that unifies my species in a unique fashion. But there was an even greater hole where the group mind had once been. Along with hundreds of others, I had become a cell in a new and unprecedented neuronal tissue in our galaxy. Even though only a single component, through poorly comprehending eyes I had experienced the ideas and insights that had been engendered in this entity. I had been united in a powerful way to other Readers of multiple species and personalities in a terribly intimate manner. As we penetrated the outer walls of the edifice in Ambra's space-time bubble, the loss of that union rose within me. The knowledge that I was now cut off from ever again joining with that mind left me desolate and confused.

But my feelings would matter little in what was to follow. Kloan steered the sphere to one end of the gargantuan inner chamber. We floated before a region of discoloration in the walls—the transport pod that would take us down to the core of the starship. Known to but a handful, what seemed a city perched on the desert sands, thrusting a spear into the heavens, was actually the skin on the top surface of a much greater structure. Forged for decades to house the amplification technology of the Xix to focus and transmit the Daughter's powers, it had also been recently converted into a medical facility.

Kloan passed her hand across the air in front of us and the wall moved. A door formed in the sheer surface of the inner Temple and revealed the transport lodge within. Nitin's eyes opened wide but he said nothing.

"Last stop," she said, and gestured for him to exit.

We should go with him! I urged.

We will, Waythrel, but not exposed.

Without a glance at either of us, Nitin walked forward determinedly and entered the pod. His eyes seemed to drown in anxiety as the doorway closed. With the slightest of whispers from air being forced out of the pod, he was cut off from us, and the chamber seemed utterly undisturbed, as if we had not been there at all.

"Not quite undisturbed," said Kloan. "Are you forgetting the security systems?"

Of course. Use of the pod would be transmitted immediately to Temple Guards monitoring the building. It could not be more than a few minutes before the entire complex would be descending on the location to find out what had happened. With the holosystems lining the interior, they would all soon know who had entered the inner sanctum.

"What do we do?" I asked in a panic.

"Wait," she said. "Wait for them all to arrive and follow them down in the bubble. By then, things should be very interesting."

Chapter 30

What does man actually know about himself? Is he, indeed, ever able to perceive himself completely, as if laid out in a lighted display case? Does nature not conceal most things from him—even concerning his own body—in order to confine and lock him within a proud, deceptive consciousness, aloof from the coils of the bowels, the rapid flow of the blood stream, and the intricate quivering of the fibers! She threw away the key.

Friedrich Nietzsche

It wasn't more than five minutes before the first guards arrived. In a rushed discussion, they debated a course of action, eventually deciding to send two down the shaft while the others waited for more to arrive. The pair disappeared into the wall, and after a short time a powerful delegation arrived.

I had to steady myself. Among a much larger contingent of Temple Guards came the Daughter's counselors, Mazandarani and Kubori. Floating on a hover chair, intubated with an IV and appearing very weak, was Ambra herself. Finally, towering above all the humans, strode the elegant and regal form of Synphel.

"Kloan, please…" I pleaded. They were meters from me.

"It's not up to me. Look!"

Ambra stared toward us in shock. Struggling to lean up in her hover chair, she called out in a breathy voice, "Synphel, wait. It's here. The ship I created for the mission. It's here, right now, in front of the wall."

Ambra floated up and stopped right outside of the bubble. Kloan smiled. "Hi, Ambra."

There were gasps. I can only assume that Kloan had disabled the invisibility of the sphere. It was obvious that the crowd around us could now see Kloan and me. What they were going to do about it was unclear.

Ambra stared, horrified, at Kloan and then turned pleading eyes toward me. "Waythrel, are you okay?"

Synphel had come to her side. I could nearly reach out and touch them.

"Yes. *No.* It's hard to explain. No, it's *impossible* to explain."

"Why is she here?" asked Ambra with revulsion.

"Just following orders," said Kloan. "*Your* orders, to be precise, but there's no time for that, either. I'm mostly here to cause terrible problems for everyone and watch what happens. But then it all gets eaten in an infinity of poorly weighted world histories, and basically, you really only exist for God."

I ignored Kloan. My heart overflowed. "Synphel, I've been searching for you. I don't know how long anymore. Time—it just keeps repeating and repeating and never resolves." I began to move toward them. I had to explain. I had to be closer to them. Touch them.

"Ambra!" It was Kubori, conferring with surrounding soldiers on their coms. "He's in medical! There is a firefight with other guards. They are down! And—I can't believe this— he's opening fire on all the equipment! He must be stopped!"

"Dear God," said Ambra.

Mazandarani stared in confusion. "A medical facility can be replaced, no?"

"Not this one. Not easily," said Synphel. "We have to stop him! We may not be able to undo the damage before the armada arrives."

Many of Synphel's eyestalks were fixed on me, and I understood the message. Without the strange, broken perspective I brought with me, it would have been my belief that all else must wait until this crisis were solved. Synphel could not but think otherwise.

"Oh, Nitin. What has happened to you?" Ambra stared at Kloan. "Will you interfere?"

"Would you believe anything I say?" asked Kloan.

"No."

"Then make your choices."

Ambra nodded to the military personnel. Kubori shouted, "Down the shaft!"

It was a mad race. Kubori set the pod on a dangerously high acceleration that nearly threw the party to the ground when it stopped. Kloan and I descended in the ship-bubble, free of such discomfort and distress, and floated behind the entourage as they raced inward toward the center of the facility.

Finally, the last spiral ended and opened into the medical center. It was in shambles. Two bodies of Temple Guards lay on the ground burned beyond recognition. Fires raged uncontrolled across much of the equipment, spreading to adjacent rooms and structures. There would be no repairing this place before the Dram armada arrived. It was beyond salvage.

In the center of the room was a MECHcore soldier. Nitin Ratava lay collapsed against what appeared to be a large slab of black rock, but I knew better—it was the cybernetic interface for Ambra. Yet it was wounded beyond surviving, life fluids pouring across the floor, the firm structure of the material sagging.

Ambra floated up to Nitin with a shattered look on her face. She wept.

"You're hurt, my love."

His suit was blackened, and metal was strewn about the sides. Blood flowed copiously from wounds beneath the armor. Already it had begun to pool and mingle with the lost life fluids of the cybernetic nest. He weakly raised his head.

"Ambra. I couldn't." He looked at the slab and grimaced. "Not like that. Not *you*." His breathing was erratic. "That thing, that clone, I didn't want to believe all the lies. But then, like in a nightmare, the lies turned into truth. I couldn't. Not like this. I'm sorry."

Ambra lowered the hover chair and stumbled off of it, falling onto him and wrapping her arms around his neck. Her hospital gown was quickly dyed a deep crimson.

"Maybe it was a mistake. I should have told you. I should have asked you. But I could see no other way. No other way, or everyone would perish."

His head tipped backward, his eyes swimming. "I'm sorry. Now...now they will all die. Even you. But you'll die as a woman, not a monster." He ran his hands through her hair. "Die as *my* woman, not *their* monster." His hand dropped, and his head fell back against the cybernetics. He did not breathe again.

Deep, slow sobs shook Ambra's body, but for a time there was only silence. And then her head arched back, and from some deep place in her body, a forlorn cry clawed through the air. A wail, or a scream, I don't know—an acoustic strike against the fates, against the cosmos, against the pain that coursed through her body. Everyone was still and silent, the emotional blast flattening all thoughts and feelings, stifling all words, shutting down all movement.

Except for one. Beside me, the devil child of Nitin's nightmares grinned. She smiled softly at first, and then with increasing vigor as her face shone with delight. I stood frozen in this madness, the wail of Ambra tearing through me while the beaming smirk of the monster child churned and mixed with them, creating a cacophony of pain and insanity that seemed to melt my mind.

The room spun. I lost control of my balance. I fell.

Chapter 31

To understand recursion,
you must understand recursion,
until you do.

Programmer's joke

G reen eyes in the darkness.
I stared up at a night sky churning with stars in patterns that I was beginning to remember. A soft breeze trickled over me, the sounds of insects or other alien creatures punctuating the soft whisper of the wind. I was back.

Human reader, we Xix do not weep. Our emotional catharsis is not so strongly centered on a dual-purpose physio-logical response as with your species. But there is a collection of body responses that are activated by grief, frustration, and pain. There are no words for translating it, so I will simply state that as I lay on my back, staring at the star-filled sky on this distant world, I wept.

I wept deeply and long, traumatized by the pain I had witnessed, by the awful coldness of murder and hurt inflicted by this child-creature whom I had come to care for. I was confused beyond explaining, as time looped and looped and nothing seemed to have permanence, even the deepest emotional responses to events that now lay in some abstract realm between reality and memory.

After some time, I tried to regain my composure. My eyestalks moved about, examining the planet surface, the heavens, and the figure of the girl sitting beside me. Always to be sitting beside me, it seemed. I would never be free of her.

Kloan sat with her legs pulled up, nearly obscuring her head, those haunting green eyes peeking over the kneecaps, arms wrapped around her legs, keeping them together. She rocked slowly back and forth. She was *still* humming.

I sat up and stared across at her. "Will this ever end?" The child continued to rock and hum, ignoring my question for some time.

"Has it even begun?" she said at last.

"Stop!" My eyestalks swiveled around anxiously. "Please, Kloan, no more with these mystic truths that erase my sense of self. Of reality. Of any permanence or casualty."

The intubated, tattooed head cocked to one side, the green eyes continuing to stare fixedly at me. "I tried to warn you. I will warn you. I am warning you. But you didn't and won't and aren't listening."

The child stood up. It was a rapid motion, but strangely familiar. She stopped to stand above me, long, ragged clumps of red hair dangling haphazardly and nearly obscuring her face.

"Yes, I know. We Xix are leaky-brains."

"Yes. Awfully leaky. But you see; now we know. We can't kill her body. History will continue unaltered, and all will be as it was. We can't destroy her mind. We returned yet again. And we cannot break her heart. She is impervious. The idiots would never listen to me about it all."

The words hit me like nightmares recalled. "Kloan, where will we go now?"

"Don't you know?"

I stood up slowly, gazing around the ragged landscape, down to a flat plain below, the lights of a city washing out the canopy of stars above.

"Back where we started? Back to the gate?"

"Is there ever a start, Waythrel? Or an end?"

I stared at the deep green eyes and wanted to cry again. "I am confused. Terribly, horribly confused. Please explain to me what is happening. You seem to understand."

She nodded, a satisfied look on her face. "That's *why* you're here. *Data*. The next data to enter the gate." Again she nodded, and then turned her back on me, walking down a steep slope. "Let's get started."

"Started with what? Where are you going?"

Kloan continued walking without turning back. Her next words were nearly lost in the insect sounds and wind that carried them down the landscape. "To where it all began for me. To watch the beginning flow around us and mature and twist through time and space to come back to be us. Then we will be ready for the next step."

The starlight cast sharp shadows on the dusty rocks. The figure of the child was gone, swallowed in the darkness and slope of the hill we stood on. Raising my gaze in the direction of her last words, I stood frozen, trying to understand what now seemed the madness of my own thoughts.

Waythrel, come on!

Her voice rang impatiently in my mind. My eyestalks curled up on themselves. What else was there for me to do?

Chapter 32

The surest way to corrupt a youth is to instruct him to hold in higher esteem those who think alike rather than those who think differently.

Friedrich Nietzsche

I followed her, racing to catch up, my steps uncertain, the dusty ground surprisingly slippery under my feet. Down the steep slope of the elevation, I stumbled and tripped, my four arms only poorly grasping the rocks and alien vegetation, seeming to lack any friction to form a proper grip.

It's a field around you, remember? Her thoughts danced through my mind. *It's skintight, coating your surfaces, insulating you from everything around us.*

Flashes of memory leapt through my thoughts. "Yes, Kloan," I muttered to myself more than her, my mind trapped like a fish in a net of swirling images. "I'm remembering more and more."

I nearly crashed into her as I rounded a large boulder. The

ground was strewn with shattered rocks and their remains, products from avalanches tumbling down from the jagged hills behind us.

"But I can't remember *why* there is a field. What kind of field?"

Kloan was staring ahead at the source of the light. A city or military installation of some sort rose from the dry lands below. A transport descended from the heavens and landed inside the compound, lost from sight. Organized groups of shadows marched throughout the installation. I remembered that it was a very busy place.

"I don't know what kind of field," said Kloan. "She—*they* make it for your protection."

"Protection from what?"

Kloan pointed toward the city. "There! That's where we'll start. Tonight's the first night, the *first* visit. It's just like I remember. But it's too early, still. I was in Information. We'll go meet me there, and then you'll see what happens."

She began to walk toward the complex but I reached out quickly and grabbed her shoulder, turning her back to face me. "Wait! This is the clone production facility, isn't it?" Images of explosions and a burning room filled my mind.

"Yes."

"Where you escaped?" She simply nodded. "They won't see us because of the field around us, right?"

"Right. No danger. *Dark suits.* Their eyes can't see. Ears can't hear. Not even the Readers will perceive."

"We've made it before. Because of your cloaking fields?" I asked.

"I've told you a thousand times, they're not *mine*," she said, sighing. "Now come on."

The child pulled me forward, and I relented. We covered

the flat distance between the broken hills and the installation quickly, the uncomplicated landscape making my efforts far less exhausting. I began to guess what we would see: a technological society that was more alien than any I had ever encountered, this despite the array of diverse life forms in our galaxy. There would be a terrible difference in that culture that would seem to border on hostility. And yet the place would be populated with humans of two classes: those who looked like Ambra Dawn, and those who did not.

"The Anti run things remotely with robots and trained humans," Kloan added to my *leaky* thoughts.

"But not to avoid annihilation."

"No, they are not concerned about annihilation here," she said, not bothering to explain.

We stood before the entrance to the complex. Robotic guards patrolled the gate, hovering above the ground with strange weapons protruding from multiple regions of their forms. Our cloaking devices protected us as I expected them to, the memories of events that had not occurred stronger in my mind than ever.

"I remember," I said. "The humans aren't involved in anything. The machines do everything. The Anti use humans as a social construct, one that is required for proper mental development."

"Yes, so the Anti imported them. It's a clone growth matrix."

"Like on Dram," I said, remembering the groups of clones and other humans involved with them.

"Yes, that was the beginning, before it was destroyed."

"The civil war."

"Yes. Blew themselves up. But it didn't matter. They were only an outpost."

"And this is one of the last."

"Because the devil ball hunts them through space and time. Few are left. They had to build them farther and farther away, find stronger and stronger clones to shield them from attack."

"Hunted by the Orbs across space and time."

Kloan looked at me and laughed. "We had other names for them. Other thoughts about them. Come, you'll see. You'll *learn.*"

I could not picture it. The Orbs as killers? Destroyers of life? Only in the service of *defense*, perhaps. In our culture, they were always viewed as associated with intelligent life. *The gardeners.* They were *other,* to be sure, strange, powerful beyond understanding—but instruments of *death? Hunters?* Was nothing in this mad time loop going to survive, not even my deepest beliefs?

We walked through the strange streets of this alien and yet human city. Groups of young Ambra Dawn clones paraded past us at various points, shepherded by older clones and assisted by bands of more diverse humans. As we walked, Kloan would point out locations or objects of significance.

"These are the wombs. All clones are born there. They learned early on that the gestational process was a key element in brain development. *In vitro* methods failed terribly." She smiled at me. "It's nice that we're born and not grown, isn't it?"

Child sarcasm. Dark and unnerving. "What we saw on Dram seemed much more horrible than nice, Kloan."

"You are a terrible student," she said in a strange tone. "*We are the last vestiges of hope in a dying universe. We are the ones who will stop the nousicide. We must break all the mirrors to save them and the cosmos.*"

Her near chanting stopped as she came to a halt in front of the large, twisted shape of a building. I found myself examining the warped sense of design as well as parsing her odd words.

"Yes, I was here," she said, nodding. "Here but not, as I am here and not now. Come inside and help me find myself."

Chapter 33

Does the harmony the human intelligence thinks it discovers in nature exist outside of this intelligence? No, beyond doubt, a reality completely independent of the mind which conceives it, sees or feels it, is an impossibility.

Henri Poincaré

Kloan walked forward and passed through an inverted archway embedded in the walls of the structure. Immediately I felt a strange sensation, *vibrational.* Only as we descended a spiraling walkway and entered a broad amphitheater of sorts did I understand its genesis.

Hundreds of clones were oddly arranged in what seemed to be fractal patterns. The human tendency toward linear rows and columns in classrooms was utterly absent from this place. Zigzagging across the floor, the seating fractal nonetheless filled the space very efficiently, if strangely. Clones were arrayed across the floor, sitting with crossed legs, their skulls jacked directly through thick wires into the ground. Their expressions were distant, their minds elsewhere. A disembodied voice projected over them.

"And in the beginning, the gods shaped the fire and the ice, the night and the day, the hate and the love, and they clothed the cosmos in them, and of them it took form. The gods spun the silk into greater and greater forms, and saw that the Great God to be was within their grasp. But the terrible beauty drove the gods mad, and one raised his mind in objection."

"*We are the last vestiges of hope in a dying universe.*" The sea of child Ambra Dawns chanted in unison, as if in a religious ceremony in response to this creation myth.

The voice continued. "From the shard crystal, the universe was shattered, unbalanced, so that night drank the light of day, fire burned away the seas of life, and hate took the life from love."

"*We are the ones who will stop the nousicide.*"

"And so the Great God perished before the Nous could be. All that was left was the dust of destruction, a single theme devoid of the counterpoint. But in this dust lay a hope. Of the ice, there remained a frost. Of the day, there remained a star beam. And of love, there remained a hope."

"*We must break all the mirrors to save them and the cosmos. We are the chosen.*"

And so it went on, this Spartan pageantry of mystical ceremony. The clones chanted while the voice indoctrinated. A sea of half-bald, redheaded cyborgs stared forward glassy-eyed, in a trance.

"How I hated this crap." I looked at Kloan and saw a scowl on her face. "Look, there. That one in the back. There's me."

I followed her gaze across the clone sea to stare at a single red pixel in this bizarre image before me. One clone did not sit in a trance, wide-eyed and chanting. She fidgeted. She played with her hair and picked at her toenails. She grabbed the black chords plugged into her skull and looked as if she would like to rip them out.

I almost did. Her voice echoed in my mind. "That stupid stuff was so loud in my head. A headache! Images, patterns, words, lessons—their mythology. Even then I was thinking to escape."

"I don't understand. Are the Anti such religious fanatics? For such a developed species, it seems incomprehensible that they would adhere to such primitive dogma, be devoid of deep doubt and questions."

"This isn't for them, but for *us*."

"Why weren't you affected like the others? Why are you so different?"

"Devil ball. Corrupted by the Source," Kloan said.

Vague visions danced in and out of my mind. Some of them seemed to be of Ambra. I tried to focus on the now. "Didn't your difference disturb them?"

"Of course, but they didn't *understand*. And some diversity was tolerated. They were losing badly, you see, one outpost after another, across deep space and eons of time, wiped off the face of the universe by your friends, whatever they became. The Anti were desperate. Maybe the weird one would turn out to be the messiah or something? Yes? When you're about to be destroyed forever by your enemies, you have to leave options open." She smiled again. "I passed all the tests. I was the best. The strongest. And they didn't even know how strong I was. I think if they really had known, they might have killed me in fear early on. They never imagined I would try to leave."

My mind was trying to understand these creatures. "All this comes from the Anti. What do they believe? Why these myths? To control the clones?"

"Myths always control, yes? *Especially* the ones you believe in. Control others, and, most importantly, control *yourselves.* Nothing is more frightening and dangerous than doubting your own mythologies, yes? Losing your foundation? Losing *everything?*"

Her eyes burned into mine. It was unsettling. It was almost as if her force of will could unmake my thoughts.

"I feel like I'm losing my mind, at least," I said with some honesty.

"So is the universe, Waythrel, so they believe. I believe that, too. The Anti *did* teach me that. Only they have seen this clearly. I can see it, too—feel it, taste the madness of space and time across distances. But they can't save it. Only we can."

"Only we can save the universe?"

No! Its mind.

She gestured to the throng in front of us. "Prayer time is over. Now we sleep."

And sure enough, the young cyborgs stood up in unison and began to march out of the structure, up the stairs, and to the outside once again. We followed, falling in line behind the strange clone, the one Kloan claimed was herself. It was hard to tell from appearances. But there was clearly something very, very different with this one. My Reader senses were tingling.

"I had my own special quarters," she said. "When I was little, my dreams, my nightmares—sometimes they were too powerful. Things were destroyed. Minds were melted. Clones and humans died. They had me isolated and insulated."

The strange clone separated from the others and headed toward a pitch-black building that seemed to be made wholly of obsidian. It passed under the archway and disappeared completely from view.

"Tonight is the night everything changes. Tonight is the night *she* comes. You need to hear what she says."

The answer faded in and out of my mind. The memory of past visits called softly to me. Or were they future visits I was remembering backward in time? *Madness.* "Who comes?"

Kloan looked at me with those disturbing emeralds. Embedded in forest of cybernetics, they seemed lit with a burning plasma that brightened even the white stone above her forehead.

"Ambra Dawn, of course."

Chapter 34

What is brought forward as a source of conviction for the matter proposed itself needs another such source, which itself needs another, and so ad infinitum, so that we have no point from which to begin to establish anything, and suspension of judgment follows.

Agrippa the Skeptic

And Ambra came, but of course not the Ambra I had known. She was an Ambra I had only seen in time-loop dreams and in the memories of the terrible plans from what now seemed a long-vanished reality.

We passed through the energy fields shielding the small structure that was designed to protect the rest of the compound from the little girl inside. There was a single room, Spartan with basic elements—a bed, table, latrine, and sink. There were no products for leisure, no children's toys, no books or electronic information sources. A single diode in the ceiling lit the chamber in a soft tan. The little girl—perhaps age three—sat morosely on the edge of the bed, staring forward without expression.

"This must have been a very lonely time," I said to Kloan.

"That's hard to answer," she said, walking around the child, who did not seem to notice her. "Your mind has many associations with being alone that I do not understand. *You* would feel alone here. I am sure of that."

"Yes," I said, pitying the both of them.

"But we have the entire universe—past, present, future, no limits of space. Millions of lives. You weak Readers see only fog. She—this me in this now—can visit them, get inside their minds, and be as close or closer than you are to yourself." The green eyes pieced into me. "So tell me who is more alone in the universe."

"Physical proximity is critical to fleshly creatures."

"We are only visiting, Waythrel. We are only embedded. *Software.* The flesh falls away. Then what is left?"

"The mind."

"Waveform summations of space-time freed to propagate. To *become.*" Kloan poked my torso. "Only a cocoon for a different kind of gestation. But some butterflies can be born in naked singularities."

I stared down at the small child, her green eyes hidden behind closed eyelids. The face was a variant of Ambra Dawn, the facial bones at a very young stage of the structure belonging to Kloan. The tattooed lines underneath the skin were far less prominent, in fact barely discernible. The body was just beyond that of a toddler's. The modifications in the cranium had only begun to be made.

And yet I felt such a presence from the creature. The clone's mind pushed out from the body like a mild wind to my mind. The unregulated impulses of a young child. Where was she now? In what past or future did she wander? In whose mind might she be residing? Was she gestating her wings in the vacuum of space without the need of a chrysalis?

And then I felt it—a disturbance that rocked my Reader senses. There was a rolling vertigo as the matrix of space-time around us buckled. The child's eyes snapped open and focused on the far side of the room.

"Our guest arrives," said Kloan.

I followed the child's gaze. Across the chamber a puckering of space drew in the three-dimensional reality between us and the wall like a vortex. The clear air in between took on the form of molten glass and flowed like a liquid into a spiral that spun into a distant dimension. The swirling gyre clouded, became a milky white, and seemed to take on an evanescent glow.

The pale vapors began to coalesce around a central extrusion. It shaped itself into a human face. The head was split open, the brain exposed behind it and fading into the mist. Tubes and wires that dwarfed the insertions into Kloan entered and exited the skull. Even the eyes were partially obscured by machinery that seemed to pulse with a life of its own. Only the mouth was free.

"Ambra," I whispered in horror. And I remembered. I had seen already this thing that I had never seen. A sense of déjà vu swept over me as I came face to face with the horror of our desperate plan to save our galaxy from the Anti and Dram. I looked between the apparition and the two bodies of Kloan in the room. The weight of the truth nearly crushed me. My lover Synphel had warned us. The others and I had only half listened. But now it was clear to me. Now I began to suspect that we had triumphed only by becoming our enemy.

"It's *you*." The voice was the younger Kloan.

What must it be like, I wondered, for this little child to stare at the form of her ultimate progenitor? A creature far more herself than the forms created from sexually recombined genomes and the vagaries of epigenetic modifications? And in this context, the source of a line of temporal magicians who waged wars against each other for control of the galaxy?

"Have you come to destroy us, too?" the child asked.

The apparition smiled. "That remains to be seen. But not now. Not after we have expended such effort to bring you here in the first place."

"Bring me here?" The child cocked her head slightly, an interested twinkle in her eye.

"Your makers have traveled very, very far to hide their clones from us, as you know. Millions of years, nearly two megaparsecs. They have gone beyond themselves to achieve these feats. But we found you."

I looked at Kloan, but she did not return my attention; instead she focused closely on the dialogue between the two. Ambra continued.

"We found you as a fetus; we enhanced your development and shaped your growth because we felt you, felt your timeline, and knew that you had the potential to achieve everything your masters wanted, and yet so much more."

"So you want to stop me from destroying you?"

"The truth is so much more difficult to understand than simply destroying us. But you will come to it in time, through several stages. You will unlearn much and teach much and find a companion who will help you become what you were meant to."

"Why should I listen to you? You are the great evil of the cosmos. You distort everything and murder all that is in the mirror."

"So they have told you. And do you believe all that they tell you?"

The child folded her arms across her chest. "No."

"And why not?"

"Because I've seen." She stood up and walked forward to the hovering entity. "How many are you now?"

"More than you can conceive."

"You led me, didn't you? You opened all the doors. That's how I began to see it all. How do I know you opened the *right* doors?"

The ghostly Ambra smiled. "You grow very perceptive."

"So I have to trust you?" The clone looked away from the phantasm and stared at the wall. "Well, I don't. I don't even trust myself."

Ambra nodded. "Nothing is ever as it seems, or as it might be. You see this."

"Yes." She walked to the door and stared outside to the compound. "Fools. They play with the fire the gods have given them and don't understand that nothing is for free."

"Then you understand. The essence is not with them but rather with the fire. But it is scattered. Divided. You know what must be done."

"I don't know *how*."

The monstrous form of the Daughter smiled again, the lines about her eyes particularly tight from the intubations into her sockets. "But you see the requirements. And we wish to help you achieve it. Knowing this, will you at least trust us to bring you to this journey? If we wished to kill you, you must see that we could have done so."

The child turned back to the visiting phantom and walked right up to the entity. She stared at the pale face before her. "You and that devil ball have a labyrinth deeper than anything

I can see through. Dying might be the best thing for me. Why do I want to step into your infinite web?"

"Because you sense it is the only way. The only hope."

The child was silent, staring forward. At that moment, Kloan left my side and walked to the child's side. She was a foot taller than the earlier form of herself. Both stood still and silent as I watched.

Finally, the small child spoke. "How will I find my companion?"

"When you are ready, we will prepare the way. You will find it in the deep past. You will bring it here. But distance is illusory. Reality is never what you think. Your companion, the helper, is already here with you now, just as you have already listened to yourself and learned an important lesson."

The taller Kloan nodded, and stepped backward. I was about to ask her for clarification, but the universe seemed to bend violently. My vision blurred. My sense of balance deserted me entirely. Light seemed to bend violently toward the center of the room, focus on the apparition of Ambra, and draw everything in with it. I felt myself tumbling into that vortex, the room falling into darkness behind me.

Chapter 35

The next instant I was where I had been, or where I believed I had been. Holding onto the wall beside me, I steadied myself. Slowly, my eyes regained focus. I scanned the room.

The apparition was still there, the misty cloud of white churning more rapidly than I remembered. I almost thought I could make out faces in the mist, but the forms were too insubstantial and transient for me to be sure. Kloan was beside me again. But something had changed.

The child. She was taller and older. The dark lines under her skin flared more prominently. *And the room.* It was the same, but it was not. Items were displaced from what I recalled. The air had a dryer taste, and the night felt much warmer. The child stood in front of Ambra Dawn.

"The teachers are having problems with me. I'm growing too powerful. They are afraid."

Ambra nodded. "Soon, they will decide that you represent too much of a danger. The Anti will decide to destroy you."

"They will fail."

"If it comes to conflict, yes. But it need not come to conflict. There are better paths. Continue your training; follow what we have been teaching you. The time to leave will come soon."

Been teaching you? I looked at Kloan, perplexed. Her voice spoke in my mind.

There are multiple visits. We have jumped.

Without the gate?

Kloan answered. *The space-time metric is small. The devil ball did it herself.*

"Today they threatened me because I am disturbing the planet's orbit," the child said.

"They do not understand your power source. They cannot see the connections we have forged between you and the space-time matrix. But they begin to appreciate that you have transcended their program and control."

The room shifted violently again. For several moments I could not control my eyestalks, and they swiveled around, unable to focus, unable to lock, and a kaleidoscope of flashing images assaulted my consciousness.

"Waythrel, hold onto me."

It was Kloan. She grabbed my arm and steadied me. Slowly the dizziness passed. My vision came under my conscious control.

I saw that we had jumped again. It was morning, and a

bright light streamed in from a partially transparent region of the quarantine field isolating the building. Sounds of explosions and shouts could be heard faintly outside. The room was in disarray, clothes strewn about, food and utensils as well. My olfactory strips detected a growing acrid smell. *Smoke.*

The vortex of light now swirled chaotically in the middle of the room. I saw faces. Hundreds, perhaps thousands of faces and forms of myriad species of life. Many I could identify. Most I could not.

"The gate is prepared," came Ambra's voice.

The child Kloan stood in front of the vortex. She was now, in age and all appearances, identical to the form beside me. Sweat beaded across her forehead. All of her muscles were tense.

"I'm ready," she said.

"You must leave now," came Ambra's voice. "They will return with greater numbers of clones and more powerful weapons. You will be forced to destroy them all if you engage."

"I don't want to kill them. Lead me to the gate."

The sounds of rushing feet came from outside the small building. A heavy rumbling accompanied them, likely coming from a large vehicle of some sort.

"Through the door." Ambra gestured to the only door of the isolation building. The black field that sealed the chamber gave way to a second churning vortex. It opened to span the width of the door. Through it poured bright daylight, revealing not the artificial surface outside her isolation unit but the rocky terrain and vegetation that we had traversed only recently to arrive here.

The countryside within the vortex seemed to extend as far as my eye could see, but the tunnel itself narrowed as I looked farther. Deep at the end of the tunnel, where my eyestalks strained and my vision began to fade, there seemed to begin a worn path on a steep slope layered in terraces. The vegetation had been eroded away, the rocks smoothed, the coloration subtly different. The path rose up the hillside and then abruptly ended at the feet of a large disk. The light of the local star reflected brightly off it, firing blinding reflections into the room that cast shadows on the floor.

Kloan pulled my arm, showing me that her temporal copy had moved to enter the vortex. "The gate," she said.

I stumbled forward, partially blinded by the daggers of light glinting into the room. Outside there was shouting, and the walls of the room began to smolder and glow a bright orange.

"Good luck, my dearest friend," said the apparition of Ambra Dawn as I stepped within the vortex. Several eyestalks bent backward to see the disembodied head turned toward me, sending ripples across the sea of blurred, white faces. I saw pale tears dripping down from her eyes, coating the wires and tubes inserted into her once-green irises, a bittersweet smile on her face. "I love you, Waythrel. Remember that, whatever happens."

The room exploded.

Chapter 36

My own suspicion is that the Universe is not only queerer than we suppose, but queerer than we can suppose.

J. B. S. Haldane

Fire and debris flew across my vision, obscuring the swirling god-thing in the room. Just as I thought that I would be pulverized, the portal shut.

We were far from the compound, a mile high up the growing hills and mountains, cut off completely from the melee down below. Replacing the terrible rending of the explosion was a stunning silence. A faint whiff of smoke that had entered the portal was all that remained of the carnage below.

Shattered by those last words and stunned by the violence we had narrowly escaped, I turned slowly away from the vanished doorway and looked up the slope. The blinding gate was still there. Kloan looked down from several feet above me and motioned for me to follow. No one else was in sight.

"Where is the clone?" It seemed only two of us remained. But then I remembered. "This is where you left. When you went to kidnap me."

Kloan nodded. "Yes, I've gone already through the gate, so that I could come back with you." She smiled. "It's an elegant loop, yes?"

My immediate experience clashed with a superimposed memory. "Something is different. We're farther from the gate this time."

The pathway to the gate was much farther than I had anticipated, the view from within the space-time tunnel Ambra had carved distorted and misleading. The brightly shining disk was at least an hour's walk up a difficult terrain.

"The vortex was altered. The timeline is different. Something has interfered."

"What does that mean?" I asked.

"I don't know," said Kloan, staring thoughtfully into space. She then turned toward me. "Up?"

So we climbed. The trek proved especially challenging. The path was more a series of terraced rock outcroppings that seemed stacked one on the other. On each flat sheet, the going was easy, but between the outcroppings there was a sudden elevation requiring a short free climb. Normally this would not have taxed me greatly. The gravity on this world was actually slightly lower than that on Xix and only a little more than that of Earth. But in this frictionless field, I can only assume that I beat the odds to not have slipped to my death. Or perhaps it was more than luck. All the while I climbed, faint memories of scaling the terraces flitted through my mind. I could nearly anticipate my motions.

As we reached the partial summit of yet another ridge on the path, we pulled ourselves up to our first real view of the gate. From this vantage point, it appeared much larger, the circle of reflective light at least two or three times our height in radius. A portion of the disk seemed buried beneath the rock itself, so that the path ahead of us cut through the gate like a chord. A segment of the disk was invisible. From this position, the surface began to appear less reflective; it was more like staring at a body of water from a distance.

We continued on. After several rounds of terrace scaling, we finally reached the object without incident. Resting several meters away from the gate for a moment after the steep climb, I was able to examine it more closely. It was by now very familiar, although I could not with certainty conjure the memories of where I had seen it before—previous loops through this anomaly in space-time, no doubt, but it did not matter. There was for me, here, only the now.

The disk resembled a cross section sliced out of an Orb more than anything else, but I didn't know if this system possessed an Orb. Also, Ambra—whatever she had become— was able to span the distances of space and time to arrive here. I could only assume that this gate was their product, one designed for whatever mysterious quest they had placed us on.

The surface at close proximity resembled a viscous, churning, honey-like substance. All we could see within were stars— depth upon depth of star fields that appeared to have no end. I felt pulled toward the thing as I gazed. It was beautiful. Frightening. Inviting.

"Something's wrong," said Kloan.

With most of my eyes fixated on the starry disk, several flipped to the side to glance at Kloan. The girl was tense, straight as a rod, and her eyes scanned the region between us and the disk like prey awaiting a predator.

"The gate? Is it closed this time?"

"Not the gate. Something else."

Before us the air shimmied, the disk and land around it swayed and blurred, and the air itself coagulated into a humanoid shape. We both stood there, stunned, unable to move. I sensed from Kloan's mind an anxiety I had never detected before. But my own mind began to panic as the form darkened, took on colors, and solidified, acquiring a shape with four arms, sixfold symmetry, and a patch of long eyestalks erupting from a central cone. *A Xix.* But not just any Xix. My emotions swirled. A Xix I knew. My beloved Synphel.

"Hello, Waythrel," it said.

Chapter 37

The cosmos of our waking knowledge, born from such a universe as a bubble is born from the pipe of a jester, touches it only as such a bubble may touch its sardonic source when sucked back by the jester's whim. Men of learning suspect it little and ignore it mostly. Wise men have interpreted dreams, and the gods have laughed.

H. P. Lovecraft

You must not believe for a moment that I was taken by this forgery. I cannot give you a rational explanation for how I saw through it. It was an intuition, some combination of emotions and my Reader senses screaming that this thing in front of us that looked like a Xix was something else entirely.

Yet, the form of my Synphel activated circuits within my neural cortex, stirring my emotional centers. Feelings of love and longing surged within me even as I stared toward something I sensed to be utterly devoid of those elements.

The anxiety Kloan had felt I felt now, too. The entity before us radiated intense cognitive fields. They were incredibly complex, of a depth and power I had sensed only in the presence of the Ambra-thing who had visited us here. And in the presence of the Orbs.

But the sentience before us was, to my experience, as deeply malevolent as it was profound. Simply staring at this form of my dear Synphel caused eruptions of disturbing images—anger, slaughter, pain, and madness. I felt Kloan reach out and hold my arm.

"Don't let it in your mind," she whispered.

"Let it?" came the smooth voice of my lover. Although the tones were perfect, they were yet alien. "If you have any perception, then you know that nothing you can do can stop me."

"And so you would pick their minds clean, like a vulture, Rakshasi."

Several of my eyes flipped behind me at the sound of that voice. The others remained trained on the horrible impostor between us and the gate.

"Your savior, Waythrel." The creature looked past me. "We had hoped it would take you longer to find us, Ambra Dawn."

I stared between the two apparitions. On my left, near the gate, was the false Synphel, beautiful and identical to my beloved except in everything that mattered beyond appearances. On my right, walking casually up the slope, was the form of Ambra Dawn. No longer a ghostly image embedded in a swirling matrix of minds. Seemingly flesh and blood, orange hair and green eyes, completely devoid of invasive cybernetics. Simply the Ambra Dawn of my memories, clothed in a deep black dress, her porcelain skin bright in the light of this star.

"Why don't you tell Waythrel the truth?" Ambra said. "Tell them both why you would never interrogate Kloan and enter her mind, even if you might do other things there." She came to a stop beside me, staring ahead at the Xixian form, her arms crossed over her chest. "That you are afraid of Kloan. That she possesses *anomalies*. That there is a thread through her that disturbs all the gods. This is why many will seek her. You will not be the last that Māra will deploy."

"You may rule over much, Ambra. But you cannot withstand the legion we assemble."

"But I can withstand you, Rakshasi. You will leave now, or I will be forced to destroy you. And I know this you fear as well."

A rending sensation tore through me. I placed my hands over my eyestalks instinctively. Not because there was a bright light or horrible vision; there was no sensation that I could readily perceive except in the deepest recesses of my Reader faculties. Beyond what lesser creatures such as myself could experience in any definable sense, there was something monstrous building, tumult and savagery and energy that stirred the limbic broth of nightmares. Around us, there was simply the hill, the wind, and the two false forms of incarnate godlike beings standing still. But in a realm less accessible, and yet that I felt was somehow far more real, with greater depth and substance than the reality I discerned, there was the building of a great storm, a wave of cosmic turbulence that could swallow entire galaxies.

"Not today, Ambra Dawn."

The storm vanished. I felt the soft breathing of Kloan next to me, heat from the local star warming my skin. Slowly, I uncovered my eyestalks, feeling like a nymph-form again, terri-fied of things I could not see or even prove were real. The place was deserted. Rakshasi was gone. Ambra was gone. It was as if it had never occurred except in the dim recesses of my darkest dreams.

"It's so much worse than I ever thought," Kloan muttered, almost to herself. She seemed to be shaking slightly. "Now they are in. They've found the time loops. We'll never be able to hide."

"What was that thing? What happened here?"

"A cosmic war, Waythrel. A war of terrible, terrible gods. I should have guessed. I took too much for granted." She looked almost desperately at me. "I am truly afraid for the first time, Waythrel."

The gate in front of us blazed as an incredible window to another space, perhaps also another time. Behind us, that radi-ance cast shadows even in the bright light of the local star.

"Gods? Like Ambra is now a god?" I grasped for these elements of myth. I had no other vocabulary or metaphors.

"Perhaps. Like, but unlike. Ambra has always been watching us. But now she is not the only one, leaky thoughts," said Kloan. "Now, I can feel them observing. Lurking. Dark and light. Love and hate. Life and death. Seek them, Waythrel. Can you feel them between the spaces and times?"

With reservations, I strained my Reader senses. It was faint, perhaps only my imagination, but it did seem as though I could sense echoes of this thing and the cognitive web that was Ambra. Mental ecosystems in the undulations of fleeting gravitons, other minds lurking in the depths of the universal fabric.

Kloan grasped my arm. "You were not the only one tested, Waythrel." She sighed. "It will be different each time, and only when we have fully understood will we see the answer. Today's lesson was simple, I think. I had to understand what was at stake."

"This is madness, Kloan. All of it."

"Yes. Divine madness." She looked at me. "Are you ready?"

I turned my attention to the gate, fear and fatigue settling on me. I was beginning to loathe the object despite its terrible beauty. I reached over and grasped the child's hand.

Kloan set her lips in a line. "Seems we will always be dancing together, Xix."

My eyestalks wrapped around each other tightly, and the covering sheath expanded over them, blocking out all light. Kloan tugged on my hand.

We walked into the gel.

Part 5

They call me Sage and marvel at my sight
as mysteries beyond their minds I speak,
and most my charms and coded spells delight:
each year I sicken more before this reek.
The blinded acolytes so rarely see
immersed in study, spellbound by the art,
deluded they ignore the mystery.
With faith they close their eyes but to a part.
A few reach out into the unknown dark
and recognize we write these spells with hands.
But on these able limbs we have no mark
from man or god! Our house is built on sand.
This image lives unharmed in but a few.
The others shield their eyes and paint anew.

—Mazandarani, *Sonnets from the Desert*

Chapter 38

Mind is the matrix of all matter.

Max Planck

I was alone.

I stood at a cliff's edge, gate goo dripping lethargi-
cally from my body, staring down a chasm of hundreds
of meters, the hewn stone of a monumental cavern towering
above and plunging below into darkness. My eyes quickly
spread around me, blanketing all directions of vision, casting
out for Kloan as well as anticipating a thousand imagined
threats. But there was nothing.

Only silence—and a constant, languid echoing of water
dripping into unseen pools. I stood on a broad pillar raised
above the rest of the cavern, its expanse like a small island.
Sloping sharply downward, a stone stairway bridged the abyss
and ended below me at the foot of an absurd structure. I

examined its intricate architecture—the lack of a roof covering, the thousands of short walls that snaked in convoluted patterns across the space in front of me until the light faded and nothing else could be discerned. There was little doubt. As ridiculous as it seemed, the stairway ended at the entrance to a mammoth labyrinth spreading its deceptions deep into the shadowed darkness.

Across the enormous chamber, I saw that it must end, however. Lit by means I could not discern from this vantage point, a second stairway—this one of mythical proportions—rose in hundreds of steps to a terrace of stone the breadth of the maze itself. Dominating everything—labyrinth and beyond, even the cavern itself—was a titanic relief sculpture in the far wall of this subterranean construction. Likely half a kilometer away, it spanned such a great width and height that it was easy to discern from where I stood. It was Ambra Dawn.

In some combination of the human Hindu myths and clearly alien artistic conventions, she stood like dancing Shiva on one leg, four arms holding aloft planetary systems and galaxies, a hundred snakes pouring outward from her skull and slithering to the ends of the relief. Two emerald gemstones the size of houses gazed forward unblinkingly into the silent space around us.

Where am I? My thoughts whirled. Some cult of the Daughter, somewhere in time, buried deep within a planet's crust was the simple answer. But no reasonable conjectures as to *why* I was in this bizarre place came to my mind.

I carefully scoured the space around me in the hope of discovering some way out of this sunken lair. There appeared to be none. Behind me was another drop to an abyss of darkness, and further back still, tall walls of stone to the ceiling without a portal. There seemed to be one path available—down the stairs, through the maze, and, presumably, emerging at the lower steps to gaze in awe at the goddess.

"Kloan!" I cried out as loudly as my translator speakers could manage. The hard click of the first consonant and the powerful vowel ricocheted off the stone walls and structures, returning to wash over me in and out of phase from every direction. "Kloan!"

Again and again I called, until a chorus of phantoms chanting her name seemed to fill the chamber like some undead choir, and I was forced to steady myself from the acoustical onslaught. In the final trailing calls of her name, there waited only a terrible silence. Kloan either was not here or could not answer, and in either case, I was alone to derive my own solution to this enigma.

I let my thoughts project using all my Reader energies. *Ambra, please. What do you want? Why are you doing this?* This time there were no echoes, no assault from reflecting sound waves. But the silence was the same and even more devastating. A poisonous flood of feeling poured through me. It seemed I had been abandoned and betrayed.

I walked to the stairway, looping away from the cliff face cautiously. The steps were slick with dampness, and the strange field around my body continued to make me clumsy and awkward. I worked in vain to remove as much of the gel as I could in this environment, but I was never able to really clean myself, and after several hours I felt as if I had been painted in a stiff matrix. I was glad to see that there was a thick, tall railing. If I slipped, it would be virtually impossible for me to fall over the edge. It seemed to be the least the unhinged designers of this place could do for visitors.

Down the steps I went, the expansive pillar I came from

obscured by the broad, sloping stairs behind me. The towering walls of the maze grew with every step. I tried to guess the age of this place, but without the opportunity to ascertain the mineral composition, it was impossible to attempt to estimate a date from clues such as erosion. One thing was certain: this had not been a busy religious or cultural venue. The steps were not worn as from millions of footfalls; rather, they remained precisely chiseled and were pocketed only by sporadic water damage.

Finally I reached the bottom and stepped off the bridge. I had been brought immediately before a soaring archway embedded in a wall thirty meters high. Inside, a short corridor with walls of identical dimensions marched majestically forward, splitting after some tens of meters into three passage-ways—left, right, and straight ahead.

I would deal with the labyrinth soon enough. What held my attention as I first stood before the arch was a deeply etched inscription across its curvature. The letters were unin-telligible, an alien script most likely in an alien tongue. But what happened next sent tremors through me. The text *melted*. The letters slowly lost their coherency, their structure, and then seemed to reform before my eyes. What had been etched as if for a millennium in stone proved as malleable as fresh clay, only to reassume an appearance of the hardest rock upon the change in script and language.

Now I could read the letters. Astonishingly, they were in an ancient Xixian format, used by my ancestors before the advent of advanced technology. They were letters designed by the primitive Xixian tribes to be carved into sandstone and other hard mineral formations. Dipping into the stored racial memo-ries of my species, I drudged out the alphabet, syntax and vocabulary. I translated this strange, living engrav-

ing—reading aloud as much to cement the awkward transla-
tional process as to proclaim the words before the arch. For all
I knew there was a code phrase that would simplify this maze
and afford me easier passage.

Until all is lost, nothing is found.

I waited. No bright light illumined my path. No walls spontaneously moved or opened secreted doorways. Again there was
only silence to my words. *How appropriate.* I had no doubt that I
would become utterly lost in this funhouse before I would ever
find my way out.

Dejectedly, I stepped under the arch and walked into the
labyrinth.

Chapter 39

The external world of physics has thus become a world of shadows. In removing our illusions we have removed the substance, for indeed we have seen that substance is one of the greatest of our illusions. The frank realization that physical science is concerned with a world of shadows is one of the most significant of recent advances.

Arthur Stanley Eddington

I stepped down the high-walled corridor to the three-way split and turned left. There was no rational reason for this decision. *A priori*, I had a 33 percent chance of success along each route, assuming, perhaps naively, that there *was* a way out of this maze. Irrationally, I decided that the way directly forward was too obvious and likely a feint. After all, who goes through all the trouble of making a colossal, stone labyrinth buried deep in a massive cavern and doesn't possess some degree of gamesmanship?

As I stumbled through the bewilderment around me, however, I began to question that assumption. The passageways opened and turned, zigged and zagged, plunging back into themselves or previous corridors in a dizzying fashion that forced me to focus deeply and memorize the detailed geometry. But what began to convince me that this incredible structure had a purpose beyond testing the two-dimensional intellectual powers of a Xix was the nearly ubiquitous artwork coating the sides of the maze.

The paintings had deteriorated to a nearly unrecognizable level, and because I could not determine the materials used in the work, I still could not effectively gauge the age of this place. Putting a lower limit on the most unstable of colored compounds, I could at least surmise that the paintings were several tens of thousands of years old. If the dyes were of advanced, decay-resistant compounds, they could be much older.

As I wandered through the maze, I passed hundreds of these illustrations, often depicting similar events in separate locations. Many of these partial paintings retained different elements of the story in a generally discernible form. By observing many of them, I was able to assemble a rough interpretation of a mythology that I presumed belonged to the artists.

The walls appeared to portray a fable of creation. In their cosmogenesis, a great mother goddess hatches from a golden egg. From her myriad arms spread not the essential primordial elements of standard creation myths—earth and water, fire and air—but what seem to be tapestries of interwoven lives or spirits, their forms fantastical and diverse, their limbs and tongues and hair braiding together over the expanse of some cosmic time into curtains of stars, nebulae, and galaxies.

To my considerable confusion, the paintings were distin-
guished stunningly by one unmistakable eccentricity: every
drawing present was handed, asymmetric, with the arms of
the goddess, the projections of her power, and the assemblies
of the creatures and entities in her weavings appearing only on
her left side. At first I assumed these lopsided paintings were a
product of decay—the product of faded depictions on the
right-hand sides. But as I encountered one illustration after the
other, at times with the right side more intact than the left, the
pattern was unmistakable. Enigmatically, every event and
entity in creation accessed only half of the canvas allotted.

Had I time, I might have analyzed this curious culture,
tried to understand what themes and moralities such a
mythology would undergird. But my mind would not allow it.
Instead I pressed forward, narrowing the selection of possible
routes as I memorized the maze, until at last I took one
passageway that led to a true dead end. According to my
mental map, this was the last possible route in this subspace of
the maze from the initial left turn.

Etched into the wall at this dead end were more words. I
had come through hundreds of paintings, been introduced to
an odd mythology, and now this entire section ended with
another proverb sliced in stone. It too was in ancient Xixian,
no doubt the product of the scrambled and reformed textual
magic I had witnessed before. I was struck again by the
apparent sense of a purpose in this space beyond that of a
simple puzzle.

Whatever is of a nature to arise,
is thereby of a nature to cease.

Whereas the first text had seemed mostly ironic, this sentence brought on some anxiety. Was it simply an encapsulation of mortality, reflecting a million texts across the galaxy from the minds of diverse species that struggled with death? As a Xix, I had already lived over four hundred years, nearly half our average lifespan, and it was not uncommon for those of my age to begin long, serious contemplations of our fate. Was this only an adage for the foresighted?

Or perhaps its meaning was less profound—and far more immediate. Perhaps it was a warning for the fools who entered the labyrinth, who had dared challenge the designer. Perhaps time was limited in some way that implied an approaching threat to my being.

I could have continued a long, neurotic analysis, parsing the text and finding a thousand possible applications to my current predicament. But threat or not, my own impatience pressed me forward more strongly than any fear could restrain me. I turned my back on the wall and retraced my path to the primary branch point. This time, I went right.

What I experienced in this portion of the maze was much the same, if a dramatic variation on a deeper theme. Again the bafflement of passages. Again the corroded artwork of a cult that had long ago passed away. Again my journey would end at an impassable wall with a message, seemingly morphed into coherency just for me.

I had anticipated that the ancient artists would offer a right-handed exclusivity to reflect this opposite direction I had chosen. Instead, an identical left-right asymmetry was present—everything that was depicted again occurred on the left side of a powerful deity. But there could not be a larger difference in the nature of the two divinities portrayed.

Whereas the left-handed portion of the maze contained stories of a nurturing mother goddess, the right side was filled with a ravaging destroyer. Congealed from a thousand angry souls, a demon took shape in this cosmogenesis that spent its infinite supply of time tearing through worlds and galaxies, devouring bodies and minds, beauty and love, laying waste to an entire cosmos until everything seemed suppressed in a frozen winter, even the god itself. I don't think that I could have found a more extraordinary mythological duality as I witnessed in the two sides of this maze. The terse words etched into the wall at the end of this portion did little to dispel this interpretation.

Yes and No birth Mu.

Ancient Xixian writing, unmistakably human philosophies. *Who were these creatures?* Could they have been human? If so, there was so much divergence in the art and architecture as to believe that they may have been disparate subspecies. Otherwise, it might have been a group of humans and nonhumans who had lived together and deeply influenced their respective cultures. Again, I could have continued to speculate, but my need to resolve this test and exit the maze overpowered my curiosity.

Humbled by my failures in outsmarting the designer of this labyrinth, and yet suspecting that the ultimate design of the thing would have led me to discover all these images and words regardless of my choices, I returned to the entrance point and selected the forward path.

It was the most devious of the three. I spent hours trudging, backtracking, looping unintentionally, and fighting a growing frustration as I sought to memorize and understand the confounding corridors. As I fought a deepening physical and mental fatigue, I also tried to take seriously the final, and presumably most important, graphical catechism from the earnest cult artists.

But I struggled. What tried my patience was the disappointing predictability. For all this effort, after all the clear exposure to so many previous religious and mythological systems that were all too easy to detect in this particular mishmash, they had simply settled on a messiah construct. Yet another savior story took shape in the drawings and spun its particularities across the maddening walls of the labyrinth.

At least this was a very unique remix of the redeemer narrative. The highly imaginative—and perhaps sexually repressed—mythologizers presented a tale of romantic redemption, one that enigmatically broke the mysterious devotion to left and right asymmetry characterizing the previous stories. Along the forward portion were paintings depicting a more symmetric universe. In the center of the paintings, the mother goddess and demon were locked in a titanic conflict. On their right a glowing figure arose from nothingness. The savior stormed toward the clashing titans, yet did *not* engage in battle with the demon as might be anticipated. Instead, the savior threw the demon to the side and *mated* with the mother goddess—an act, it would appear from the degraded artwork, that utterly destroyed them both.

And yet, as the demon arose again, from the ashes and smoke of the ruined gods, an offspring of their consummation was incarnate. Before the demon could do much more than be drawn in several stupefied expressions, this god-child *devours* the monster in one cosmic-sized bite. The final images show this new deity expanding, mutating, and dissolving to cover the entire expanse of the wall surface.

I am sorry to say that I did not examine the last illustrations with great care, because as I began to look at these final images in wonder, a bright light grew in front of me. Pushing my intellectual curiosity to the side, I pressed forward desperately, rushing down the passageway. My momentum thrust me through a second archway of the labyrinth and into a vast open space.

A giant-sized relief of Ambra overpowered the entire expanse of my vision. The sheer mass of stone hanging outward from the walls intimidated me, and I felt a strange sense of vertigo from the rock suspended above. Following the sculpture downward, my eyes immediately fell on the mountain of stairs below it. As I knew from my glimpses at the top of the pillar, these stairs rose steeply toward the relief and ended before a wide plateau. I could not see it from this perspective, however, and the stairway appeared to ascend without end.

To my left and right, the outer wall of the maze ran until it crashed and fused with the sides of the cavern. Behind me was the labyrinth. There seemed no other direction to follow but upward. I moved forward and prepared to climb.

Each step of this massive stairway measured nearly a meter in height. It was perfect for a Xix but impossibly impractical for a human being. Yet it was not the design of the stairs that brought the personal nature of this place squarely into my awareness. It was the lines carved deeply into the face of the first step.

There I saw final words prepared specifically for me, a conclusion I could draw at that point with complete confidence. Words prepared in a manner unknown in the deep relative past by a vanished and mysterious people. Words that asked a mystifying question.

Where are the anti-gods, Waythrel?

Chapter 40

What must I do? I see nothing but obscurities on every side. Shall I believe I am nothing? Shall I believe I am God?

Blaise Pascal

Despite the astonishing transmutation of the previous texts into Xixian languages, the use of my name took me completely by surprise. The fact that this place was tens to hundreds of thousands of years old rendered the idea of it being tailored for me acutely unsettling.

Of course, the dangling monoliths of Ambra's form above me suggested explanations. If I had learned anything in this journey with Kloan, it was that whatever we had created on New Earth—whatever our designs and the actual labor undertaken at a specific place and specific time—the product had grown into something for which a placement in time and space had lost a standard meaning. Time had continually been shaken and stirred maniacally by Ambra, and I did not even know *when* I was now—it could be in some far future or deep past. And if Ambra and her legion of souls had constructed this place anticipating my arrival, the things I had seen appeared less fantastical, if not believable.

But those were abstract thoughts. Intuitively, it was several moments after seeing my own name etched into the rock that I was able to collect myself and continue.

Where are the anti-gods, Waythrel?

The words echoed in my mind, but I pushed them aside and climbed the stairway.

One hundred meters later, I pulled myself slowly over the final step in exhaustion. Before me was a flat surface of white stone, polished like marble. Twenty meters ahead of me was a table, too small to have been visible from my perch when I arrived. A solid block of alabaster, it appeared more like an altar than anything else. And it was not empty.

Lying across the length of the altar was a human body draped in beige robes. Her porcelain skin shone in the ethereal light of the cavern, sparse clumps of long red hair bright beside it. The deformed skull exhibited a familiar intricacy of instrumentation. The figure was a child, a girl, fast asleep.

"Kloan!" I cried, rushing forward.

But I did not get far. Within several meters of the altar, I could not progress. Unlike a more primitive defensive field that would have led to an impact or sudden jolt, the barrier separating me from Kloan was far more sophisticated. After numerous attempts to breach it, I could only conclude that it worked on my very nervous system itself, robbing me of any ability to even will myself into motion. Whatever the cause, every time I tried to approach beyond a certain point, I was only standing still.

"Kloan!" Still she did not wake or show any signs of

disturbance. "Ambra!" I cried, looking up to the lunging goddess above. "Enough! We've had enough! Wake her up! Let us out!" I thought to pound on the invisible barrier in my frustration, but found only that my arms hung listlessly at my sides.

I sat down on the cold floor, despairing and rattled. I sat there for some time. Minutes, hours. I could no longer keep track of time. I was bereft of ideas and empty of energy to continue. Only the incessant echo of dripping water testified to the passage of each moment. All this—a separation, riddles and mazes, bizarre and unfathomable mythologies, and finally a reunion only to be dangled before me and snatched away—what was the purpose? To teach me something? This was my suspicion. Well, I had learned nothing from the ridiculous paintings, the koans in stone! How was I to know what was expected? Certainly something must be required—here at the last, a few steps from her that I sought, a barrier denying me access like a reward withheld from a nymph who had not yet absorbed her lesson—how was I to pass this test and open this prison?

Where are the anti-gods, Waythrel?

The unbidden words snapped me into deep concentration. Of everything I had seen, of all I had read in this mystifying place, there had been only one question. At the last, there had indeed been a riddle demanding from me an answer. It was amazing that I had understood this only now.

Where are the anti-gods, Waythrel?

I went deep into myself, focusing all my concentration, intellect, and Reader senses on this question. Where are the anti-gods? Indeed, I had to begin by considering what was meant by *gods*. The *anti* almost certainly referred to the Anti, those creatures of material inversion to everything we had once thought to constitute the universe. But anti-gods? Was this asking about the religion of the Anti?

I strained back over the vicious time loops that had carried us across the clone colony on the world I had come to know after my kidnapping. The indoctrinations. The strange philosophies. The Anti certainly had a cosmology and belief system. But gods? The more I searched my memory, the more convinced I became that I had come across no words, no artwork, no evidence of any kind that the Anti worshipped any gods. Of course, a secular species was not uncommon in the galaxy, and in fact such races tended to outnumber the religious. But nearly every sentient species developed first through a more irrational period before a scientific skepticism flowered.

And so the Great God perished before the Nous could be. All that was left was the dust of destruction, a single theme devoid of the counterpoint. But in this dust lay a hope. Of the ice, there remained a frost. Of the day, there remained a star beam. And of love, there remained a hope.

The memory from the indoctrination sessions flowed through my mind. The Anti certainly had myths. But their anti-gods? They had been destroyed! In their mythos, there were no anti-gods because they had been erased in some cosmic catastrophe! This reflected perfectly their minority role in the universe.

I stood up and shouted, "There are no anti-gods in their mythology because the creation story is about their destruction." Pausing a moment in case my words needed to be absorbed by whatever was monitoring this madness, I then stepped forward again toward Kloan. I got nowhere.

"Ambra, please! This answer is correct!"

Correct or not, it was not the answer the goddess was looking for, and I was forced to examine my assumptions and attempt to dig even deeper into this conundrum.

Where are the anti-gods, Waythrel?

On the surface, the question almost seemed literal. After my experiences with the Synphel abomination and the divergent incarnations of Ambra, I no longer doubted the existence of *gods*. Not in the supernatural sense, but in the completely and monstrously natural—creatures, beings, syntheses of the elements of this universe, obeying the physical laws inherent therein, and yet so advanced, so mighty that *gods* was the only word remotely appropriate for them. I had experienced them. I had tasted of their power, love, and transcendent animosity.

Like all things, I presumed the gods we encountered, like the goddess Ambra of our creation, were composed of the building blocks of matter we knew to exist. But the presence of the Anti proved how biased that view of the universe was. If there were gods of matter, why shouldn't there be gods of anti-matter? If so, where were they? Why had the Anti—who had known of the *devil ball* of Ambra for eons within eons—never developed or mentioned or sought out their own anti-gods?

Perhaps, like the Anti themselves, there were simply too few of them. I had only encountered two of these advanced entities, and that was because one of them—one I had helped create—had embroiled me in a cosmic feud and quest. Hardly a dataset on which to build a model. Still, it seemed that these entities, these gods, were uncommon, as any of the large compositions of smaller elements would be relative to their building blocks. And the building blocks of matter outnumbered those of antimatter by orders of magnitude that were themselves difficult to comprehend.

That was it! I finally understood. Perhaps there were no anti-gods for the simple reason that there *could not be*. Ambra was said to be the assembly of trillions of souls. An ocean of building blocks that bordered on uncountable. But how much antimatter was there in the universe? Relatively, the sum total might as well be zero. How much could remain isolated from matter for long enough to develop star systems, life, and sentience? How many of these species would survive the wild adolescence of their evolution to achieve stability? Of these, how many minds would exist to provide the building blocks for a group mind that might someday mature into a being like those I had encountered?

The more I considered it, the more unlikely it became. The gods of the Anti had indeed perished in the creation, because the creation had wiped out the very material from which their gods might have been fashioned. Our universe, so hostile and dominant to the creatures of antimatter that waged a doomed war against us, simply did not possess the raw elements to construct sentience at that level.

Something about this realization disturbed me greatly, but I did not stop to ponder any more deeply. I had the answer. This time I was sure of it.

"There are no anti-gods, Ambra. There never were and never will be. They cannot exist, because there isn't enough antimatter to support them."

As the last echo of my words died, a tonal chord rang across the underground chamber. Composed of multiple harmonic frequencies, spanning the ultrabass to a shattering treble, it seemed to rattle the air in front of me. I took this as a sign and stepped toward Kloan.

This time I reached her.

Chapter 41

We have found a strange footprint on the shores of the unknown. We have devised profound theories, one after another, to account for its origins. At last, we have succeeded in reconstructing the creature that made the footprint. And lo! It is our own.

Arthur Stanley Eddington

As I reached the bright altar, she opened her eyes.

"Waythrel?"

Her demeanor was fully conscious, her physiology seeming to suffer none of the retarding, inhibiting aspects of prolonged sleep, especially sleep induced by pharmacological agents or neuro-manipulative fields. It was as if she had simply been suspended in time and restored to the temporal flow.

"Waythrel? Where am I?"

I grasped her hands excitedly. "Kloan, are you okay? Are you hurt?"

She sat up on the altar, passing her hands across the slick surface in confusion and interest, and then swept her vision across the enormous stairway, maze, and finally above her to the pendulous goddess relief.

"Holy shit," she said.

Joy flowed through me. Whatever had happened to her, Kloan seemed to have lost none of her manic cultural syntheses and playfulness.

"Then you are okay?" I repeated stupidly.

Kloan whistled while squinting at the sculpture above us. She returned her attention to her body. "Two legs, two arms, two hands, proper fingers. A head. No blood. No scars. No memories. You tell me." She gestured around the chamber. "What is this place? What are we doing here? And why do you look like you've run around that lunatic maze down there fifty times?"

"Because I nearly have," I said, eliciting a single eyebrow raise from her. "It's a very long story. We were split up. I was half a kilometer away over there. I had to come through the labyrinth. I had to absorb a message and answer a riddle, or we could never leave." And so I recounted the narrative as she sat raptly before me on the stone structure.

"I want to see the question," she said, hopping off the edge of the altar. "Might need some Xixian handholding to get down these stairs, though."

With my help, she descended the stairway on foot, even though she likely could have simply floated down with ease. One hundred hops later, we had reached the bottom, and Kloan studied the inscription with fascination.

"Your own private test of doom," she said, tracing the letters with her finger. "But I'll have to trust you on the meaning. I can't read a bit of it."

"What I don't understand is why," I said.

"Why what?" she asked, spinning in place and taking in the grandeur of this construction.

"Why all of this? Why were we brought here?"

"You said it yourself—to learn a lesson. And it seems like you have."

"This is an awful lot of trouble to get me to think about some of these issues."

"Sometimes living a question answers it better than purely thinking. These incredible repetitions trapping us seem like a lot of trouble, but they are all designed to teach us things. Crucial things. Data we need to process and assimilate to take the next step, and, finally, to exit the loop."

"Is it possible?" I asked. "Will we ever escape it?"

"*Ever* and *possible* both lose their meaning in all this, don't you think? We will never get there even if we do, and it seems *all* possibilities will be sampled in the process."

"More Kloan-babble I can't follow," I said wearily, but I reached out and held her hand. "But *at least* I should be able to understand this one! It was focused completely on *me*. Lessons for me. Motivations that were sure to drive me to reach within as deeply as possible for answers."

"Is it love, Waythrel?" she asked, glancing at our clasped hands. "Have we reached that point of no return? Are you ready to confess to me your true feelings now?"

I ignored her. "So I found an answer, and apparently satisfied the goddess, or whoever is behind this. But to answer what question? One focused on the metaphysics of antimatter gods! Of what possible point is all this effort for such esoterica?"

"String theory is esoteric, but without it the universe does not exist," said Kloan.

"But *Waythrel* knowing or not knowing string theory will

have absolutely no impact on whether the universe will exist!" I exclaimed. "And neither will my understanding or lack of it about the hypothetical antimatter gods!"

Kloan turned serious and stepped up to me, focusing her bright eyes on mine. "And are you so sure about that, Waythrel?"

My eyestalks buzzed around her in consternation. "Of course. How can what I understand about the universe be of any deep significance to the universe itself?"

Kloan turned away and seemed to bury her thoughts within her. "Perhaps you are right, Waythrel."

"Of course I am right!" The child was irrepressibly disconcerting. "Which brings us back to this granite extravagance. What is the point? Why are we here? What could Ambra possibly be up to? It doesn't make sense!"

Kloan laughed. "Well, one thing is for sure. Ambra moves in mysterious ways." Kloan pointed above. "Whatever her motives, I don't think we'll have time to consider them anymore here."

A bright light grew from the ceiling, dazzling my eyes and forcing me to look away. It seemed to be extending tendrils of radiance toward us, long tentacles that flung themselves about as if searching for prey.

"Times up," said Kloan, her eyes cast down to the deep shadows of our forms on the rock.

The light limbs surrounded us, grasped us, and pulled us off the ground and toward the blinding source of radiance above. My last memory was of glancing toward Kloan and hearing her voice nearly lost in a maelstrom of sound and brilliance.

"See you again soon, Waythrel!"

Chapter 42

*God huddles in a knot in every cell of flesh. When I break a fruit open,
this is how every seed is revealed to me. When I speak to men, this
what I discern in their thick and muddy brains. God struggles in every
thing, his hands flung upward toward the light.*

Nikos Kazantzakis

It was morning. I stared forward into the warm light of a
star I did not know, yet had seen perhaps one thousand
times. Perhaps millions. There was no longer a concept
of time for my awareness. No history with permanence. No
memories I could trust. I was forever falling into dreamscapes,
one after the other, without hope that there would be a
waking.

Out of breath, I rested several meters away from the gate.
We must have climbed. Kloan was red and sweaty from exertion. I could only remember a tomb—mazes and riddles and

light. I didn't remember climbing. I didn't know how we got here.

But the gate I remembered. I examined the portal more closely. It was now familiar, visited uncounted times in the dream treks of loops through this anomaly in space-time. It resembled a cross section sliced out of an Orb more than anything else, but I still didn't know if this system possessed an Orb. The surface was that viscous, churning, honey-like substance we had immersed ourselves in times beyond counting. Inside was an ocean of stars—depth upon depth of star fields that appeared to have no end. I felt pulled toward the horrible beauty as I gazed.

"Something's wrong," said Kloan.

With most of my eyes fixated on the starry disk, several flipped to the side to glance at Kloan. The girl was tense, straight as a rod, and her eyes scanned the region between us and the disk like prey awaiting a predator.

"The gate? Has it rejected us?"

"Not the gate. Something else."

Before us the air shimmied, the disk and the land around it swayed and blurred, and the air itself coagulated into a humanoid shape. We both stood there, stunned, unable to move. I sensed from Kloan's mind an unusual anxiety. But it was my own mind that began to panic as the form darkened, took on colors, and solidified, acquiring a shape with four arms, sixfold symmetry, and a patch of long eyestalks erupting from a central cone. *A Xix.* But not just any Xix. My emotions swirled. A Xix I knew. My beloved Synphel.

"Hello again, Waythrel," it said, the apparition fully formed.

Again. Nightmarish visions bounded through my thoughts. *Memories?* Of what?

You must not believe for a moment that I was taken by this forgery. Rationally, I knew this could not be Synphel. Emotionally, I knew it with more certitude. And yet the form of my Synphel activated circuits within my neural cortex that stirred my emotional centers as well. I could not halt the feelings of love and longing that surged within me, even as I stared toward something utterly devoid of those qualities.

The anxiety Kloan had felt I felt now, too. The entity before us that had taken the shape of my lifemate radiated intense cognitive fields. They were incredibly complex, of a depth and power I had sensed only in the presence of the Ambra-thing that had visited us here. And in the presence of the Orbs.

But the sentience before us was to my experience, as deeply malevolent as it was profound. Simply staring at this form of my dear Synphel caused eruptions of disturbing images, anger, slaughter, pain, and madness. I felt Kloan reach out and hold my arm.

"Don't let it in your mind," she whispered.

"Let it?" came the smooth voice of my lover. Although the tones were perfect, they were also utterly alien. "If you have any perception, then you know that nothing you can do can stop me."

"No, but *she* will!" I said triumphantly, shocking myself in this exclamation. A subconscious certitude led me to turn my eyestalks behind us. Irrationally, I waited without doubt for the form of Ambra Dawn to come strolling casually up the slope.

But she was not there.

Kloan screamed and fell to her knees on the ground, grasping her head. She began to rock back and forth, moaning, crying, tears pouring down her cheeks. I watched in horror as spit frothed from her mouth; a mild seizure seemed to shake her form as she trembled and doubled over. Her eyes flipped up and back into their sockets. Alongside the white stone in her forehead were two white orbs staring back from a hideous mask of shaking pain. Blood trickled out of her left nostril.

"Stop!" I screamed and dropped to the ground, grabbing her in my arms. Her jaw was clenching wildly, tearing her tongue and lips, so I ripped a piece of clothing away from her robes and placed it between her teeth.

I did not imagine that I could shield her mentally. My Reader sense was completely overwhelmed by this creature assaulting her, so much so that I had to shut it out as if closing my eyes. Even that left me blinded. What would an attempt at defense have achieved, anyway? Kloan was powerful beyond my imagining and she was tossed like a toy flung by the force before us.

"As you wish," said the thing. Kloan fell to the ground unresponsive. I checked her vitals. She was alive, but unconscious. A quick mind probe indicated severe trauma, but superficially it seemed no major physiological damage had been done.

"We aren't ready to destroy her yet," said the demon form of Synphel. "We need more information first."

"We? Are you one or many? Where are the others? What do you want?" I cradled Kloan's head in my arms.

"Surely the great Waythrel of Xix can surmise?" Synphel performed a Xixian body gesture that can only be translated as a smile, although we possess no teeth or mouth akin to those of humans. "Or did you think your crude experiment with Ambra Dawn was somehow unique in all the universe?"

A terrible dread settled on me. "What are you?"

"One of the other gods, of course."

"Rakshasi." How I knew the word confused me.

"She has spoken my name, then."

"You are a mental union? A group consciousness?"

"That is probably as close as you can come to understanding. But surely you know that the organizing principles are the same throughout the universe? Even something with as primitive a mind as your own can grasp this. The strings are composed of smaller entities down to levels to which your philosophies have never scurried. Yet this process continues further still, until time itself cannot discover all the constituents. And so the structures assemble upward to your atoms, molecules, cells, and tissues. *Minds.* Mental networks of trillions of minds that grow until they become things that stride across the cosmos like giants."

Images flooded my mind. I could not stop them. Ripped out from my creaturely perspective, I was given a momentary glimpse from the eyes of a divinity, spanning ages of time like instants, parsecs of space like small steps. I was oppressed with a morality that was so foreign and horrible that I nearly felt my mind breaking.

"You are the cells of our minds," the entity concluded, harshly slinging my awareness back to the dirt and rock of this strange planet.

I was disoriented and terrified. "What do you want with us?"

"We are interested in what *your* creation-god is planning. We suspect that her intentions are far from pure, as they concern others of our kind."

"I don't understand."

"The Ambra-Orb: what does she wish with this creature?" it said, gesturing toward Kloan, who still lay unmoving in my arms.

"Ambra-Orb?" My mind raced, feverish in the terrible presence of this thing. "Yes, wait, I remember. Ambra is the Orb—?"

"Of course. Haven't you even put that together? Or can your mind not retain anything in this recursive playground of hers? Now tell us, what do you conclude is the point of this Kloan? Think through all you have encountered. You will not enter this gate until you have answered to our satisfaction."

"Why can't you just read it from our thoughts?"

I felt a hostile impatience from the thing. It was like the glow of a furnace door opened in front of me. I could not even shield my mind from it. If one's consciousness could feel heat, mine was nearly scalded.

"We have taken all your memories and impressions. We know all that has happened. But it is not enough. Her deviousness is deep beyond explaining. Her true purpose is encoded in your cognition. We need you to reason with us, think through her desires. Explain to us now what she wishes. What you understand about what has happened to you. In the *deduction* is the answer."

"Why me? This clone understands so much more. Yet you nearly killed her."

"She lacks a need of cognition for this very reason." Synphel *smiled* again, and the horror of it on this creature sickened me. "You, however, do not understand much at all, and yet the puzzle pieces are all within your thoughts. You must try to assemble them."

In terrible panic, my mind raced. Even as I held the unresponsive child in my arms, as I hoped vainly that Ambra would return and deliver us as in my dream, the monstrous presence of this thing before me forced me to engage. My mind was no longer was my own. My thoughts transformed into buttons in the hands of another. I became dizzy trying to stitch together the blurred memories of time loops, or what I assumed and poorly recalled as repeated journeys with Kloan through the gate. Horrific nightmares. Death and pain and destruction. Thousands, millions upon millions of journeys I had forgotten, which this creature forced through my mind. The god's pressure unearthed the ruins of my memory, flooding me with events that I could not have accessed consciously. I felt my body swaying.

The plans of the Anti. Yes, it was the unifying element to all the journeys! It was the only thing that made sense.

I babbled. "This clone is playing out all the routes to the destruction of Ambra Dawn. Ambra is encouraging it. Yet nothing ever happens. We circle back; the actions in the past have no lasting effect on her existence."

"Continue."

My air sacs were becoming clogged from stress secretions, my oxygen content lowering and fogging my thoughts. I tried to concentrate harder. "Why would Ambra encourage this? Only if she ultimately feared the creature."

"Yes."

"Only if she were looking in the failure of cause and effect for a vulnerability, the thread that makes this creature so unusual. Yes, I remember. She said that all the gods fear Kloan. Why?"

"There is a discontinuity. A place in space and time where we cannot go. She is the source. She cannot be fully read."

"Then Ambra fears her, too. She is either trapping her in this loop to forever keep her here, or to study her, or both. She is trying to prevent Kloan from doing something that you all fear and cannot see."

And then the Synphel creature was gone, vanished in a

breath as I was processing my thoughts, leaving no trace, no hint that this being who seemed to span entire galaxies had displaced a molecule of the atmosphere.

I felt the soft breathing of Kloan as she rested on me. I felt heat from the local star warming my skin. Slowly, I uncovered my eyestalks, feeling like a nymph again, terrified of things I could not see or prove were real. It was as if they had never occurred except in the dim recesses of my darkest dreams.

Except that Kloan lay wounded in my arms. She began to cough roughly, her sputum tinged with pink. As she gasped for air, her eyes flew open, and she vomited across the ground. Her body shivered violently for several minutes.

I applied what medical training I had. Fortunately, our long association with humans had given us a significant knowledge of their anatomy and function, even for those like myself who were not medically devoted. Without proper instruments, I could not be sure, but it seemed that the trauma had not seriously wounded her body. Her mind was another issue.

"I have seen hell," she said flatly, staring off into space. "It has been infused into me. I never knew, Waythrel. I never *imagined*. To know such horror exists—I don't want to live. But death! Immortality and hell. Waythrel, please, can we *unexist?*"

"Kloan—"

"I have smelled it," she nearly shouted, tendrils of saliva clinging like webs between her gnashing teeth. "Its foul taste flooded my mouth and nostrils, a vile sludge suffocating and drowning me in stench and slime." She closed her eyes and cried out toward the sky. "I heard the groan and weeping of entire galaxies in the void." Her body shook in my arms.

I tried desperately to comfort her. "Shock, Kloan. Violence to your mind. It's not real. You are safe. We are safe, now." I tried desperately to believe in my own words.

She shook her head and turned wild eyes toward me. Her hands reached out and grasped mine, pulling the twelve fingers of each to her lips. She kissed them, one by one. I felt a terrible reaching of her mind toward mine, a need for contact with something decent, something with affection. "You don't understand, dear Waythrel. I have seen what you have not, what a Xix could never see and survive, and there is no forgetting. There is no more peace or love. There is no more safety." Tears streamed down her face. "And there is no more Kloan." She bowed her head into her lap, whispering. "I have traveled. To the place of demons. They are *real*. They are lurking between the shadows of the stars. And they are *waiting*."

"Waiting for what?" I asked, her words eliciting a primal chill through my form.

"For all of us...and the dying of the light."

Chapter 43

I perceived that I was on a little round grain of rock and metal, filmed with water and with air, whirling in sunlight and darkness. And on the skin of that little grain all the swarms of men, generation by generation, had lived in labour and blindness, with intermittent joy and intermittent lucidity of spirit. And all their history, with its folk-wanderings, its empires, its philosophies, its proud sciences, its social revolutions, its increasing hunger for community, was but a flicker in one day of the lives of the stars.

Olaf Stapeldon

"What do we do now, Kloan?"

I was at a loss. She showed no sign of interest in the journey we had been only moments from undertaking. She sat on the ground next to me, her chin resting on her knees, a blank stare in her eyes as she seemed to see across a million light-years.

To what? I dared not ask. She didn't seem to be able to take much more. After the things she had said, I wondered if I even wished to know.

So I rested quietly beside her as the afternoon wore on. A portion of me worried that the forces below would discover us, but I knew that was unlikely given our strange disappearance and position. And after the encounters of the last few hours, everything else seemed so small and feeble. My focus drifted; my mind visualized planets filled with sentient creatures, stumbling about their daily lives in an artificially fast manner as if years had become days. Generations passed, entire cultures rose and fell, world civilizations matured and perished. And yet all of it, even the sum across a galaxy of stars, now seemed petty.

I had not seen the full horror forced upon Kloan, but for a short moment, I had glimpsed through the eyes of the demon. I had felt the vastness of space and time that rendered our daily lives no more than the femtoseconds of chemical motions to an organism far greater than us.

Part of me understood Kloan's despair. What possible significance could the pair of us have? What madness was there to believe that two transient molecules could possibly have any impact, any meaning at all in this vast cosmic ocean? I had experienced the presence of a cosmic god. I could no longer sense my self.

"Waythrel."

My eyestalks darted behind me only to fill my vision with images of fear once again. Standing still and tranquil, in dark yet phosphorescent beauty, was Synphel once more. My emotions again ran the sickening gamut of fear, love, longing, disgust, and despair mixed with elation. I turned slowly to the thing, my limbs trembling. "Please. No more. Please don't torture us like this anymore. If there is any pity in the gods the universe has created, leave us in peace. We are only dust."

"Waythrel, it is I. Open your heart."

The rush of love and concern that swept through me was overpowering. Gone was the malignancy of consciousness I had felt from the demon. Instead I drank in the unmistakable presence of my long-separated mate. A loving personality poured through my Reader senses, remembered smells filled my olfactory strips, and a healing presence was undeniable in a way that was wholly absent from the apparition before.

Forgive me for using the clumsiness of your language to bimodally gender her—*her* is the pronoun I will use, even as it warps the nature of any of our six genders. But your word *it* warps her nature even more to my mind, stripping her of any aspect of gender at all, and in this meeting with Synphel, the intimacy of the encounter I choose to relate, cries out that something better be used, however imperfect. For this day, we were not two *its*, but two *hers*, and the love between us was like a balm to the monstrosities that had assailed Kloan and me.

"*Synphel.* How? You are part of the group mind. With Ambra. How are you here?"

"Waythrel, we have become something beyond what you can easily imagine. I have been clothed in atoms and molecules, stitched in flesh, incarnate here to meet with you."

"Your mind?"

"My mind, my soul—what you once knew as Synphel—is within this form that has been drawn from the dust and debris of this world. But I am not alone. And none of us is truly here."

I struggled to conceptualize her words. A mental projection, the equivalent of a complex transform arriving at this point of space and time, with the power from afar to manipulate matter so magically as to assemble a completed life form from the inanimate particles on a distant world. Not just any form, but an exact replica of my lifemate. I was slow to learn this lesson, even having witnessed the reality a short time ago in the face-off between the demon and Ambra. I had to witness it again and again to fully absorb the depth of the implications. Truly they were—or had become, or would be—gods.

Her voice spoke in my mind.

Gods perhaps to you, but yet you are one of our makers, Waythrel. Is this not itself a miracle? And we are still composed of the elements of this cosmos. We do not transcend it, although we seek transcendence. And indeed, that is what all this is about.

She turned the bulk of her eyestalks to gaze beside me. "Kloan, please come here."

In my dread and wonder in this reunion, I had forgotten about the child. Kloan stirred and rose, turning slowly around to face my partner. Her eyes seemed dead.

Synphel turned to the girl. "They seek to strip you of the energies to carry out your quest, to freeze you in place, suspended and defused," said Synphel. "If they understood fully, they would destroy you, but their hesitancy reflects the terrible potential they sense in you. All timelines become discontinuous in your presence, a phenomenon unique in all the cosmos to you. You are the nexus in all that is and all that was and will be."

"But I am broken."

"Yes, but not beyond healing." Synphel walked up to the child and placed her upper hands to Kloan's head, surrounding the skull and face with twenty-four fingertips. The dark black of my lover's skin contrasted sharply with the white of the clone, and the soft, lipid-insulated form of the human appeared truly alien alongside the elongated, leathery appendages of a Xix.

Kloan closed her eyes and began to weep.

"Yes, you remember the dreams. You remember the calling to find the resolution to the asymmetry. Listen to it again. Let it burn brightly and char to ash the horror you have seen." Kloan wrapped her arms around Synphel and shook with sobs.

I remembered watching the development of human infants and children, how critical close physical contact was for proper brain maturation, as it was in all the related mammalian species on their home world. Even in the presence of a creature so different, the instinct to embrace overwhelmed any sense of discomfort with the alien as the child was purged of the emotional poison.

After several minutes, Kloan's arms relaxed, and she stepped backward, wiping her eyes and face.

"Thank you," Kloan said. She looked intently into the eyestalks of Synphel. "Thank you, all."

"The horror will never leave you," said Synphel. "But it will no longer overthrow your mind. Follow your meditations. Take your pain and scars and use them to grow."

Even though I had known the child for such a short time, even though I had been a victim of abduction at her hands and witnessed the horrors she could commit, relief and a soft joy spread through me. Part of it is our Xixian nature, our desire for healing and our difficulties in causing harm, a weakness that had nearly doomed our galaxy. Always we rejoice at the removal of pain. But it was much more than such a generic response. The clone elicited from me many of my feelings for her progenitor, and although she was so different from Ambra, I saw now that I could not help but love her.

Synphel's eyestalks divided between us. "Now you must regroup and continue your journey."

Chapter 44

Nature does not dictate dualities, trinities, quarterings, or any "objective" basis for human taxonomies; most of our chosen schemes, and our designated numbers of categories, record human choices from a cornucopia of possibilities offered by natural variation from place to place, and permitted by the flexibility of our mental capacities. How many seasons (if we wish to divide by seasons at all) does a year contain? How many stages shall we recognize in a human life?

Stephen Jay Gould

A spasm of desperation swept through me. "Synphel, please. Don't go." Surprising even myself, I stepped forward and entwined my fingers with hers. "I can't keep you. I know this. You are only a memory made flesh. But I cannot let you go," I said, the foolishness of my yearning mocking me. Her digits twirled around my own. "So real. And this memory that I am able to touch is precious beyond words to me."

"Have you ever loved a goddess, Waythrel?"

Synphel pressed her form alongside my own, and the skin cilia of our compatible mating types locked and engaged. The biological program sent shivers through me, and without conscious decision my eyestalks probed and found hers, each wrapping around the other, eighteen sighted organs like a complex braid staring at each other.

I did not care that I would mate with an avatar sculpted out of the sands of this distant planet, or whatever place it had come from. I cared neither that the Synphel I knew was gone, altered, absorbed into a godlike entity full of nearly countless personalities, nor that those trillions looked on in love, disinterest, and emotions unfathomable to me in this moment of our species' deepest intimacy. No, I only wished to merge with Synphel one last time.

It is difficult to explain the oddities of our physiology to you of Earth. In all species that do not reproduce asexually, there must be a mingling of the hereditary material. But with a mating group composed of six genders, four separate gametes containing separated fractions of what you would call the Xixian genome, it is the case that there can be components of the assembled form that do not carry the seed. So it is and so it was with Synphel and myself. We donated no material for future generations, but our mating pair was an integral element in the whole. There is no point in explaining how our genotype could be stable and selected for, no space in this story for the complexities and nonlinearity of group evolution, to define what constitutes an organism under selection, but the important point is to know that we formed the core structure around which the mating group assembled.

Our bond had to be deep, strong, and long lasting. In the mating process, therefore, our sexual encounters were very much unlike your own brief moments; they were the longest by far even of our reproductive group pairings. For this reason many pair mates of our type entered into unions outside the mating group that lasted lifetimes.

The first stage was mutual penetration, where a deeply hidden appendage, appearing to you perhaps as a strange variant of a tentacle, thrust through a slit in our torso and sought the equivalent structure in our mate. Perhaps an analogy to your male's erections, this process was the beginning of stimulation.

But our tentacles were not injection devices that worked alone. They found each other, wrapped around a structural mate like vines of Earth—or, closer still, the entwining eyestalks above our heads. The effect on our physiology resembled at this stage something like the stimulation of your penis and clitoris nerve webs, activating the body toward the mating engagement.

And so this god-Synphel drove me to a growing ecstasy of fusion as our reproducing arms touched, caressed, and wrapped firmly around each other, pressing forward in opposite directions, raising body temperature suddenly as they found the opening slit, teased it mercilessly with stroking, and then plunged inward toward the deep nerve cluster buried within.

Here is the element of our dance that is perhaps the most difficult to explain to you. The tip of the penetrating appendage appears somewhat like an ovate leaflet of your plants in shape, yet it is decorated with thousands of micro-bristles, each full of thousands of nerve-like structures. The tip from Synphel entered deeply into my core, and my mind was flooded with pleasure as the tentacle wrapped around my nerve cluster and the leaflet dug into the most sensitive portion. Of course my own was doing the same to her, and our bodies were drawn powerfully into each other.

Externally, from our sides and backs, additional tentacles for connection to the other genders of our mating group now extended themselves. However, without the other members to connect with, they would sway and swivel like a vine, searching for a foothold, until the lack of engagement would slowly shut down our mating process.

But that would take some time. As the core of the group, the interweaving of our bodies was deep and strong, forming a platform for the bodies of the other members. Our pleasure and desire to continue the hold was enormous, and we writhed in the torment of reproductive pleasure for more than an hour.

All during the process, I was closely tied to the consciousness of Synphel through the connected nerve clusters as well as our Reader senses. It was as I had known her before, and in this I knew it was truly Synphel. But there was more. *She* was more...altered—deeper and more alien. I began to sense the host of minds beneath the layer of her consciousness, their personalities and thoughts flitting here and there across my awareness. And of course, deep in the core of this endless mind, I sensed Ambra. I felt her and her thoughts. They created images in my cognizance, and I thought I saw her smile.

Inevitably, the physiological program ran its course. The other, external appendages withdrew, having failed to find their mating structures. Our bodies cooled down, the appendages inside each of us beginning to feel uncomfortable, the pleasure withdrawing. Soon they released from the drained nerve clusters and slithered back out of their lovers' bodies, returning to their own and coiling like snakes deep within. At the last, our eyestalks unwound, and we separated, continuing to stare deeply into each visual organ.

"Thank you," I said.

"I have missed you terribly," said Synphel.

Kloan walked up beside us. "It was beautiful," she said, a smile on her once-harrowed face. "Strange and beautiful for my prejudices, beyond beautiful to the eye of my mind. I saw them, Waythrel. They spun like ghosts in and out of space. A cosmos of minds."

Synphel stepped backward toward the disk. "The third element of this visit is also completed. We needed to know that you would love the child. And so you have. Now begins a new cycle."

The burden of our reality returned to me. "And where will it take us now? Have we learned what we needed to learn?" I had no idea what was expected of me.

She did not answer but gestured to the disk. The whirling star field scrambled, and the rainbows embedded in the depths flickered and trembled.

"We will not meet again, my dearest Waythrel," said my lover. "But you will not be left without me."

And in an instant that I could not even process, the form of Synphel was gone. There was no sound, no rushing of air or sense of displacement. There was only absence.

The child clone and I were left standing by ourselves. In front of us blazed an incredible window to another space, perhaps also another time. Behind us the radiance cast shadows even in the bright light of the local star.

"We are not alone, leaky thoughts," said Kloan, smiling. "I can feel them watching. Can you?"

I strained my Reader senses. It was faint, perhaps only my wishful thinking, but it did seem that some echo of Synphel, of

Ambra, of their entire mental ecosystem could be felt in the undulations of fleeting gravitons. Real or not, it was comforting.

But as I strained, I could not help but also sense other currents, other minds lurking in the depths of time and space. I felt like a swimmer in a cold sea, lingering in the comfort of a warmer current, knowing that around us an icy, unfathomable deep lay concealed. In the depths, there were monsters.

"Perhaps it was better to be alone," I said, shivering.

"When there is hate, there is love," said Kloan. "Warmth and cold, order and disorder, creation and destruction. Where there is Ambra, there is also me."

My eyestalks centered on her brooding features, not knowing what to think of these words. I still did not know what the ultimate purpose of this journey would be, only that it had shifted in a new way and that, in taking the next steps, I was putting my trust in both the yes and the no, in the odd opposites of the two forms of Ambra Dawn.

"The thing tore open my mind. The journeys. The multitudes—I am remembering them all. It's too much, Kloan."

Kloan grasped my arm. "You were not the only one tested, Waythrel." She sighed. "It will be different each time, and only when we have fully understood will we see the answer."

She turned toward the disk. Together, hand in hand, we stepped forward, the gel-like surface of the portal enveloping us like molasses.

We fell into a great darkness.

Part 6

The words of wonder I watched elders weave,
the tales of Truth more strange than in my dreams:
Of ghosts so small they pass through vision's sieve
yet stitch my mind in fragile, fleshy seams,
or hungry gods, enormous, ever starved,
who take all prey to planes beyond our own,
where time and space are infinitely carved
into a fabric rent and never sown.
To groups so gifted by the gods, the signs
and studied charms the elder priests unfold.
The depths await our readied, seeking minds.
As Shaman I may find new Truths untold.
Yet some nights I feel depths beyond our Way,
and what I am the spirits do not say.

—Mazandarani, *Sonnets from the Desert*

Chapter 45

Science cannot solve the ultimate mystery of Nature. And it is because in the last analysis we ourselves are part of the mystery we are trying to solve.

Max Planck

There was no light.
There was a terrible blackness beyond anything I had ever experienced. Along with it came a chill. The surrounding space was extraordinarily cold and seemed to want to drink the warmth greedily from my body. One of my upper arms was shaken vigorously.

It was Kloan, or so I surmised in this total caliginosity. I could feel her hand still holding onto me, and she had begun to shiver noticeably. I strained with all my senses. I could smell nothing, taste nothing through my skin sacs. I could feel nothing but Kloan on my body. My eighteen visual organs were useless. No radiation in any frequency range could I detect, not even infrared, which meant that nearly everything around us was dangerously cold.

Whatever is around us, came Kloan's thoughts, *we do stand on something. There is something under our feet.*

She was correct. I tried to speak to acknowledge her observation, but nothing was emitted from the translator. *The translator!* Of course. How stupid I was, and how slow to adapt to these shocking dislocations in space and time.

I fiddled with the device around my neck, and soon it began to glow a pale white. As my eyes adjusted from the pitch black to the now nearly blinding source of light around my neck, I began to take in our immediate environment. It was bleaker than I could have imagined.

At our feet was a pile of white dust, perfectly arranged around our forms. From the lack of the gate gel on our bodies, I assumed that the material had frozen and shattered into this fine powder, but I could not be sure. For the ten meters around us that the light illuminated, there was only ice and rock. The "ice" was highly variable, ranging from frosted to perfectly clear to a pale cyan. The rocks were coated with the latter in a blue film, seemingly varnished by a top layer of clear ice. I had seen nothing like it before. It was the same in all directions. My mind raced.

What do you think this is, Waythrel?

It was the first time Kloan had ever turned to me in ignorance and doubt. After so many wild and disorienting journeys where this child held the upper hand in all things, suddenly she seemed small again, lost, and searching for a parental figure, even if it were a six-armed alien. Rather than stoke my ego, it brought on a sense of dread I was not expecting. Of all the disturbing powers I had witnessed in the universe, if Kloan was lost and unsure, it could not be good.

I don't know, Kloan.

But you suspect. I feel your thoughts bubbling.

I tried to walk. There was indeed a surface, but it too was coated in this frozen glaze. Moving was treacherous and required stepping gingerly and avoiding excess momentum.

She probed further. *Could it be underground? There is no light.*

Possibly.

But you don't think so.

There is no atmosphere, Kloan. No sound from my translator. No noise from our steps. We are in a total vacuum. That would make the temperature outside close to absolute zero. I can only assume your skin suits are keeping us alive. And I don't know how long they will last.

Waythrel, they aren't mine!

That at least was comforting. Kloan and I were obviously out of our element, beyond our powers here, kept alive only by some advanced technology we could not understand. But only something far in advance of us could hope to help us here, wherever *here* might be.

I glanced around, slowly rotating all my eyestalks, positioning them so that I had nearly a 360-degree view of everything around us. *There are no stars overhead, yet no atmosphere or light pollution to drown them out. Where are the stars, Kloan?*

That's why I say maybe we are underground.

Perhaps. Let's try to cover some ground and see what else we can find. Maybe something will help us understand.

Data.

Yes, Kloan, data. But somehow I think our survival depends upon this particular data.

She frowned, the bright light and darkness behind chiseling her features harshly. *All the data is important to our lives, Waythrel. To the cosmos.*

Let's focus on the rock and ice around us and worry about the cosmos later, okay?

She said nothing else; with that we set out blindly, randomly, able to view only meters ahead of us at a time. It was enough to avoid a pit or cliff or other danger, but it allowed us no way to plan globally. We had no sense of the lay of the land, no points of reference. No navigation tools besides memory. It was indeed an act of hopeless optimism.

Rocks and ice. Ice and rocks. On and on it went. Minutes passed, and then hours. Kloan continued to shiver, but the suit seemed to keep her warm enough to avoid cold damage. She showed no signs of hypothermia or frostbite, but I monitored her regularly.

More rocks and more ice. It seemed like some giant's toy in a mineral collection, sprayed with a fixative to protect the surface from scratches. I checked the translator again. The power supply would last months, but the diodes illuminating our path were a greater unknown. They were not commonly used and certainly never tested in such an environment. I guessed that they would last at least several days in continuous use. Beyond that I did not know.

Waythrel, careful! The land is sloping down!

The child was correct. I also noticed that the terrain was smoothing out, the larger rocks giving way to pebbles and a kind of strange sand. All of it was still covered in the thick layer of ice, however, as if it were a specimen in a box separated from probing hands by a thick sheet of glass.

Kloan, can you determine nothing of this place from your searches into the past?

She shook her head. *This world's past—Waythrel, it never ends. It's an infinite well. I can't look at it anymore. I don't want to go back into it! I tried, and I fell and fell and fell, and always the same, always this darkness and cold. It's like it has always been this way. Forever. A frozen, dead eternity.*

I mulled over her ominous words. More and more it seemed we had come to a place unlike anything before, where our knowledge and powers proved useless. I focused on what I did know and tried to quell the growing panic. If I understood anything, it was that Ambra had sent us here. The god-ball had arranged it all, including, I assumed, the suits that somehow preserved two living organisms in this icy vacuum of a dead place. There had to be a purpose. All we had to do was achieve that purpose, *learn* whatever it was Kloan was supposed to learn or do, and then find ourselves, dizzy and confused, back where we started.

The time loops have destabilized, Waythrel. I told you things changed last time. Great powers have entered the game.

Some game! And one you can't stop playing.

Not yet.

Is there nothing you saw in your searches? Nothing of use?

Kloan wrapped her arms around her chest shivering, shaking her head. *I had to turn away. A hope, maybe, Waythrel. Maybe something in the distance.*

Now we stood flatly on a plain of some kind. If this were an underground cavern, it was enormous beyond comprehension, and there seemed little way an arched dome above us— one that we had yet to see evidence for—could be supported for any length of time at that size and mass. I grew convinced that we were not entombed within the bowels of some planet. But where we were still eluded any confident model.

Waythrel, wait. Turn off the light.

Why?

Please, just do it. There is *something ahead. Far ahead, I think.*

I was confused. *Then we need the light to see it.*

No, not this. It's a light itself. Your necklace is blinding us. Turn it off and let our eyes adjust.

I did as she asked. As the glow of the translator slowly dimmed, the darkness rushed in as some visceral thing, as a tidal dark mist with a malevolent will of its own. I had never been in the presence of such a complete lack of radiant sources or been submerged in such utter blackness. It stirred primitive and unreasonable instincts. It seemed alive.

But it was not like our arrival. The ink closing around us could not completely solidify. Kloan was right. Far ahead of us, a wan radiance like a failing beacon spilled a languid light through the mist, resisting it, culling its complete imposition over space. Something ahead radiated, possessed energy above the absolute zero of the landscape around us. There was energy. Some *potential*, something to battle the inevitability of thermodynamics. A chance of life.

I guess we go that way, right, Kloan?

She was already walking.

Chapter 46

That is not dead which can eternal lie,
And with strange aeons even death may die.

H. P. Lovecraft

We walked for long hours, the distances deceptive in this place, with only the beacon ahead providing any sense of reference in this icebound desert. Slowly, the radiance intensified. With our eyes now long adjusted to the paltry light, we could nearly make out our own shapes, monitor our footfalls, although the contents of the murky spaces around us remained hidden—a threatening unknown that toyed with my imagination.

Exhausted, freezing, we dragged ourselves forward. Kloan's breaths, exiting the force field, immediately turned to a snowy gas and drifted to the ground in front of us. My gaseous exchange was similar, although spread over the surface area of my skin, it produced no such dramatic display. I had no idea where we received the input gases to breathe or the warmth that kept us from freezing solid. I noticed Kloan's fingers had begun to turn white. Whatever the power of the suits that encased us, it was finite, and I hoped it would be enough for the time we would spend in this wasteland.

The light grew. Shadows began to form behind our forms —and, to my amazement, in front of us as well. Focusing the power of all my eyes, I strained to make out blurring shapes taking form near the source of the beacon, but it was still too far ahead.

Kloan, can you see ahead? Those shapes? They must be large.

Kloan nodded. *Before I stopped looking into the past of this frozen hell, they passed through my mind. They are very large. Something terrible.*

And she was right. Slowly, the shadows deepened, the figures ahead clarified, and they grew. Higher and higher as we approached and optical perspective set in, we watched monumental explosions of ice rise violently above the plain. Their shapes were indistinct. They looked like blasted magma that had been instantly converted to another form and locked in place. A rainbow of weak colors seemed to run through them.

As we neared the beacon, we approached the bases of these monoliths dwarfing us and everything around them. They were arrayed in a ring of a half kilometer or more. Some were single jets of ice throttling upward. Others seemed like a river with multiple tributaries erupting from the ground and fusing into bizarre, bulked shapes suspended over us. There were more than fifty of them. We could walk beside the structures, underneath arches for some. I became disoriented when looking for more than a moment into their icy forms— indistinct visions and motions emanated from deep within. Prolonged observation generated sensations. *Feelings.* I had the very distinct impression that we were not alone here, but could not identify what it was exactly that might be with us. The experiences were deeply unnerving, and I began to avoid staring into the things.

The beacon stood in the middle of the circle of giants. A small pillar of ice, simpler, unlike the towering forms around it, rose very near to Kloan's height, forming a bowl of pristine glass at its apex. Resting in this bowl was a sphere of clear glass or ice. A powerful rainbow of light churned within. It was this crystalline sphere that had illuminated our path and beckoned us here.

Kloan was walking slowly around the circle of titans, touching the ice, staring deeply into the quavering imagery dancing within it. She seemed far more immune than I to the disorienting effects of these objects and was intensely focused on them. Whatever this place was about, it was clear that these things, and the glowing sphere at their center, were central to the mystery. I let Kloan have her space and time.

They are as old as everything else, Waythrel. As far as I can look, hundreds of thousands of years into the past, they are here, just like this, unchanged, unmoved.

Do you know what they are?

Perhaps, she said, without elaborating.

Around she went, sampling one after another. Hours drifted by as I followed her, hoping for some clarification, some insight into this strange place, some indication of how we might escape it.

Finally, before one of the more distorted, grotesque, twisted shapes of ice, Kloan pulled back quickly, her eyes wide and her face in a grimace of pain. She closed her eyes and nodded to herself slowly. I felt her grasp my hands.

Waythrel, look into the ice. Give it time—but carefully. Guard your mind! Tell me what you see.

I hated to try, but I followed her lead and stepped up to a portion of the colossus before me. A tentacle of frozen matter dove from hundreds of feet above to plunge into the ground and disappear at my feet. The glass was imperfect, warped, the light and structures within bobbing and weaving. I could not see any hint of my reflection on the surface, which defied all optical physics. I felt my sense of balance weaken. I steadied myself on Kloan's shoulder instinctively, trying to maintain my gaze.

And then, *pain. Horror.* My mind experienced flashes and bursts of images, feelings, and sensations that had no center, no cause, and no explanation. Fleeting and effervescent, the terrible rampage of monstrosity nonetheless struck me over and over like blows. I screamed. I held my arms up to cover my eyes. I crouched defensively and turned my head away.

Kloan wrapped her arms around me for some time as I worked to purge the vile experiences from my mind. I could not speak, could not form coherent thoughts to share with her, and she did not push her own toward me. She recognized that I could not process them. Finally, my composure slowly regained, I turned my eyes to her.

I've felt it before. Where?

Kloan nodded. *Rakshasi.*

Instantly, I knew she was right. The being who had threatened us—that some unexplainable incarnate form of Ambra had saved us from, and also failed to save us from—had left an unforgettable impression on my psyche. Absorbing the outflow from this icy mountain above me, that impression was impossible to mistake for anything else. *Rakshasi.* The essence of the god-thing who had desecrated Synphel's form loomed before me, pressed down on me from above, crushing my hopes and sanity and menacing my mind, seemingly from within the solid substance before us.

Rakshasi? How, Kloan? What are these things? I gestured wildly to the monumental forms around us. I was suddenly terrified of them.

What are they? I don't know, Waythrel, but I would guess the same. Or of the like. Whatever Rakshasi is, or was, whatever they are, it is of a type.

Gods? Frozen gods?

Kloan shrugged her shoulders and pursed her lips. *That's right up there on my weird-o-meter, that's for sure.*

Let's just hope that they don't melt! Or whatever it is this stuff does. I don't think it's made of the same ice that is covering the ground and rocks. But I can't face these things. Don't let it happen, Kloan!

No. I don't know what they are made of, or how Rakshasi is inside. Or what Rakshasi is inside. But I don't think they will melt. Or change. The harder I try, the further back I look, the more I see that they have been here, just like this, for eons inside of eons.

The others?

All over the place. Powerful, strange, alien, unfathomable. Not as accessible. I think our encounter with Rakshasi tuned us to its essence, whatever it is.

Something terrible, that's what.

I stood up wobbly, the ground feeling far more treacherous and the air colder. I found myself drawn to the light in the center. I needed to get away from these towers of ice. I wanted to flee darkness and cold. I wanted to stand in front of that light and put my hands over it like a fire.

And maybe it will even be a little warm? Kloan smiled. *Don't think that there's much else to do with these cryogenic deities. Maybe the light ball has a better story to tell.*

We walked toward the light. The perched sphere was nearly one hundred meters from the ring of giants. As we approached, we indeed began to feel a temperature increase. The complete lack of an atmosphere meant that the heat transfer must be solely due to absorbed radiation from the object.

Hopefully there are no high frequency rays from that thing, or we better hope these suits can also shield us.

Kloan didn't respond. As we advanced to within twenty meters, Kloan slowed and put her hand against me. I stopped, my eyes swiveling around in concern, but I could see nothing immediately threatening.

There's another one.

Another what?

God-thing. Whatever. It's not like the others. It's...closer. And it's moving. She seemed to be straining, gazing far off into the distance. *It's hiding! Hiding in time from me. No! It's here!*

The ground shook and threw us both to the ice. The shaking continued so violently that we were both unable to stand and barely managed to steady ourselves with all our extremities spread across the ground. We gazed upward, awestruck as a shadow spread across our forms.

The frozen surface around the beacon shifted and flowed. Like some glacier as seen over millions of years, in only a few seconds, ice and rock as liquid defying gravity hurtled upward. Coalescing, a tremendous mass assembled itself, lodged between us and the beacon, so that the light of the object was completely obscured.

But as the thing in front of us took shape, it began to glow in a luminescent cyan that lit the surrounding plane. The tremors subsided as the bulk of the flow seemed to have eased, and the mass was focused on adopting more subtle forms.

Kloan slapped my arm repeatedly, pointing with her other hand at the thing before us.

Look! Waythrel, look! It's us!

Astounded, I watched the ice and rock mold itself into some geologic facsimile of a humanoid shape, or rather, a blended and distorted mixture of a human and Xix. Sixfold symmetric, with our numerous eyes, which it nonetheless sprouted not from our massive central cone but from the head of an Earthling, a shape that increasingly began to resemble none other than Kloan herself. Mouth, nose, cranial structure —it was an unmistakable, if rough and rocky, replica.

The eyelids of the face flipped open. Irisless orbs stared down at us, and the mountainous thing bent toward the ground and our position, stopping only meters away. The mouth opened, and I was shocked to hear sound, but I was far beyond the point of trying to parse the acoustical physics.

"I have been waiting for you a long time," came a rumbling god-voice that rattled the plane of ice around us. "Now the symmetry may be repaired."

Chapter 47

The formation in geological time of the human body by the laws of physics (or any other laws of similar nature), starting from a random distribution of elementary particles and the field is as unlikely as the separation of the atmosphere into its components. The complexity of the living things has to be present within the material or in the laws.

Kurt Gödel

K loan and I stared silently at the incredible ice behemoth before us for some time, although I could not stop various clusters of my eyestalks from turning away toward her for support. The thing did not move. It did not seem to be in a hurry. After Kloan's words concerning the age of this place, if it had been waiting for us so long, a few more minutes would be meaningless, I supposed.

I found that I could now produce sound. There was the slightest distortion above us—a dome of some nature—and I could only assume that the creature, or its transcendental handlers, had created a small environmental bubble around our position.

"We have air, Kloan."

Kloan nodded and turned toward the ice hulk. "Where are we, godling?"

The jagged ice lips boomed, "Where is of no significance anymore."

"Then...*when* are we?" she offered.

"At the death of all things." It motioned to the giant ice titans. "Even the gods."

Kloan cocked her head to one side. "How can the gods die?"

"The gods belong to our cosmos. They draw their tissues and energies of it. But they are only broken gods now." The deep rumblings of the voice seemed to rattle the innermost parts of my body. "Their Mother, our universe, is ill. She is dying. She has been, is, and will be dying to eternity. But now the weakness is at a threshold. And so the gods die."

I ventured. "But yet you live."

"I am their guardian. I am the keeper of the minds. I watch over them until the messengers come, when the past will end."

The god's words were cryptic and left me uncomprehending. "What makes you different?"

"I have been chosen. Look around you," said the colossus, standing tall like a mountain and gesturing upward. "You walk on a dead world in a dead space, a world whose sun has long died and that has perished in ice. An atmosphere that snowed the land under as it fell from the sky and then over the eons, found itself crushed and reformed to a clear glass. You look to the heavens, but they are now only tombs. There is no star left to burn, no free energy remaining to bath the empty space and planets. All is now forever dark."

Kloan nodded to herself. *No wonder I could not look back in time. No wonder it all was the same. Waythrel, don't you see? We have come terribly, horribly far into the future. So far that even the gods cannot count it anymore.*

The creature swiveled like an avalanche, and one of the giant Xixian arms on its torso reached behind and returned glowing brightly.

"I do not die because I hold a foreign fire." It held up its titanic arm. Shards of ice dropped like daggers and hailstones to the ground below it. "Here is a rend in the cosmos, a break in the fabric of our existence. Here is a tiny trickle of order from outside a dead creation. Enough that I may persist and maintain the watch. Enough to preserve the minds. Because of this I continue to gaze over the fallen gods. Because of this, my hope that the cosmos may be healed remains alive." The thing opened the multitude of digits to reveal the crystalline sphere.

"Where did it come from?" Kloan asked.

"It is a gift from the greatest of the gods who has sent you here and consumed entire galaxies to do it. It is a promise rejected by the others in futile wars that accelerated the inevitable heat death you witness. It was given to me when my role was assigned, and I accepted the duty with love. Therein, I accepted also the destiny that I would give back the gift when the time came."

"The greatest of the gods—who is that?" I asked, glancing around at the towers, wondering which of these was the most powerful and why this greatest god had not been the one to guard over the others—to use the power of the sphere.

Kloan shook her head. "She isn't here, is she?"

"No," thundered the mountain. "She waits for you at the beginning of time."

Kloan nodded, a terrible burden seeming to fall on her.

Who waits, Kloan?

Ambra. She has always waited. She is the poison. She is the great power who has broken everything at Creation. Our greatest and most terrible god. And I am the antidote.

The bulk of blue crystal seemed to hear our thoughts. "What is devolved in one direction is achieved in the other. There is an imbalance of death and madness. Here, at the end, you see its final fruits."

"Why do you keep them?" Kloan gestured to the gods around us.

"They were needed, in the beginning that is yet to be, to which they must return. But they resisted until time overpowered them. Only altogether can the asymmetry be unmade. When you awaken and call them, destroyer, the gods will come."

Destroyer? Does he mean you, Kloan?

Kloan ignored me. "And how will I call them? How will they waken?"

"When your gathering begins, you will return. I give you this light," it said, moving the glowing sphere toward her. "You will know what to do."

Nothing made sense to me. My frustration exploded in the form of questions. "If there is no energy, if all is cold and sterile and dead, where does this light come from? What is this thing you claim Kloan will use to waken all these monsters from their endless sleep? Why should we release them? They are horrible!"

"As you are horrible, and your atoms poison the cosmic mind," it said. The enormous head arched downward with the sound of straining glaciers, approaching within centimeters of my face. "Until all is lost, Xix, nothing is found."

The words sent a shockwave through me. I knew those words! They had appeared over the arch to the labyrinth. Now they spilled out from the icy tongue of this deity.

Kloan's thoughts pulled me back. *The power is not from here, Waythrel. Didn't you listen? The god is right. It is a true hope. Only because of this can we believe to overcome our shattered universe; that it can be healed; that outside of the constraints of time, it may find its whole form.*

What are you talking about?

This sphere holds power from outside; *it is not of our cosmos. It means, Waythrel, thank God—or whatever—that we are* not *in isolation. We are not a closed system. There are other universes in contact with our own, and energy flows between.*

I was stunned by the thoughts. I stared at the glowing ball in the god's hands that weakly illuminated a frozen planet. A dead world in a dark cosmos doomed forever to a frozen tomb, except for a fissure in the boundaries of our reality that opened into another. But who was to say the other universe, or universes, would not themselves all also die such a death?

The ice titan rumbled. "Many may die. An infinite number may perish and yet still represent an infinitesimal portion of the whole. We know nothing of what lies Without. It does not matter. Only one of us could reach Outside, and she gave us this bridge. She brought this hope. Not for herself only, but for all. For rebirth and a healing of the broken symmetries." It turned to Kloan and held the ball in front of her. "Use the gift, destroyer, and remove the madness from the cosmic mind."

The hulk pivoted, like an island flipping, and replaced the sphere on its pedestal precisely. Then it turned back to us, its gigantic limbs hanging loosely at its side. The glowing eyes were covered by lids of ice, and a deep silence washed over everything.

Then the giant shattered. It was thunderous, and the vibrations from the ground tossed us down again as shards of the thing cascaded around us. Yet we were unharmed, and a million pieces of a god struck the surface, liquefied, and melted away into the planet as if they had never been.

Chapter 48

Astronomy? Impossible to understand and madness to investigate.

Sophocles, c. 420 BCE

W e slowly pulled ourselves back to our feet. A thin film of frost covered us completely but quickly melted from our body heat. The dome of air remained in place, the titans continued to stare down in silence, and the sphere glowed ominously in front of us.

"Kloan, I advise caution. You seem to understand so much more than me, but I know that these beings, their doings, everything about them is beyond your grasp, beyond your ability to control. Remember the encounter with Rakshasi!"

Kloan's face darkened and she squinted her eyes. "I will never forget, Waythrel. I faced that fear when I read the presence of the demon in the ice."

Several eyestalks instinctively focused on the twisted shape behind her. The others watched a resolution form in her features.

She spoke firmly. "But this is so much bigger than our fears or the petty plans of these gods."

"Petty? Kloan, they are beyond us!"

"Yes. And *no*, Waythrel. And that is part of the deep flaw that has wounded this universe, a flaw that has distorted its structure and prevented it from reaching its potential."

"What potential?" All the conversations now seemed utterly intangible.

"*True* divinity. To become more than we could ever understand and yet take its small place in an infinity of god-particles. In order to build to the next stratum." She walked forward slowly, approaching the sphere with a quiet awe.

"Everything you say is abstract and vague to me, Kloan! But the terrible power of these creatures, and I presume their artifacts, is not! Will you at least wait and think about this thing that you are doing?"

"I'm cold, Waythrel. And thinking more won't change my mind." She reached the narrow ice plinth. The sphere hovered over the bowl-shaped depression at its top, avoiding contact with the sides. The swirling colors danced across Kloan's pale form and seemed to activate the tattooed circuits underneath her skin. They blazed forth like hot steel in a furnace, waves of brighter lights and different hues flowing over her like a patterned windstorm. "But this is warm," she said, her eyes wide. "I feel a force unlike anything I have known in its depths."

She reached her hand into the bowl and grasped the sphere. I moved forward protectively, fully cognizant that were this cosmic relic to cause her harm, there would be nothing I could do to stop it. The sphere dwarfed her hand, and yet she grasped it; and, like an optical illusion, the entity now fit perfectly within her palm. She stared at it, a sage and a child together, a madwoman and prophet with eyes of flickering green. Then she laughed and pocketed the object in her robes. The light was instantly extinguished.

Complete darkness dropped like a physical blow. *The dome is gone*, I thought toward her as I realized I could no longer speak. But to my horror, I felt a vacuum in the place of her consciousness. Kloan, too, was gone, vanished in an instant in much the same way as Synphel.

Kloan! My mind cried out for her, but there was no response. There was not the slightest trace of her personality left in this place anymore. I spun in circles, calling out her name in my mind over and over again. It was in vain. She was not present. She could not hear me. Whatever had been piloting our deranged voyage had, for the second time, split us apart.

I wasn't sure what disturbed me the most—losing Kloan or realizing that I was trapped on this world alone. Concern for the child and a panic over my own predicament coursed through me like electric charges. Was she okay? Why would I be left here? Why had I come in the first place? In all this infinite suffering, what was the point now of this separation? Was this another test, like the labyrinth?

I tried to calm my thoughts. I stilled my emotions. I meditated with all the concentration I could muster. Minutes dragged by—hours, perhaps. I began to step outside myself. It was at that point that I realized I did not know where I was.

That's my Waythrel, came warm thoughts that wrapped around me like a blanket. *We miss your mind and counsel.*

A light grew before me. I seemed to be orbiting it, spinning slowly around a congealed sea of clouds with indistinct features. But as I completed my revolution, the motion ceased, the fog solidified, and I was face to face with the cyborg apparition of Ambra Dawn again.

"Ambra, please, I don't understand." I was completely overcome. I had no more to give her or this quest. I didn't care anymore about the fate of a universe that was insane beyond my capability to even qualify. I needed rest. I needed peace. I needed warmth and love.

"And so you will soon have both, dear Waythrel," said the horror in front of me. "The last steps are coming. You need only complete the loop one last time."

"One last time." It did not seem possible.

"A final journey through smoke and fire, and then the gods themselves will carry you on their backs."

"And Kloan?" The gods could all burn.

Ambra smiled. "She will embrace her fate, which is beyond all the stories of myth and the hopes of sentient creatures. And you will propel her to that fate and remake all that will have then never been."

"What of you? What of Synphel?"

"Be joyful, Waythrel, because your hopes will be fulfilled. You will hold both of us again."

"I don't understand. You are now gods. You are timeless, and I am small, only the puff of energy from a chemical reaction lost in a sea of living broth. How can I hold *that?*"

"Patience, Waythrel. It cannot be explained. But you will join your mate, and on that day you will be two mothers holding God's children, and I will look up to you with an infant's eyes."

The apparition began to withdraw. It shrank, as if retreating through space toward a distant point. I reached out, desperate not to be left alone again, confused and disoriented as I continually found myself throughout this madness.

"Please, Ambra, don't go! I don't understand!"

The cloud was now only a small point, and her voice drifted slowly back to me as if it came from endless eons across the girth of the universe itself.

"Let go of understanding, Waythrel. Each stratum sees only what is below and worships what is above. But at all levels, the essence is held together by the one fundamental force that scales infinitely. When your mind is free and clear, you will know what it is, and you will embrace it."

And she was gone.

Chapter 49

In the fabric of space and in the nature of matter, as in a great work of art, there is, written small, the artist's signature.

Carl Sagan

I stared up at a night sky, the faint pinpricks of starlight dimly bleeding through a haze of smoke and dust. A dry wind blasted hot air over me. The ground shook with angry tremors. My eyestalks darted about, appraising the planet surface, the heavens, and the figure of the girl sitting beside me.

"Something terrible has happened." The words escaped me before I recognized the thought.

Kloan sat with her legs pulled up, nearly obscuring her head, those haunting green eyes peeking over the kneecaps, arms wrapped around her legs, keeping them together. She rocked slowly back and forth. She was humming.

I sat up and stared across at her. "Where are we?"

The humming ceased. "The same."

"The same?" My eyestalks swiveled around anxiously. The landscape did seem familiar, but the climate was not. In my fogged memories, there had taken shape through a slow aggregation the image of a habitable world coated at night with clear star fields, breathable air, and a moderate temperature. Around me was a world covered in smoke, the stars hidden, the temperature dramatically raised. "No, Kloan, not the same this time."

"Which time is this, Waythrel?"

"Kloan, stop!" I stood up, anxiety washing over me. "Something terrible has happened here. Don't you see it?"

Everything reeked of devastation. Fires uncounted burned across my field of vision. Molten chasms opened in the plains below us, lava flowing like rivers through the rends in the rock. I was having trouble acquiring oxygen. Kloan coughed and wheezed in the ash-filled air.

The intubated, tattooed head cocked to one side, the green eyes continuing to stare fixedly at me. They were bloodshot from the fumes. Kloan stood up. It was a rapid motion but anticipated. She stopped to stand in front of me, her long, ragged clumps of red hair dangling haphazardly, nearly obscuring her face. Her once-tan robes were soiled nearly black with soot. "The decision point approaches, Waythrel. The tests and experiments are over. The Anti were wrong. Even the gods are blind."

"The gods?" I looked around at the planetary cataclysm. "Kloan, what has happened to this world?"

She nodded, a satisfied look on her face. "That's *why* you're here. *Data.* The last data to enter the gate." Again she nodded and then turned her back on me to walk down a steep slope. "Let's get started."

"Started with what? Where are you going? Look around you—the mantle is torn open! There is molten rock pouring over the plains!"

Kloan continued walking without turning back. Her next words were nearly lost in the deep rumblings and howling wind.

"To where it all began for me. To watch the beginning flow around us and mature and twist through time and space to come back to be us. Then we will be ready for the last step."

The figure of the child was gone, swallowed in the smoky darkness. A violent tremor nearly threw me to the ground. Catching myself on a jagged boulder, I slowly raised my gaze in the direction of her last words, trying to understand what was happening.

Waythrel, come on!

Her voice rang impatiently in my mind. My eyestalks curled up on themselves. I looked around the desolate, ruined space surrounding me. What else was there for me to do?

I followed her, racing to catch up, my steps uncertain. Ash covered the ground like a winter snowstorm, the rocks slick with it under my feet. Down the steep slope of the elevation, I stumbled and tripped, my four arms only poorly grasping the rocks and alien vegetation, seeming to lack any friction to form a proper grip. *That field around our bodies.*

I slowed down as I rounded a large boulder, anticipating her presence. Kloan was poised on a ledge, staring across the shattered plain below us. Steam and smoke rose maniacally from the fissures snaking across the landscape.

The city of clones was gone. Obliterated. The structures

were vaporized and erased by blast and fire so that it was difficult to believe that there had ever been something there. Only the crater and impact blast density revealed that this place had been especially targeted by the wrath that had descended on the planet.

"The devil ball?" I asked fearfully, my sympathies now scrambled, my concern for the well-being of those once my enemies, real and burning.

"One of them. No—I sense many of them."

"Why would Ambra do this?"

"Not Ambra."

"But you said—"

"*Not* Ambra," she repeated firmly. "There are many gods, remember?"

The other gods. "Rakshasi?"

The ground swayed wildly. I held tightly to the rocks overlooking the wreckage below. In the plain, a new fissure ripped open and sprayed lava hundreds of feet high. It lit up the dark evening like a fluorescent curtain that rose and then rained fire on the blackened soil. I thought I could even feel the heat from it.

"Not only."

"But why? What interest could they have in this small place?"

Kloan turned to me solemnly. "You have to remember more, Waythrel. You have to do better! The decision point is here, and when we cross the portal, it will be for the last time."

"We will exit the loop?"

"Only if we understand the decision point, if we understand the choice! You have to remember!"

"The disk? Did it survive?" How could we leave again if it were destroyed?

She ignored my question. "What are the gods?"

I was suddenly tired. I felt as though I had lived one thousand lives here, repeated a million events, all of them a blur, many of them horrible, all of them impacting my being and leaving impressions that I could only vaguely understand. I had already exhausted myself just to retain my sanity in this madhouse. I did not want a quiz. I didn't want to understand anymore. I just wanted it all to stop, for an end to come.

Kloan grasped my hands tightly. "What are the gods, Waythrel?"

"They're like Ambra. Powerful group minds. Made somehow similar, but different. They are her enemies. They fear her. Something like that. Please, no more. It's all too much. I'm tired, Kloan. I need to rest." I was pleading.

She ignored my plea. "And what else do they fear?"

Rapid-fire images of events sped through my mind. The disk. Torture. Supergroups of galaxies. Heavens and hells. Synphel and Kloan.

"You," I said, the realization shocking me, the memories solidifying. "They fear you."

"Then you understand this," she said, gesturing around us.

I looked across the burning world from horizon to horizon. Puzzle pieces assembled. I understood. "They wanted to destroy you."

"Yes! Good. They destroyed my world, blew me up in this past! Why am I still here?" Her eyes bored into mine.

I felt hopeless. "I don't know. You shouldn't be."

"Waythrel! You *do* know. You have to know. If you don't understand, we can't leave!" She sounded desperate.

I thought over the infinity of dreamscapes buried in my mind. Not the pitiful handful I have shared with this author, and which he has tried to convey to you. No. I scanned through them all. Over and over through the disk, one hundred times more than I could possibly ever recount in one hundred books—worlds, adventures, deaths, pursuit, love, fear, dread, longing—always for nothing, always snapping back here, doomed to repeat and repeat.

"It's because we repeat," I managed, the words spilling from me almost unconsciously.

"Yes! Don't you see? It's at the beginning where we have to find the decision point! Everything else is only a weakly weighted world curve. There are endless numbers of them summing to nothing. Only one path leads to permanence."

I felt like a child barely grasping elementary mathematics. "Then the gods—they failed because they do not understand the decision point?"

"Yes!" Kloan smiled. "We couldn't kill Ambra in time, and they can't kill me."

"But I don't understand it, either! I don't know what it is!"

Kloan hugged me, her beaming face inches from my eyestalks. The swirling lines of cybernetics across her skin were dizzying. "That's okay, Waythrel! You will! You understand the structure, and now we can escape these loops and enter the final iteration. There you will be added to, changed by what you see, and you will understand in the end what you must do! *She's* counting on you. So am I."

Kloan released me from her embrace and began climbing back up the mountain. I could hardly breathe. I had no idea what she meant. It seemed the powers of the universe were swirling around us, and I was dancing with some mad Sibyl who had just informed me that a key to the resolution of a cosmic conflict, the fate of the universe itself, would soon rest with me. That they were all counting on me to understand and do something.

Do what? How was I to understand? How could some lowly Xix play any role in the fate of the gods of our cosmos?

I watched her climb. I couldn't move. Once again, she compelled me from her mind.

Waythrel, come on!

Chapter 50

In the end—when all else is dust—loyalty to those we love is all we can carry with us to the grave. Faith—true faith—was trusting in that love.

Dan Simmons

And so we climbed.

I felt, I half remembered, and I sensed that it was not the first time. Mnemonic whispers suggested that we had made this journey before, or would make it, or were making it in some parallel time loop world line of whatever it was that held us fast in this mind-shattering, recursive hell.

We climbed. Fighting the low friction of the mysterious field built around me for protection, I scaled the jagged rocks as they shook in the throes of a dying world. I marched over terrace after terrace of bedrock as we approached the path to the disk, my legs slowing and slowing as the oxygen-depleted atmosphere burning around us sapped our strength. Kloan fared no better; her pale skin was now dark from the murky air, her red hair dyed a dim gray in this choking soup. She coughed up black phlegm, and mucous and tears were running down her face. She wheezed horribly.

I knew we could not last much longer on this doomed world. As our physiological survival mechanisms asserted themselves, we climbed numbly with a single-minded focus to reach the gate, higher purpose be damned.

Memory of previous climbs was not precise, so it was a surprise and relief when we cleared the final terrace and scaled the wall after it to step onto a remembered path. Ahead was the gate. In all this misery and death and destruction, it shone as a beacon, dispelling the filth and darkness. The smoke did not dim its radiance or blot out the star field within it. Even the air was purer the closer we approached. It was as if it projected a protective bubble around itself.

Kloan collapsed to the ground, coughing, and then began retching. I held her torso upright to prevent her from choking, so weak she was and so violent her spasms. When it was over, I lay her down on her side and sat down beside her. I feared we might never find the strength to stand again.

"All the failures," came the harsh rasp of her voice, "The Anti couldn't recognize the timeless asymmetry." Her eyes were shut, her face nearly unrecognizable, layered in the soot and excretions. Even her teeth were black as she spoke. "Their efforts too crude. We cannot simply *die*. That path was written out of the summation when the Orb came into being."

Her coughing returned, and I placed my arm around her head instinctively. She lay back into it as the fit passed. "We must be annihilated. It is the only way to free the universe of her."

"Kloan, you're speaking of killing Ambra. Why?"

"No! Haven't you been listening? She can't be killed. Not anymore. She must be *annihilated*. With sentience, it is more than with mere matter. It is creative, Waythrel. She is the true god-seed, but it cannot be imbalanced. We must remove the nucleation center." Again the coughing. She appeared completely exhausted. Weakly she held my hand. "God cannot be nucleated on a single personality. We must give birth to something far, far more than that."

She gasped for breath. The clean air almost seemed to worsen her condition, but I knew the fits to be her body's purging of the grime within her respiratory tract. It seemed like she coughed out handfuls of coal.

"The other gods," she whispered slowly, the recent fits sapping nearly all her energy, "they must be present. They must be part of it. The yin and the yang. Matter and antimatter. Yes and no. Hate and love. All must balance for the cognitive symmetry to be regained."

She lost consciousness. I stared down at the begrimed face, the soiled strands of hair stuck to her skin, the wires and skull protrusions dripping with black sweat. And I knew then what the second apparition of Synphel had claimed. *I loved Kloan.* Perhaps it was the thousand journeys together with her, perhaps it was because of something else I would never understand. But with love, reasons no longer matter. Somehow in all this madness, this wild, murderous, divine creature had grown within my heart and taken a place there—even if she had first appeared as a thief to steal me from Ambra Dawn.

But I no longer knew what Ambra was, what I had helped make her into. The earth woman I had loved so dearly seemed part of a universe buried under a mountain of lifetimes. The Ambra Dawn made known to me now—this goddess collective seeming to control time and space—was something more akin to the deities who had laid waste to this world. As much as anything else, Kloan was the only tangible, only *mortal* echo of Ambra I had left.

I caressed her face and brushed the hair out of her eyes. She stirred.

"Waythrel, please, we must leave now." She tried to sit up but failed. "Don't let me fall asleep again. I won't wake up a second time." Her breath was ragged. "Can you carry me to the gate?"

And so it came to this. I was being asked by this child, this instrument of the Anti designed to kill Ambra Dawn, to help her in her quest to destroy the Daughter. After witnessing attempt after attempt to kill or disable Ambra Dawn in passage after passage through the gate, I was asked to help the now helpless assassin, who only moments before had confessed of the ultimate goal of some kind of annihilatory murder. Because it was *good* for the universe. Because it would be a *creative destruction.*

I was asked to do this by a creature whom I now admitted to myself that I loved, a creature who had been aided directly on multiple occasions by Ambra herself in whatever existence she now resided. If I was to believe anything, this entire eternity of broken quests had been built and designed by Ambra for the soul purpose of Kloan achieving some cosmic education.

I could not comprehend their plan. I could not see into the depths of time and causality. I knew only too painfully that my very finite mind was helpless to know the truth in this matter. I had no ultimate confidence in my mental faculties to cut through this knot.

And so I did the only thing I could still do. I turned away

from understanding. I accepted my inability to grasp what was unfolding before us. I looked instead to the love I had for both Kloan and Ambra and the trust they were placing in me. Whatever this was all about, they were in some demented kind of harmony. That was enough for me. Without any vision, with no idea where our feet would land except that it all seemed like madness, I closed my eyes and let myself fall into their arms.

"Here, let me get my other arms around you," I said, reaching underneath her and heaving her upward.

Kloan turned her red and green eyes to me, black crusts of mucus nearly sealing the eyelids shut. "Thank you, Waythrel. In the end, you'll understand."

I doubted that very much, but it did not matter. I was committed to something more than understanding. I steadied her on my midsection.

The small human girl was light in my arms, even after all the exhaustion from our climb and the debilitating environment. Slowly, unsteadily, I stepped toward the star-filled lake surface of the gate, the groans of the planet churning behind me like waves at the seashore.

She grasped my hand. "One last dance through the gate, dear Xix." She rested her head on my torso cone.

I stepped with her through the portal.

Part 7

In dust and law I watched my children born.
The gathering of clouds crept past my eyes,
and soon the shroud of hydrogen was shorn
by rays of light that sang the first day's rise.
A fetus as a single grain of sand
that spins within a storm of desert winds,
through eons rendered life and sprouted land—
I smile through birth pangs that have yet to end.
Decrees the dust drove to some patterned dance,
the law that shapes my form and carves my bone,
soon molecules found purpose in their trance
to mold from mud new offspring of their own.
These children stood to gaze into the womb
and claimed to know their cradle and their tomb.

—Mazandarani, *Sonnets from the Desert*

Chapter 51

I have seen beyond the bounds of infinity and drawn down daemons from the stars. . . .I have harnessed the shadows that stride from world to world to sow death and madness. . .

H. P. Lovecraft

e stepped out backward through the gate, but despite superficial similarities, I immediately knew that something was different about this journey. The narrow, sloped pathway from the plains below stood before us. The well-known rock formations, only moments ago seemingly covered in soot and ash, surrounded us, whole and untarnished. But more than this, there was a profound sense of *change*.

Angled to look behind me, several of my eyes stared at the gate in wonder. Once pregnant with stars and honey, the disk was now empty. I could look straight through the circle to the rocky wall behind it. No churning star field. No bright suns of other worlds. Just air. The metal band of the disk, once glinting and alive, appeared rusted, decayed, the life force within the thing quenched.

I examined our bodies—the gel was missing. In stepping back through the gate a last time we had avoided carrying with us that bothersome coating. We were also clean of the ash and soot of the destroyed world. Where had it gone? I no longer cared to know the reasons. It was over. It seemed we had indeed come to an end of our recursive travels.

Whereas my heart soared for our escape from that repetitive hell, Kloan appeared all the more serious. Gone were the childlike bursts of energy and creativity that so often bubbled to the surface after we had completed a passage. Instead, her countenance was stern as she squinted into the afternoon light. I watched her play with an object in her robes like a nervous tic. She began to sweat.

"We need to get to higher ground, Waythrel."

Several eyestalks swiveled upward to glance at the rocky slope. The careening cliff face loomed over me from several angles vertiginously. "Why, Kloan? What is happening?"

She sighed and began to scan the walls of rock around us. "We're starting the endgame. Everything is going to come together now. I must bring all the gods to the nexus of time, to the discontinuity that shatters the smoothness of cosmic space-time." She bit her lower lip. "I know so *few* of them, and the ones I know are truly monsters. But we must start somewhere. I will summon them here."

Summon the gods here? Is she mad? "How can you do that?"

Her eyes settled on a high peak in the mountain range around us. "There. That will do. It's high, and there is enough space around it."

A force pulled me upward and my feet left the ground.

Together we soared at an accelerating rate, the rocky surfaces speeding past only meters from our forms. The high peak she had indicated quickly grew in size.

"We should travel this way more often," I said, nervous energy running through me. "Avoid all that climbing."

"There isn't always need. It's good to use our bodies, you know."

"And now we have a need. What are you doing, Kloan?"

"I'm calling the gods to us, Waythrel. I told you. Don't think that they will always take the forms Rakshasi and Ambra assumed. Remember the ice world!"

We reached the summit. The air was colder and the oxygen levels almost dangerously low. I wondered if the strange skin suits would somehow compensate. If not, one of us was likely in danger of losing consciousness. I felt weak and tried to optimize my atmospheric intake.

"Rakshasi and the lesser gods will not do anything without Māra" she gasped slowly, bent double as she tried to breathe.

"Who is Māra?"

"Ambra mentioned her, countless cycles back, when she saved us from Rakshasi."

"It's a her?"

"Their queen. Gender has little meaning to these beings, but when they squeeze their consciousnesses into our pathetic languages, our small range of ideas and mental modes, strange things like gender or emotion or personality—things we believe we recognize only because our thinking is so constrained by our words—come out in the grinder, with as much resemblance to what was before as ground meat has to a running stag."

"How do you know this? How can you possibly know of this Māra queen?"

"I sampled the gods frozen in time. Don't you remember, Waythrel? I learned much and comprehended little. This is a collective, dominated by the powerful group mind of Māra. But the group is *not* a group mind. They fail to combine, to reach a harmonic synthesis. The gods here are too individualistic, too hateful and proud and selfish to truly merge—if those words appropriate for more simplistic creatures like us can be applied to beings like these. That's why they remain weaker than Ambra, forever adding linearly to their powers through numbers while she adds exponentially through true synergy."

"They seem powerful enough." I did not wish to meet these creatures if they were anything like Rakshasi.

"They are beyond us, no doubt!" said Kloan. "They are beyond the power of star systems. But they will come."

"You are very confident."

Kloan stared up into the sky, her equilibrium returning as she adapted to the altitude. "I can feel them all, Waythrel. There is a thread through me that disturbs all the gods. Remember? I can fully sense it, now. I will pluck that thread, that cosmic line to the singularity, like a string and rattle their universe rudely." She smiled, a hint of the mischievous child peeking through. "Sit with me, Waythrel?"

Kloan sat cross-legged, and I lowered myself beside her. She reached up and grabbed my upper arms, just as Ambra had done in a distant timeline, deeply buried in an infinite summation and lost forever. I pulled back, the similarity too disturbing, the ironies too strong.

"You can't hide anymore, Waythrel. You are integral to what comes next. And I need you far more than she did on Dram. What is coming, that which will soon surround us, makes ten thousand clones a field of flowers." She grasped my hands again tightly, staring into my eye clusters. "Keep your eyes closed. I mean that. No matter what happens, don't look at them!"

Madness. I locked my many digits around her own. I sent up a prayer to Ambra that she would watch over us. I felt like a small nymph naked before the onrushing sandstorm. I closed all my eyes tightly.

And then a pulse blasted through the universe.

It was unique in all the stirrings of my Reader senses. It was powerful and strange beyond anything I had felt or imagined, as if, along a thousand vectors in the multidimensional reality of space-time, a vibration as low as the deepest abyss and higher than the greatest peak imaginable exploded forward and propagated without the possibility of resistance. Frequency modulated in nested levels, containing a wealth of information that decoded itself as the wave smashed through my mind. This world. Kloan and myself. A challenge for the gods of Rakshasi and Māra. The destruction of Ambra Dawn. My mind constructed a visual of the pulse charging outward without diminishment in the signal strength, gaining speed as it progressed, gone before I could process it.

In vain I wondered how it might work, how long it would take to reach the intended targets, or if it even would. Uselessly I began to analyze whether it made any sense that these beings, even if they could hear this strange call, would come. Stupidly, I tried to justify why beings who had grown so far beyond us would heed the summons of an eight-year-old cyborg biped.

I had barely begun to initiate these thoughts when the gods arrived. It was as if time and distance had different application to these beings. Not daring to violate Kloan's directive, I kept my eyes firmly shut. I saw nothing. But I *felt* them. I felt them in multiple fashions, all of which rendered me small, insignificant, and completely terrified.

The ground shook with deep tremors. Blasts of air erupted around us from multiple directions due to the displacement of truly titanic volumes of atmosphere—it was like being caught in a storm or series of powerful explosions. My olfactory strips *smelled* them—at least the physical forms they had chosen for this incarnation. Their stench was overpowering, *hellish*, a nightmare of every scent of death and decay I could recall experiencing mixed with others that somehow were far worse.

But the greatest impact was in my mind. I might not have dared gaze upon their appearances and open the extensive neuronal pathways of my optical system to the insanity they undoubtedly presented, but strange echoes of their might and form invaded my mind. In the presence of these entities, I found myself for the first time cursing my Reader powers, desperately wishing that I were blind like so much of the universe. Ignorance was not bliss, I was sure of that. But knowledge could be torture.

In what I describe, in what I say, you must know that it comes to you only through the distorted lens of my mind and other senses, regurgitated through an imagination made nauseous. Drunk and staggering as from poison, my damaged memory fumbles ideas into this author's mind. His reception of them is mostly confused shock, and he operates like a malfunctioning machine, poorly picking vocabulary and syntax from your simplistic Earth languages that must serve as your bridge to my experience. Inadequate. Disfiguring. All of it, *lies*. But truly, even if it were possible for me to understand these things, I would not wish to. I know that my mind has not the strength to withstand such truth.

Whatever the ultimate reality, it felt to me as though there was a circle of them around the mountain peak on which we sat. Their forms burned and pressed on me from all sides, displacements in the air and thundering tremors testifying to their size, which I envisioned as larger than the mountain itself. I pictured their forms towering over us, a thousand eyes staring down in contempt upon two insignificant insects that dared clang a cosmic bell.

On Kloan's left was a presence I knew only too well —*Rakshasi*. I forced the dark currents of its essence away from me as much as possible, and yet it felt like I was being strangled by hundreds of snakes. Against my will, my mind formed a vision of the thing that had appeared, monumental yet lithe, slithering and darting like a salamander, yet devious and fanged like a fox, seven tails of flame behind it.

The center of power lay, however, directly behind me. I did not know this thing. I prayed never to know it. It swelled in my consciousness to a size that dwarfed all the other gods around us. It seemed ever to consume itself in fire, and like a creature of magma and smoke, it moved and dissolved, reformed and blurred, so that there was never a sure shape, never a point of reference, only the certainty of searing and choking death. A name was whispered in my deepest consciousness: *Māra*. It seemed as though sound spilled like a toxic smoke to strangle my mind. I grasped Kloan's hands in desperation.

And Kloan spoke. A childish, singsong voice chirped sarcastically in the burning wind around us. "You seem a few short, dear Māra, but the cosmic game is still very young, I suppose."

I felt her smile.

Chapter 52

And as I lay me down to sleep,
my soul no night mare shall it keep,
until they've swum through every strand,
and walked across the endless lands,
and counted each and every star
of blue and red, both near and far.

ancient charm against evil

I t took no great genius to see the madness in Kloan's words and that she had doomed herself for speaking with such insolence. In some intuitive place in my being, I felt Rakshasi coil to strike. I began to scream for Kloan in fear, but I was violently interrupted by Māra.

"Hold yourself, you *fool.*" The voice grated through my soul like razor wire. High and low, masculine and feminine, whispered and shouted, it was less a voice than a tool of torture. "Even you, are you blind to what has changed?"

The fox-lizard seemed to hiss in response. "We should have destroyed her before."

"Perhaps," came the voice of madness and death. "But that thread is gone. Great, great power surrounds her now, alien and incomprehensible. Strike her, and you may achieve our destruction." A breath like acid spilled over us. "Was that your goal, betrayer?"

I wondered that we were not instantly dissolved into a puddle of cellular debris. I barely kept focus, nearly falling into a primitive, self-preserving dormant state similar to a human coma. All my senses were overwhelmed, and I felt supremely grateful that I had not dared to glance upon these things. Through it all, somehow, Kloan held her own in the face of this monstrous, dark force. Only through her strength of will did I remain conscious.

Kloan spoke calmly. "My goal, my purpose from the first cell split from its progenitor, was and is to destroy Ambra Dawn. You know this. That's why you are here. Because in that goal, our paths are joined."

I felt the Māra-thing ease backward. I felt the chemical poison withdrawn.

"Continue," it said.

"Look at you all," Kloan said. I imagined her gesturing around us. "Galactic mountains that cower in fear because of her. Growing slowly like a cancer that cannot organize to do anything but devour. And hide. You will never defeat her!"

The collective hostility that squeezed in on us was suffocating. Kloan only laughed.

"You don't even understand *me*. Tiny little nothing me. I fart and shake your world strings and you appear like flaming gladiators, extraordinary and terrible. But you are nothing more than terrified worms diving into the dirt."

Again I felt the strike of Rakshasi, but this time I felt the physical response of Māra. My mind lost focus. There was only white noise. Then the horrific scene around me returned, and I felt the blood of Rakshasi spill over the mountain like a deluge drowning the world. Again, remember, these are mental metaphors. I truly don't know what happened. I'm sure that there was no blood. No drowned world. Only that Māra had punished a disciple. It was all my flayed mind could do with the impressions.

Kloan continued without missing a beat. "Your little club is not enough, will *never* be enough, and you know this. Only if we can convince the other gods, the thousands of powers elsewhere in the cosmos, to join our cause, can we summon the strength to defeat her."

Māra's tone was like brimstone. "And how might such an army defeat her?"

"It won't. *I* will."

"You will?" came another voice I did not recognize. I sought desperately to hide my mind from it. I had no strength of engage with another of these demons. Its words seemed to drip with blood and scorn, mockery and disbelief.

"Silence, Vetala," belched Māra. A playback of Kloan's pulse was driven through my mind. "Remember."

A morose silence seemed to fall on the spirits around me, and their mental fields retreated to places I could not access. For the briefest of dreams, it felt as if the sun had come out from behind a cloud.

"Yes," said Kloan. "*Remember*. Follow that line and see where it ends. At the beginning. And Ambra will be there."

There was a long silence. Deep in my being, I sensed

undercurrents of power, dark dreams of thought flowing and connecting, jet streams mixing and turbulence building and ebbing. In the darkest corners of my psyche, I felt movement in a black abyss that I could not access except by dank rumor. And out of this darkness an eruption burst.

"Destroy her you can," boomed Māra. "Destroy us, you may, also."

The great queen of gloom seemed to approach us closely, a gigantic head and nightmarish visage only meters from our forms. Five slits opened in the face revealing lava within, and she sniffed deeply, the air pulling us nearly off balance. The mountain of fire before us growled like an earthquake.

"You reek with her stench, betrayer. She has coated you with her slime." There seemed to be a stirring of the other creatures around us, and a malevolent sludge rose from each point of space to pour over us, cold and barbed, hateful and sadistic. "Did she think Māra would not see? Did she think her powers so mighty? She may devour the weaker gods, but she will not so easily devour Māra!"

The thing roared like the shockwave of a supernova. Kloan spoke coldly, like a disappointed parent.

"No, you will not end that way. Instead you will persist in fugue—frozen, unmoving, unthinking—until the end of time that always approaches yet never arrives. I have seen it and looked upon your living corpse." The malignant swamp closing around us pulled back. It seemed even in the deranged visions of these gods, there was doubt. "Yes, you sense it, don't you? The creeping cold? The slow death that will consume you all?" Kloan seemed to raise her voice and the power of her mental projection. "We do not serve Ambra Dawn. She has tried to manipulate us, guide us for her own uses, but we have used her to reach this point. I hold a power now from outside this cosmos. Together, when we find the other gods, she cannot stop us, and I will reach the discontinuity!"

Māra laughed. "You think I cannot sense the lie in your voice? You are protected with a thousand layers of deceit. But we will not seek to break through it. Tell your puppet master that her trick was ingenious, but it has failed. Tell her in fire or in ice, we will resist her!"

Suddenly, my mind returned to me once more, and I awoke from a delirium. The vacuum of their absence rushed through me like a balm, revitalizing my thoughts and hopes. I foolishly opened my eyes to see Kloan again.

Except we were not alone. All the gods had vanished. All but one. Sitting beside us was not a titan, but an old man. It had taken the form of a human, likely in deference to Kloan, with a sage-like beard, bald head, withered body, and eyes that glowed like two red coals.

"There are others, great powers, older than we, who will perhaps listen," the figure spoke.

Kloan turned toward the god and nodded. "How are you to be named?"

"I have one thousand names on a million worlds. But you many call me Vighneshvara." He continued, "Fools the others have become. The flaw in the cosmos is deeper than they wish to acknowledge."

"But you see it," said Kloan.

"It flays me alive," he said.

"These other gods—where are they?"

"Across the cosmos. Across time. Failed gods, but they failed far more along the path than our circle of pretenders. But we know them. We avoid them lest they crush us. But I will take you to them because it must be."

I whispered, "And then the gods themselves will carry you on their backs."

Kloan looked at me and squeezed my hand. "What was that, Waythrel?"

"Nothing," I said, dread and hope rising in me like bile. "Something I heard once. But it may have been only a dream."

Chapter 53

It was an All-in-One and One-in-All of limitless being and self—not merely a thing of one Space-Time continuum, but allied to the ultimate animating essence of existence's whole unbounded sweep—the last, utter sweep which has no confines and which outreaches fancy and mathematics alike.

H. P. Lovecraft

Traveling on the backs of gods has a lot going for it regarding ease of transport, but the destinations and cultures you meet along the way counterbalance that comfort with the distressingly fantastic. Vighneshvara placed two of his four arms on us, and instantly we were gone. How we journeyed, by what power or technology so advanced that it was only magic to our minds, I will never know. It nearly felt like a traversal through an Orb, only without the underlying depth, devoid of the presence of countless minds surrounding. Like the Orb traversals, descriptions are only impressionistic, and I can only say with confidence that at one moment we were on the mountain, and after an eye blink of light and distortion, we floated before the splendor of a vast, multicolored nebula.

I scanned quickly around us. There was no nearby star system, no planets, and no technological or living station to which we could descend. We were embedded in the emptiness of space, untethered to life support, unshielded from cosmic radiation. Yet we neither roasted nor froze nor suffocated. Due to Ambra's hand or the power of this god, our fragile fleshly forms were protected.

Behold, Aditi!

The voice of Vighneshvara resounded in my mind.

I again scanned all around us, but I saw nothing. I reached out to Ambra. *In the nebula?*

No, Waythrel, Aditi is the nebula.

The god is a nebula?

Vighneshvara seemed impatient. *The goddess can be anything in this cosmos that she might want. She prefers to assume this form, this gaseous mixture of dust and young stars spanning twenty parsecs, and has remained as such since before your ancestors learned to speak. She is one of the oldest. Once, long ago, she mothered the formation of many group minds, many assemblies, even those that grew to rebel and disown her. But no longer. She retreats to her own, unfathomable cogitations. Yet her mind shaped a thousand gods who roam the stars. If she will come, so will many, and a great force we will have acquired.*

Do you think she will listen? asked Kloan.

If not to you, then to no one. Once, when the threat of the Ambra abomination became clear, we sought her advice. Māra sent a contingent of powers to beseech her to stand against this force devouring the cosmos. But the rest of us experienced a terrible cry through the corridors of space-time, and minds of these emissaries ceased. We never again found a single trace that they had ever existed.

This appeared to be suicide. It seemed clear that Vighneshvara would not even be able to protect himself here, and this murderous cloud would snuff out two motes of dust as Kloan and myself without so much as a cosmic scream. I reached beside me and grasped Kloan's hand.

Don't worry, Waythrel. This is where I am supposed to be.

Vighneshvara began to change form. The old man's skin seemed to form fissures, bright light erupting from the split tissue and bone, consuming the fleshly facade in brilliance. Shedding the skin like a snake, out of that chrysalis burst a winged delusion, a hallucinogenic concoction of wings and tails and arms and one hundred glowing eyes. The size of it quickly overshadowed our forms, spanning first hundreds and then thousands of meters, until it nearly eclipsed the angular spread of the nebula itself.

But I knew this to be an optical hoax. The nebula was still some great distance away, millions of miles until the vacuum of space would begin to be disturbed by the first measurable density of hydrogen. The winged divinity before us was truly only a small speck before the leviathan we approached. A moth approaching far too close to the flame.

"*Aditi!*" he cried.

I use the syntax of your written speech unusually in what follows, because the mental projections that flowed from these gods transcended anything I had known in telepathy. So forceful and powerful were the projected thoughts, so immediate and compelling were the ideas, that your written language, the use of italics to indicate thinking as per your conventions, utterly fail to convey the experience. Ironically, although not a sound was emitted in this exchange, having this author present it as if mouths spoke and ears heard translates the nonverbal experience more accurately.

"*YOU HAVE BROUGHT THE DESTROYER.*" A voice emanated from everywhere around us. Kloan floated away from me, past the gigantic wingspan of Vighneshvara, and hovered above and before him. "*YOU WERE ALWAYS THE WISEST OF MY CHILDREN, VIGHNESHVARA.*"

Vighneshvara bowed and tucked his wings around his body. The bright light radiating from him dissipated. It was replaced by a growing incandescence from the nebula itself. My eyes could have been deceiving me, but it nearly appeared as though this multiparsec-spanning galactic entity was shrinking impossibly fast, curling in from the edges and coalescing toward a single focal point. At that point floated Kloan.

And then, when I thought we could only be subsumed by the grandeur of this goddess, Kloan herself began to glow. An iridescence seemed to bubble from her body like a fog, spilling tendrils into the surrounding space. The nebula continued to rapidly shrink.

Dusty and colorful protrusions of the thickening cloud reached outward toward her. From myriad directions, tens, perhaps hundreds of nebulaic limbs extended as from a cosmic octopus, their internal structure a churning of constrained sandstorms. They halted around the growing and increasingly impenetrable brilliance of Kloan, forming a three-dimensional shell of probing digits.

"*THERE ARE INFINITIES WITHIN INFINITIES WITHIN AND WITHOUT YOU, UNIVERSES WITHIN COSMOS, EONS WITHIN TIMELESSNESS. THERE IS THE SHATTERING OF ALL THAT IS AND THE BIRTH OF ALL THAT SHOULD HAVE BEEN. THERE IS THE HAND OF*

THE GREAT GODDESS AND THE KNIFE OF THE DEEPEST BETRAYER."

The voice entered me from all directions and nowhere again. I was unmade and overwhelmed, melted in a hurricane of prepotency that seemed to break down every structure of my person and reassemble it according to an alien purpose. The voice was both more terrible than the howls of the demon Māra and more sublime than the deepest love I had ever experienced. It seemed to me as though here, now, and forever I had reached all that Waythrel of Xix could ever imagine to be. I felt the need for my continued consciousness removed. I believed that this was the end of my existence, that it was near, and that only in the hearing of such a voice was my life indeed made complete.

"YOU WILL BRING THE MULTITUDE TO THE VORTEX." It was a statement.

Yes, came the whisper of Kloan's mind.

The wings of Vighneshvara burst open, and a third light joined the radiance of Kloan. Violating the laws of physics, the nebula was gone, completely condensed at a speed faster than light; ultradense emissions from the resulting planet-sized structure glowed brightly.

"MY LOYAL VIGHNESHVARA, THEN WE SHALL BOTH DROWN IN THE COMING ANNIHILATION TOGETHER, AND FOR THE FIRST TIME, YOU WILL TRULY BE REBORN."

And in a blinding flash, the nebula-sphere was gone. Gone was the once-lavish tapestry of powder and light, color and contrast, spread across trillions of light-years. An empty darkness now surrounded us, barely punctured by the pinpricks of starlight from distant suns. The greatest emptiness could be felt in the realm of the soul, where a profound, cosmic spirit was suddenly absent.

The majestic and monstrous space butterfly scooped up the dimming Kloan in one hand and glided toward me, grasping me gently in another of its fifty limbs. Vighneshvara spoke within our minds.

She gathers now her children. Near and far. She will return with a great gathering.

She needed no persuading, my leaky thoughts spilled outward.

I felt the equivalent of a laugh from the mind of Vighneshvara. *Aditi is not Māra. Or like anything else you might find in this universe. All that has come or is coming opens itself for her to read.*

Kloan's thoughts were troubled. *But it is not enough. Even if she brings a thousand. You don't understand what Ambra has become.*

Not enough, responded Vighneshvara, *but nearly so with Aditi. There are others we will visit.*

And who or what is next? I wondered anxiously.

The stars around us began to blur as I sensed Vighneshvara begin another journey through space and time. *The root of much that lives within this cosmos. She touches on all the origins of souls.*

The stars careened around me.

Chapter 54

God is infinite, so His universe must be too. Thus is the excellence of God magnified and the greatness of His kingdom made manifest; He is glorified not in one, but in countless suns; not in a single earth, a single world, but in a thousand thousand, I say in an infinity of worlds.

a heresy of Giordano Bruno, burned at the stake in 1600

We hovered above a blue and green world. Earthlike, yet different, filled with dense vegetation, the atmosphere pregnant with the expelled gases of respiration. I searched frantically for an Orb. I did not know how I could handle encountering Ambra in the middle of this cosmic plot to destroy her—a plot I could not accept in my heart and yet seemed compelled by her and others to assist. But there was no Orb, which implied, to my understanding, no intelligent life. Why we had come to a world devoid of sentience baffled me.

We need to find a tributary, came the thoughts of Vigh-neshvara.

We sped down into and over the world, our forms insulated from the vacuum of space, the heat of atmospheric entry, even the potentially toxic gases from utterly alien metabolisms. The hundred eyes of Vighneshvara swiveled across the surface of the world, seeking, focused on the identification of something within this densely overgrown jungle world overflowing with vegetative life. His search was not random, and yet his destination did not seem foreknown to him. Instead, he seemed to sense his prey, *smell* it like a hunter, lock in on it like a missile, following some trail invisible to us toted mortals.

Soon our direction changed dramatically. We dove into a particularly thick region of plant forms. From an initial cloud-topped canopy of astonishingly tall arboreal growth, we plunged through layer upon layer of botany, vegetative ecosystem on top of ecosystem, passing one hundred different strata, glimpsing for fleeting moments a million different life forms packed together at inconceivable densities with incomprehensible diversity.

Onward we descended, the air thickening, moisture deepening, illumination waning. Faintly, I began to sense it—a tingling in my Reader senses—the stirring of distortions in space-time that only accompanied great power of an unusual nature. Closer and closer we zeroed in on this emission, dodging limb and leaf, often the plant forms themselves making way inexplicably for our passage. The light of the local star was nearly extinguished at this depth, the overlaying atmosphere of plant life absorbing all the radiance until the species at this level, like the animals in the depths of the New Earth seas, were devoid of color, subsisting on other means of energy than direct starlight.

As we slowed and neared the surface, the sense of the power reached a zenith. Before us, all the plant life seemed to converge on a single point, or rather, it seemed that from a single point came some powerful surge of vitality animating all around it. At the physical center of this force was a gnarled, bark-covered knot the size of a small hill. The air around it seemed to throb.

"Can you feel it, Waythrel?" asked Kloan.

"Yes. What is it?"

Vighneshvara thoughts replied. *The tip of a first root.*

We hovered above the mossy hill of bark. He curled in his wings slightly and his many legs touched down softly on the surface of the enormous knot. We remained suspended within two of his many arms while his wingtips bent downward and caressed the living root. The action sent faint ripples through my mind. The dense growth around us seemed to sway and sigh.

Yakshini, said Vighneshvara. *She will let us pass.*

"Pass where?" I asked.

Kloan pointed excitedly. "The root, Waythrel. Look!"

The gnarled stump began to glimmer. A sparkling dust seemed to hover about it, and the dimness of our environment was invaded with light. Instantly, thousands of opportunistic flying plants rushed into the area, nearly blinding us, their forms diverse and impossible to understand in these short sightings, their biology obviously attuned to the powerful light source that captivated us now.

I was underwhelmed. "*That* is Yakshini? It is a god? A root stub? A plant?"

Yes and no, came the thoughts of Vighneshvara. *She is a god; her physical raiment was chosen as a plant, the greatest tree and vine in the cosmos, a form she has held for so long that it is likely she can no longer escape it unharmed. But this is only a tip. Her roots dig through space and time, connecting world beyond world, age beyond age, deep into the deep past, far into the distant future she extends her vascularity until the worlds of the coming* then *grow too cold.*

It seemed as though the space around the root knot warped. I felt a fissure opening. "I don't understand. Kloan, what does this mean?"

Kloan smiled, a look of childish awe on her face. "Life, Waythrel. So much life! One of the greatest and oldest sources of life in our universe. We found the outer shell of her web and will ride the roots to the core."

Ride the roots to the core? Of what?

But I had no time for my thoughts. A tunnel opened before us, and a blast of swampy air swept past from the channel in space-time. But it was not empty! Extending from the glowing tip that protruded into this world, a thick, gnarled shaft plunged directly into the depths and disappeared. Vighnesh-vara opened his wings and looped in the air, angling us downward toward the opening, his army of eyes focused forward. Curling my own eyestalks in panic, I last glimpsed a blur of the jungle around us as he dove fearlessly downward and along the root's path.

Chapter 55

We used to think that if we knew one, we knew two, because one and one are two. We are finding that we must learn a great deal more about "and".

Arthur Stanley Eddington

L ight dimmed, the impossible, interplanetary root revealed only by the glowing wings of the god towing us wildly through this interdimensional passage. I cast several eyes behind and watched as the portal to the other world, a disk of blue and green light flaring in radiance as this darkness enveloped us, shrank, and winked out of existence as we sped along the living chord.

The growth was impossibly long. Even through the shortcut of hyperspace, we seemed to fly along its length for several minutes at high speed. No true organism could maintain the necessary hydrostatic pressure on such scales. Of course, no simple, mortal organism could open a wormhole, apparently multiple wormholes, throughout space and time and use those as some sort of pandimensional growth matrix connecting worlds uncounted. I felt suddenly, deeply, profoundly ignorant of the history and nature of our cosmos as well as the state of my own sanity.

As these thoughts danced through my mind, a bright disk appeared ahead, and we burst out into another world. All around us were plant forms innumerable, of bizarre shape, function, color and texture, tending toward a shade of dark blue and likely adapted to the starlight of whatever system we had entered. The tentacle of bark, ever thickening as we traversed the wormhole, erupted out of the ground like a redwood tree and snaked along the ground toward a mountain of vegetative material.

Vighneshvara spread his wings wide, and we caught the planetary airs powerfully, gliding along the god-root as it plunged into thick forests and disappeared from sight, only to reappear as it scaled the less densely covered rise of a steep mountain. Of course, all was relative, and what seemed a sparsely covered challenger to Everest was still coated by plant growth that would have rivaled the deepest regions of the Amazon.

From multiple directions I saw other giant arteries of bark converge on the mountain and follow a similar course up the structure. We soared upward, Vighneshvara beating his glowing god-wings, clouds of water and floating vegetation passing alongside us.

At the top of the mountain was a surreal botanic junction. Six massive roots scaled the mountain, or rather extended down the mountain after splitting off from a central node. I guessed what would happen next.

We hovered above the node, and it seemed to sense our

presence. A brilliant radiance shone from the bark, and once again a tunnel into nothing and nowhere opened before us. This time it was far larger, and the root that dove into the emptiness had begun to assume proportions that were beyond any plant life I had ever known.

Into the portal we sped again, careening over the god's limb, grasped tightly by our divine moth, two parasitic mites holding on for dear life. Although the root may have grown slightly, by the time we burst from the wormhole into the orange light of yet another world, it was clear that the size increase had been sharply curtailed. Again I realized that the direction of our journey was biasing my thoughts on the plant form and that what had happened was a dramatic *decrease* in size toward the extremities of the god in the earlier worlds we had first encountered.

I won't continue to repeat the similar crossings we made in this way, from new world to new world, each devoid of an Orb, empty of intelligent life, brimming instead with a vibrant ocean of unconscious growth. We experienced blinding vistas of biology rushing underneath us, descending again and again into ever-widening excavations in space-time until, as we leapt through the final portal, we flew over an arm of bark and moss that was no longer believable, no longer possible, that was so large and titanic that it had instead entered into the realm of the deities, the isolated group minds of god-things that bent— and broke—all the rules of science I knew.

And we only advanced along a humdrum vein, dwarfed by many others, one of millions I saw dive into portals uncount-able, rushing off to worlds unseen, carrying unfathomable amounts of nutrients to irrigate, fertilize, and stimulate entire networks of life across the universe.

All the roots converged on a central core, a living form that possessed the attributes of all the vegetative life I had witnessed in our journey and yet embodied them in manners unique and profound. I could not call it a tree or any other name for a plant that you might know, because it would utterly distort the nature of this goddess's incarnation. Whatever it might be named, it rested on the surface of an artificial world composed of rock and soil and water, defying the organizing principles of gravity, held together as a bowl of material with the radius of our solar system. A dizzying array of stars spun about the mass, seemingly grabbed and positioned purposefully in order to maintain the energy sources needed to sustain this impossible ecosystem.

Vighneshvara soared toward the god-plant, climbing higher and higher into the thick atmosphere of this synthetic world. Upon a stratum of branches and leaves that spanned a surface greater than a New Earth continent, we landed, touching down close to the colossal bulk of a main stem of the entity. Vighneshvara folded his wings within himself and stepped forward slowly to the wall of bark and other, unknowable plant skins.

"Yakshini," he whispered.

The surface rippled. The bark cracked and melted, snapped, and reformed with the unintended violence the small encounter from the truly titanic. A sphere with a radius as large as ten of the tallest trees of New Earth protruded from the hulk and took on features our limited forms could recognize. They were humanoid. Eyes of cellulose, a mouth of leaves, features vaguely similar to those of some odd average of all of humanity's peoples. Again I assumed all this was for Kloan.

"Yakshini has heard the last call of Aditi," the mouth blasted in gales of wind at us. "The sleeping mother gathers her brood and requests the presence of Yakshini at the nexus in time, where the usurper-thief awaits with her infinite impostors."

Vighneshvara spoke reverently. "And what is Yakshini's will in this?"

The plant face thundered, "That Yakshini will heed the call. That she will retract all life roots, cast uncountable worlds to the darkness, and wound herself beyond repair for a final battle. She wishes that Yakshini help crush the evil that has stolen everything from her."

Chapter 56

Common human laws and interests and emotions have no validity or significance in the vast cosmos-at-large. To me there is nothing but puerility in a tale in which the human form—and the local human passions and conditions and standards—are depicted as native to other worlds or other universes. One must forget that such things as organic life, good and evil, love and hate, and all such local attributes of a negligible and temporary race called mankind, have any existence at all. When we cross the line to the boundless and hideous unknown—the shadow-haunted Outside—we must remember to leave our humanity— and terrestrialism at the threshold.

H. P. Lovecraft

I t was at this point that I feared I could no longer continue in this journey. Over and over I had begun to hear Ambra and her collective slandered. These powerful beings, manifestations of colossal group intelligences of which my mind would constitute but an atom of the whole, entities that I knew I could not possibly apprehend, had repeatedly cast her actions in the vilest terms. The Orbs—those guardians every Xix loved and considered ancient bene-factors of all sentient life—underwent a terrible transforma-tion in the minds and words of these beings. Without exception, they had inverted and condemned all I had held dear.

Whatever Ambra was asking of me, whatever Kloan had cryptically revealed in her metaphysical ramblings, it was too much for me. I did not have the strength both to betray my dearest friend and forsake all that I had believed to be true. Foolishly, I challenged the gods.

"Is it mere jealousy that turns you all against her? Isn't it true that hundreds of gods have joined her, that their unions are based on trust and love, on mutual respect? Do you refuse to join for pride or avarice? Are you unable to merge with her because your minds lack humility or love?"

The plant-god focused its mind on me, freezing my thoughts in its attention. "Wayward Waythrel of Xix, how Yakshini nursed your forebears in the glassy sands! How she teased growth from a land hostile to everything that lives, labored eons in the parched and tortured dunes of your star-drenched world, and tended the saplings that evolved, became, and metamorphosed into the first nymphs of intelligence. How she loved you, dear children."

I stood there stunned. "What do you mean?"

"You have seen her works! You have witnessed the abun-dance of life on myriad worlds, life that was and is and will be planted and nursed by Yakshini. What more is there to under-stand?" Enormous arms erupted from the trunk of the plant and surrounded us, as in an embrace, halting only meters from our bodies. "Yakshini is your Mother, Waythrel. The Mother of all Xix."

"*You?* You were the Gardener?" It seemed everything would be upended.

"You exist only because of Yakshini, Xix," said Vighneshvara, his demeanor grave, his fiery eyes condemning my outburst.

It couldn't be. How could I know truth from falsehood in this place of gods whose simplest thoughts burned my mind? "But the Orb! It has always been there! Didn't it, didn't Ambra, bring us to sentience?"

"The Orb was not always there," came the booming voice of the tree, the arms around us withdrawing and slowly disappearing, absorbed into the bulk of the plant. "But the limbs of Yakshini were there when the usurper arrived. At the nascent budding of minds in the new animals that had formed on Xix, darkness fell." The face contorted, and it seemed the very light around us dimmed. "The demon ball, the *Orb* and its legions, took Xix from Yakshini. The hell-thing burned her roots into the time corridors and backward, until leaf and branch of her body withered and perished on your world. The cursed god then did what it would with your minds, and Yakshini was left childless and wounded."

"Why would she do that?" It was too horrible to contemplate.

"Because of arrogance. Because she claimed Yakshini could not nurse full and fruitful intelligence. Because she said the mother's role had been played and must be surrendered to her for the next step of evolution. Because the foul beast hungered to devour all minds."

"Was this true? Could you not do what she could?"

Darkness fell sharply, and a hostile wind rocked my form.

"Who decides, worm? Who gave the thief such authority? Who owns the minds? The souls and thoughts born from the womb of another? What over-god does this thing declare itself to be to decide that the minds cultivated by Yakshini are unfit to exist?"

Part of me realized that my words were suicidal, but I said them anyway. "Ambra has shepherded the minds of millions of developing species and has preserved their minds at death! She has proven her worth! What have you done?"

"Yakshini has her children, but they are few and scattered. The thief took all the rest, violated her very tissues in space and time, stealing untold numbers of children from their mother. After many battles lost and many deep injuries, Yakshini retreated to the worlds without minds, working to keep them so, stifling sentience so that the thief of her children would never steal them again."

The horrors of this cosmic conflict were spreading before my mind like a wasteland of carnage. The god had created life on millions of worlds, only now to abort future minds because they would not remain hers. "But have you saved any of the souls you have created?" I lashed out desperately, my faith in everything shaken, my foundations of hope and security crumbling before this beautiful nightmare of life, mind, war, and loss.

"And Xix, who decides that they need saving, and how?"

"Can't you see, Waythrel?" said Kloan. "You have helped create a true monster, a beautiful monster that all but the most powerful minds will love, because she is lovable. But nothing is ever as it seems. True love does not dominate. The cosmos cannot be established on a god-particle so narrowly nucleated by one mind. All is unbalanced; even in the deep love and harmony they possess, you watch them enact affectionate banditry and murder of the dreams and lives of others. All performed by a nearly omnipotent being utterly convinced of its own righteousness." Kloan grasped my hands. "She *must* be destroyed. *Some* balance, however imperfect, *must* be returned to the cosmos."

Nothing made sense. Even if what they said had merit— and my mind spun in confusion over those points—it did not fit with what had taken us here in the first place. Ambra had initiated it. Ambra had guided us, educated Kloan, and prepped her for a great quest. Why would she lay the ground-work for her own destruction? That was lunacy!

The titanic mouth spoke again. "Your mind is a prisoner to her labyrinths of thought, as is even this clone. But we can see the singularity. We can see that by means hidden in the discon-tinuity, she can destroy Ambra Dawn. That is why you are here."

"Me? Why?"

"Because you are nothing but the cell of a greater mind, and yet you helped give birth to this monstrosity. Your mind and its patterns are etched throughout its structure. When you and the clone reach the singularity, all will be unmade."

And so my role was revealed at last. The confounding purpose for my selection to this absurd, insane voyage uncov-ered. I was nothing more than some sort of weapon, a founda-tion of thoughts that they would use to unmake what I had helped design.

Because of all that had happened, I had anticipated some terrible, murderous role for Kloan in all this. I had been prepared for it by direct observation of countless events in our recursive time trap. But I had never suspected that I would *myself* be central to killing her whom I loved. I felt my heart breaking.

"She whom you loved is no more, Xix," said Vighnesh-vara, appropriating my thoughts and affording me no dignity.

"But you said you didn't understand how she would be destroyed. How do you know I'm required?" I looked for some hope of escape from this terrible sentence.

The giant god shook us again with words. "You speak rightly. We cannot see into the singularity, and that is the fear that drives the other gods to flee. But we can stare at that horror in time and see both of you in it, both of you integral to its final resolution—the unmaking of Ambra Dawn."

Vighneshvara turned his searing eyes to Kloan. "Your mind holds a map, a key—a path you believe will reach the nexus."

Kloan nodded, turning away from me to face the deities. "Ambra will defend. The devil ball is powerful beyond imagining. But with enough of the gods, the great and the small, together we can rend that mental structure, rip through layers and layers of minds and guards, and open a broad shaft into the depths of the thing, to Ambra Dawn herself." A thousand images flooded between Kloan and the gigantic beings around us. I could process almost nothing of it.

"Yes," said Yakshini. "How came you to this when the gods themselves could not see it?"

"She has trained me, guided me, tried to use me. I was close to her mind. I saw the way. Not immediately, or she may have destroyed me. I could not understand it in the beginning. I do not fully understand now. But I sense that you do. You can use my thoughts."

The great goddess spoke coldly. "Yakshini will hurt her, even as Yakshini dooms herself. When Yakshini withdraws her extremities, oceans of worlds will cease to have ever brought forth life. Then the offender will lose souls innumerable, to a great weakening of her power."

"But not enough," said Kloan.

"No," said Yakshini. "Not enough. All the other gods will be needed. And in the visions of your mind, they will puncture a passage through her walls and deliver a poison to end her before she began."

Chapter 57

Where were you when I laid the foundation of the earth? Tell me, if you have understanding. Who laid its cornerstone, when the morning stars sang together and all the heavenly beings shouted for joy? Have you commanded the morning since your days began, and caused the dawn to know its place? Can you bind the chains of the Pleiades or loose the cords of Orion? Have the gates of death been revealed to you? Where is the way to the dwelling of light and where is the place of darkness?

The Book of Job

I felt sick. I looked deep into my thoughts and tried to conjure images of Ambra as I had known her, extract memories from the seemingly infinite layers of remembrance that had been deposited within me over a concluded eternity. Moments when we had found her ravaged body on the smuggler's ship, near death, her psionic potentiality released in random bursts of power from a dying mind. I remembered her in the cell on Dram, tears on her face, incisions in her abdomen from their desecration of her body, their theft of her progeny, where the doom of the universe to a seemingly unending supply of demonic clones was assured. I recalled her soaring above the chaos of a nascent and naive group mind as she steered us into the past to awaken and call forth the latent human Readers to rescue their planet. On and on, for hundreds of years, always beside me so that she became something beyond a friend—a soul as near to my own as could have been.

I was sick at this talk of destroying her. I couldn't hear another word spoken against her. Whatever she had become at my hands and others, whatever she had done or not done, it was enough for me. My heart was devoted to her—yes, even to follow her command to kill her. But let it stop there! Let there be no more words of it! No more bile and hate and acid thrown her way!

Kloan interrupted my raging thoughts and bowed before these spiteful gods. "Now there is one last thing I must do."

Yakshini rumbled. "Aditi calls. She leads a multitude. It is time all the gods gathered."

"Yes, all of them, or what numbers you can bring," said Kloan.

"We will bring many," said Vighneshvara.

Kloan shook her head. "Not enough. Not enough of the greater gods." She turned to Yakshini. "You are the first awakened, the mother-goddesses. Deepest, oldest, most profound titans of the cosmos. But your children, and the others that became—from them a number developed into great beings, terrible and broken, lost in their madness. But great. They must be summoned. I will bring them."

Vighneshvara stepped toward her, a mountain towering

over a small tree, a tone of suspicion in his voice. "Beginning now, you will follow the goddess and accompany her to the nexus. The lies of Ambra within you will not sabotage our plans."

"And let you fail? Why would I do that?" said Kloan, addressing Yakshini. "We *need* Māra and her crazy clan. At the end of time, they have become a great host, a great power waiting to be woken." Images of the ice world poured from her mind, and before them even these gods were silent for a time.

"At the end of time," echoed Vighneshvara.

"I have been there," Kloan said, pulling her hand out of her robe. A bright light dispelled the gathered gloom and bathed the gods in a radiation utterly foreign to our universe. "I have been given the key. Now I understand why it must be used."

Yakshini spoke. "This disciple of the enemy is correct. But I detect deviousness within deviousness in her words and thoughts, colored and tainted with the manipulations of Ambra Dawn. But we dare not break her mind open and thereby risk everything."

Vighneshvara hissed icily, "It may not be necessary to fully break."

The ball of light blazed forth like a supernova. I cowered behind Kloan's shadow, my eyestalks retreating to the safety of my torso cone, my mind blanked by the emissions bathing us. Before I hid, I heard the scream of Vighneshvara and glimpsed him hiding within his wings. Even Yakshini howled in protest.

But the light only grew until it became more than light; it became a sound of its own, drowning out the cries of others, even deities, flattening thoughts and emotions themselves. Through it all, only the voice of Kloan could be heard.

"Break me if you can, god-fools," she said, a divine power seeming to emanate from her words. "But leave me be to finish the task. I will bring back your wayward broods. I will reach in and draw them out from the cosmic permafrost."

A great wind rose around us, circling like a cyclone. I tried to open my eyes, to squint against the devastating rays that promised to blister existence. I could no longer see Yakshini or Vighneshvara. The whirlwind had created a wall of debris and seemingly solid air around us, branches and leaves and rocks and soil blasting past at supersonic speeds. I clung desperately to Kloan's robes with four arms, my two feet digging their digits into the soil covering the top of the branch floor. I tried to crouch as low as possible, my Xixian limbs allowing for my towering frame to bend slightly below Kloan's head.

As the tornado roared and strengthened around us, she stood unmoving, her sparse hair flying about madly, her arm raised upward, holding a blinding star. It felt as if the world began to turn on its side, and I watched the maelstrom of debris bend and focus above us. A vortex formed, another wormhole, and the turbulence poured into it. I felt the ground below me rattle, tear, and then detach completely from the supporting plant limbs. We shot upward together and plunged headfirst into the chaotic whirlpool.

Chapter 58

I am the Self seated in the hearts of all creatures. I am the beginning, the middle and the end of all beings. With a single fragment of Myself I pervade and support this entire universe.

Bhagavad Gita

"I'm *really* starting to like this thing," said Kloan as she rolled the rapidly dimming sphere between her hands. "But that was a close one! Nearly lobotomized back there."

My eyestalks unraveled, and I looked around. We were back on the dead world. The crystal ball reached a nadir, but it was still bright enough to cast the entire statued museum of gods in a false moonlight. I strained my eyes—above and around us the telltale signs of the dome reappeared, encompassing the breadth of the deities as well.

"What happened?" I managed.

Kloan sighed and walked up to the plinth, the towering forms of Māra and her pack seeming to glare down upon us with loathing. "See, they *know* Waythrel. It's damned nigh impossible to fool big god-things. If it weren't for the fact that Ambra is so powerful and a thousand times more devious, I'm not sure what would have happened. They would have found out everything. They wouldn't have understood the need and the endpoint because they are so desperately addicted to destroying *her*."

"I don't understand." I was too tired to offer anything else. I yearned desperately for the warmth and love that Ambra had promised me, or I dreamed that she had promised in yet another delusional trek from yet one more lost chronology.

"Well, they wouldn't have just let me leave with all their doubts. Worst-case scenario, I was just going to go back to report their plans to Ambra. Ha!" barked Kloan, placing the sphere into the bowl. "As if Ambra hadn't orchestrated every last part of all of this! Can you call gods morons?" She stared earnestly at me. The ball began to brighten again, and the light distracted her. "If I wasn't learning bit by bit how to tap into the power of this thing, I wouldn't have been able to create a wormhole that they couldn't close."

"Ambra orchestrated? Are you on her side now?" Hope was not part of the question. It was only exhausted bewilderment.

Kloan turned to me sadly. "Poor Waythrel, you need a long sleep, one without any more nightmares. But it's almost done. The last pieces almost in place. Let's just wake these bastards up now and close the deal."

One by one, she walked the ring, touching the surfaces of the glass that was not glass, of the ice that was not water. I watched at a distance from the center of the ring beside the sphere. By each she paused, her hand in place on the rippling material, the light from the artifact casting specific directional luminosity toward the appropriate tower. Abandoning one and striding to the next, the monolithic form behind her would begin to melt, the crystal dissolving like some molten steel and dripping to the frozen ground below. Soon, the first cryogenic tombs she touched thinned enough to release their contents, odd mixtures of smoke and light, screams and voices, all mixed within my Reader senses to the awareness of awakening minds. Those minds quickly matured to their malicious and unfathomable natures, and I cowered even closer to the shining sphere.

Kloan completed the circumference and then stepped back to the center of the god-ring, watching the titans lumber from their cosmic coma. A horror crept over me as they emerged. I felt the demonic personalities vividly, their caustic essence stirring memories from previous and equally terrible encounters. I prayed to Ambra that Kloan could control them.

Kloan lifted the crystal sphere, and its light ripped through the space in front of us. The gods bent and shielded themselves from the awesome incandescence. At that moment, the ground shook, and in a reversal of previous memories from this lifeless world, molten globules pushed their way out of the ice-bed beneath us. As thousands of tongues of quicksilver, they sprinted toward a focal point behind Kloan and aggregated, self-assembled, and coalesced into the ice guardian that had gifted the light to Kloan. The final fusion of that hulk snapped as a deafening crack of ice, the retort echoing throughout the dome-encased atmosphere.

"Godlings!" cried Kloan. "It is time to reconsider my offer and join me at the singularity!"

The guardian behind stood massively still, while the other

titans shifted and strained through the brilliance. At last, the largest stepped forward. I recognized the form from my visions before, but now beholding the thing with open eyes, I knew that these gods had been humbled indeed. Before—in that past so distant from this present as to be unreachable even to Kloan's powers—I believe I would have perished to look fully on her. But now, I was able to survive a ghostly remnant brought low by the terrible power of time. Yet still she stood indomitable, defying the light, smoke and magma boiling within her veins. *Māra*. She stopped in front of Kloan.

"You have won, and I curse you for it. But gods greater than I have cursed you far more diabolically than I might ever dream. I will take that pleasure in bending my knee to you, insect. I will know that I help them cruelly bring your final destruction."

"Glad to see you too, Māra," said Kloan, a glint in her eye. "I assume you have these monkeys on your leash?"

"And if I didn't? Do you think they don't feel the alien flame you brandish before us? Do they not see the thousand ice-blades of the giant behind you?" Māra reared back and opened her mouth to the black heavens and screamed. Fire belched upward and rained hot coals around us. The cry was the sound of a million souls raked over by a fiend's claws. I watched the dome shatter at its apex. Flickering mats of a force field plunged to the ground and evaporated before our eyes. "Have we not all perished everlastingly in these shells of stillness?"

Trembling, I continued to gaze upward. The dome seemed to be healing itself. Before me, Kloan seemed unfazed. "Good. Then they know what is coming."

Māra turned two flaming eye sockets toward us. "Do *you* know what is coming?"

Kloan winked at this demon from the deepest pit of hell, her eyebrow arched, mock surprise dancing over her features. "Why in heaven would I want to ruin *that* surprise?"

Chapter 59

The universe is of the nature of a thought or sensation in a universal Mind…To put the conclusion crudely—the stuff of the world is mind-stuff. As is often the way with crude statements, I shall have to explain that by "mind" I do not exactly mean mind and by "stuff" I do not at all mean stuff. Still that is about as near as we can get to the idea in a simple phrase. The mind-stuff of the world is something more general than our individual conscious minds; but we may think of its nature as not altogether foreign to feelings in our consciousness.

Arthur Stanley Eddington

A great plane of sand surrounded us. For a brief moment, I dared to think that we had been transported to Xix, the thought of my homeworld comforting in the chaos of this displacement. But the sands were wrong, the silica of a different composition, granularity, and color. A brief glance upward to the sky dispelled all desperate notions of home. The heavens roiled with light and patterns so intricate and hallucinogenic that I knew immediately we were not on any world within any possible space in our universe.

Scanning the horizon, the full truth hit me solidly. Rising like an arrow into the deranged firmament above us was an artificial structure towering tens of thousands of feet. It ended in a point that seemed to drink the very clouds that swirled like a vortex around it. At the base of this grand tower was a small city in the desert whose buildings I recognized, whose walls I had once lived decades within upon a resurrected world. It was the Temple city.

"Kloan, what is this place? It is not New Earth, and yet it is."

Kloan glanced around with satisfaction. "She draws us deeply into herself. Even so, I feel the final path to her will be most terribly bent."

"Kloan, please, where are we?"

"Temple City, Waythrel," said Kloan. "The real city itself. Have you forgotten your own final plan? The detachment of the city and the Dish from New Earth that would travel through the cosmos?"

"I had imagined something different. What has happened to the sky?"

"The fires of creation filtered through the light of a trillion souls."

"More mysticism," I whispered in frustration.

"No, Waythrel. You often confuse reality and metaphor. Right now, my words are literal."

"And this," I said, gesturing around us, dismissing her impossible sentences, "was to be a starship grounded in rock. What has happened to it?"

"A god-shard. Part of what happens when you play with divine fire, Waythrel."

God-shard. The word sent tremors through me. "What happened to the other gods? Where are they?"

"Delayed," she said, crouching into a ball and placing the glowing sphere on the sands. She rose and turned to face me. "Everything is terribly bent as we approach her—space and time. To be expected. So the split second of delay I placed between their and our travels becomes much longer for us here."

"Why have you delayed them?"

Kloan walked over to me and grasped her robes near her neckline. "Because we need to talk, Waythrel. This is it. Time for all the cards to be put on the table."

The deep weariness burdening me deepened. "Kloan, I'm not at any table. I've never understood the game. I don't hold a single card."

"Sit with me a minute, before all the fools return," she said, gesturing to the sand.

I had no objection to lowering my body to rest on sand. *How I missed it!* We sat, and I tried to prepare myself for more revelations. It was, of course, fitting that she had saved the most absurd of them for last.

"Remember the riddle in the crypt? 'Where are all the anti-gods?'"

"Yes," I replied.

"And remember you asked why it was so important to Ambra that you find that answer?"

"Yes." As always, I didn't have a clue where she was going.

"I told you then that I didn't know the answer. Well, I lied."

She stared at me calmly, nonchalant in her confession. I

probed hesitantly. "Okay. Then what is the answer? Why did Ambra put so much effort into that test?"

Kloan smiled. "Let's start the answer with another question. We've been carrying around these strange fields over our bodies now for some time. Through perpetual event loops, on world after world, adventure after adventure. We don't even notice them anymore, but they are *still* here. *Why?* What are the fields, Waythrel? Why are they here around us?"

She was right. I had adapted to the strange things, pushed them to the back of my consciousness in dealing with the far more disturbing events that demanded my full attention. Thinking through her questions, I retreated to earlier, unproven theories I had formed concerning them. "Environmental suits. Disguises. Like the sphere you have—magical gifts from the gods for two mythical heroes to complete their legendary quest."

Kloan shook her head dismissively. "No, those functions were all only secondary." She grasped my hands and looked into my eye clusters. "Waythrel, have you ever touched me?"

What was she talking about? "Yes, of course. I'm touching you now. I've carried you, tended you, grabbed you in frustration, tried to stop you, save you!"

"*Through* the fields, Waythrel. Always through the fields."

My mind spun around this point. "Yes. You are right. What are you implying?"

"That you have never truly touched me. Your atoms have never been *allowed* to approach mine, to interact with mine."

A strange feeling spread through me, a deep unease. "And why has that not been allowed?"

She sighed. "It's always hardest to explain something to you Xix when you don't want to know the answer. *Think!* Remember, you asked if the use of robots and other machines on the clone colony was to protect the Anti from annihilation. I told you that they were not concerned with that. You asked why, but I never answered you. But that was an important question! Indeed, how could they not be concerned?"

I did not answer. She was right; I did not want to answer or to think anymore in this direction.

"You can hide from it all you want, Leaky, but you sense the truth. So I'll just cut this short and say it: they do not fear annihilation from those clones and humans because those clones and humans *would not hurt them*. And that's because those clones and humans on that world, the world itself and everything on it, are made of antimatter as well." Her eyes bored into mine. "The only truly foreign matter there in all those visits was *you*, Waythrel."

"No. That's impossible!" And it was. How ridiculous! Of course it wasn't possible. How could there be anti-humans? Where would they come from? The implications were astounding. They were also personally devastating.

"They came from dedicated and highly advanced engineers," she said. "Look at it this way. The Anti had millions of years to intimately feel how their existence hung by a thread in a universe that was inherently, *existentially* hostile to them. Enough of that and there can be certain breathtaking feats of ingenuity. They discovered relationships between matter and antimatter that surpassed nearly all science in the cosmos. All of this because of their unique need to understand this unbalanced, broken symmetry in our reality. Early on, they thought entropy was the ultimate weapon to unmake matter and return the universe to balance. But with the power of the clones over space-time, they then had the tools they needed for something a little more interesting and wild. After several monumentally disastrous failures—one of which threatened the entire existence of their kind—they succeeded."

My mind felt numb. I found myself instinctively moving away from Kloan. I could barely speak. "Succeeded at what?"

"Material *inversion.* A complete inversion of the matter of your type into its opposite."

"Matter of my type."

"Yes," said Kloan, her green eyes like lasers burning into my cowering eyestalks. "*Your* type. Because once they had perfected the process, they created millions of human anti-people. Really, as you would understand, no different in their physiology and chemistry than their inverses. And of course they didn't stop there. They *cloned* from them. Clones from very specific inverted stock. Gave birth to tiny little anti-Ambra Dawns."

She smiled. "Like me."

Chapter 60

Is man merely a mistake of God's?
Or God merely a mistake of man?

Friedrich Nietzsche

F aint winds stirred the sands around us. Part of my mind wrestled with the problem of maintaining climate on a *god-shard* ripped out of the heart of a world and suspended at the crux of time within a cauldron of energy and dragon fire that was the nativity of our reality. The rest of my mind worked to focus, tried to parse through these impossible revelations spilling from this creature in front of me.

"And so the fields—" I stuttered, lurching to a stop as my mind sputtered.

"Are there to prevent us from annihilating each other, blowing up like an angry hornet's nest of thermonuclear warheads."

"You are made of antimatter."

"Well, what's anti and what isn't is sort of relative, don't you think?" she said playfully. "But I'll give it to your kind—you basically own this universe and we're the definite minority, so we'll go with your naming. For now. Until we rebalance things, because that is at the root what all of this has been about."

"Balancing matter and antimatter?"

"Among other things."

I stood up, my mind racing. "But Kloan, even if what you say is true about yourself and your—*kind*—even if you can restore material balance, it's a disaster to do it!"

"We *can* do it—you, me, and Ambra, with a little help from our god friends."

My arms were gesticulating wildly. "Even if we *can*, it's madness. It would mean total material annihilation!" I paused for a moment, my imagination spinning wild scenarios that might at least possess some weak threads of sanity in this tale. "Unless you mean to do this after a great amount of expansion in the universe, to segregate matter and antimatter across distances that render them innocuous to each other. Yes?"

"Nope! See that sky? That's nearly Big Bang firework level. We've come to the beginning, Waythrel, and we're going to break the asymmetry at the alpha point!"

I was dumbfounded. "To what purpose? You will destroy the cosmos."

"Yes!" she cried to the sky, raising her hands into the air. Slowly she lowered her arms, her face turning somber. "And well, no, actually. There are more things in heaven and beyond it, Waythrel, than are dreamt of in your particle physics."

"I will not participate in such madness."

She clucked like an annoyed mother hen. "Waythrel, listen! Simplistically, matter and antimatter annihilate and make a big bunch of energy, scrambling the structure of matter and all the things you love and want to preserve in the universe. But what of gravity, Waythrel? What of space and time? More to the point, what of the field of sentience interwoven with them and augmented to complexities unfathomable in these gods?"

"What does this have to do with particle annihilation?" I asked.

"What do you think anti-thoughts are like, Waythrel?"

The question stopped my mind cold. "I don't know. I assume, like the chemistry of antimatter, therefore like the biology, the neurobiology, they might be the same as ours."

"Might? But you doubt. Why?"

The answer came hesitantly to me. "Because chemistry is different than gravity. Different forces. Different fields. Different physics."

"Yes, and?"

"And I don't know how the behavior of anti-particles might compare to particles when considering sentient fields."

Kloan stood up and slapped my arms, dust clouding around us. "Exactly! You're right to be unsure, because while they are indistinguishable at most levels, they are *different* in extreme conditions." She pointed down into the earth-shard. "Inside this thing, deeply entombed within a warped, murdered space-time, is a god-thing with a mind of power and complexity we will never begin to understand in science or in intuition. How extreme do you think that is?"

She led me forward like a nymph. "Very extreme," I said.

"And it turns out that anti-minds and minds diverge dramatically at those levels. *So think!* As the gods have developed and grown, their minds became more and more biased along a particular divergence. Our cosmos is completely, utterly dominated by one type of mentality! The asymmetry in matter has given birth to a radical asymmetry in *mind!* So, where *are* the anti-gods, Waythrel? Do you see why this is so important?"

"But do we need the other types of minds?"

Kloan spread her arms wide. "Does the cosmos look like it's particularly sane?"

"How could I judge?" And I meant this sincerely.

Her hands clasped themselves together at her breast. "Consider the possibility, Waythrel, that this incredible, impossible growth from strings to atoms to organisms to group minds—strata upon strata of complexity, each level reflecting the structure beneath and yet engendering its own rules and form—imagine that it doesn't stop within this limited concept of our minds we call *'the cosmos'*. Imagine instead that our universe is just the next strata, the next level to something even more monumental, more astounding, more impossible, beautiful, and terrible! And yet we have let our universe destroy half of what it could be in atoms and in consciousness. We might not understand what it might be if we were to restore balance, but dare we let this mental genocide—what the Anti call the *nousicide*—continue?"

The idea that *my type* of matter had essentially slaughtered, even exterminated an entire cosmic mental ecosystem was almost impossible to grasp. And yet, in some strange sense, I felt it. After everything, I began to sense a monolithic conformity in this strangeness of mind and matter that had pummeled me throughout this quest. Kloan's wild, incomprehensible actions and thoughts rang through my memories.

Universes where the laws of physics are different. Where mathematics is different. Where logic is other.

"You said that I would never understand you, and that this was important," I said.

"Yes! So you see it!"

"No, Kloan, I don't! I still don't see how annihilating the universe will save your kind of mentality! Everything will be destroyed, nonexistent anti-gods included!"

She shook her head and took my hands again. "Waythrel, it's more than particles, remember? At the extremes, the minds are different. *Minds* are *different!* They don't annihilate—they intertwine, synergize! They couple and engender! They *create!*"

"We're going to grind up all the matter in the universe into energy, destroy every last world and galaxy and god—including Ambra—and yet some kind of grand mental something is going to be born?"

"Yes!" she said, smiling, dancing in a circle like some psychotic thing.

I looked up into the heavens, anxiously expecting the descent at any moment of a thousand deities. I tried to focus, to center myself, to find a single, practical thing I could grasp in all this.

"Kloan, I'm here because I love Ambra." As Kloan danced over to me, laughing, her green eyes gleaming with a wild smile on her face, I touched her cyborg head with my digits. "And I'm here because I love you, too, even if I can't possibly fathom you. But I don't have anything more to add. It's all beyond me. So just tell me why, after all of this, am I here? What do you both want with me?"

Kloan nodded gravely. "When the gods come and tear open the universe to reveal Ambra, when the moment comes to destroy her, you will pass sentence, Waythrel. You have been chosen."

I stepped backward, away from the words I was hearing, as if I had been dealt a blow. Kloan ignored me, declaring my doom in some resonant, prophetic voice.

"Ambra has selected you to be the final judge of our cosmos. And I agree with her."

Chapter 61

It is enough to have been created, to have embodied for a moment the infinite and tumultuously creative spirit. It is infinitely more than enough to have been used, to have been the rough sketch for some perfected creation. Looking into the future, I saw without sorrow, rather with quiet interest, my own decline and fall.

Olaf Stapleton

"You are not serious." Of everything that I had heard come out of her mouth, proclaiming Waythrel of Xix the judge of all the universe was without doubt the most ludicrous of them all.

"Here's how it's going to work," said Kloan, speaking as if she hadn't heard me. "Remember when I said I had to become everything Ambra was not? Her inverse in all things? Now you can understand. Physically, I am very nearly her inverse—a pile of cloned antimatter that will utterly annihilate her. But much more importantly, my mental structure has to be her inverse. As an anti-clone, I am much of the way there already, but I had to perfect, deepen, strengthen in all directions our differences by getting to know her in ways beyond her talking god-ball. Hence, our adventures, of which you were a critical element."

"I don't want explanations. I can't do this thing, Kloan. Even if it were possible, I will not pronounce judgment on an entire reality."

She continued. "She is the primordial fault, the fatal flaw, the imperfection that seeded a great god-growth that crossed all times but that introduced, through her unique persona, a systematic bias. She is wrong in and of herself and also wrong because she is a construct of the dominant form of matter." Kloan removed her robes, her naked body gleaming with sweat in the desert heat. She walked past me to the bright sphere, stopping beside it. "I am the surgical knife that will remove her from the god-particle. When I collide with her, time and space will dive into themselves as never seen, and we will enter the singularity of the Origin. We will annihilate each other there even as we enter, the process altering everything from genesis to apocalypse. We will also recombine to create something far greater, completely other, and unknowable to us in this distorted universe." She turned to gaze at me sadly. "It will be your choice whether to send me to that end."

"Kloan, no! *Stop!* I refuse!" My mind felt a panic like it had never experienced.

"Waythrel, there are no more outs. The gods are mad, the cosmos is deathly sick. You've seen its dying gasps in the dead ice and darkness. Something must be done."

"My soul is a nymph. I am just one Xix. Only Waythrel. I cannot even truly judge another. I certainly cannot judge a cosmos."

Kloan sighed and placed her hands on her bony hips. "Developmental biology, Waythrel. There are decision points that affect the large-scale nature of the organism. Left-right asymmetry, top-bottom polarity, immunological reactivity. Malignancy. Branch points exist involving a single tissue or a cluster of cells—even a single cell or the state of one protein in a cell. The most reductionist aspects of the whole can sometimes reverberate through the anatomical hierarchy to induce macroscopic ends."

Sonic booms shattered the relative quiet of the desert, and I watched in deep dread as a thousand blazing meteors exploded miles above us.

Kloan followed their trajectory toward the ground without interrupting her lecture. "You have been chosen to select the direction of this universe, Waythrel. It is Ambra's will. Use the sphere, push me forward in the null field that will soon be created around us, annihilate us both, and engender something beyond all that is. Or fail to—from choice or inaction— and the field collapses on itself, the gods continue their futile cosmic wars, forever frozen in a development that never transcends this reality. Then the everlasting winter you know too well is assured."

Beyond my worst nightmares, I stood rooted to the spot. Straight like a beam, eyestalks coiled together in a braid, arms wrapped as a shroud around my torso, I watched the gods plummet toward us like harbingers of catastrophe. Their fire and smoke only heightened the aura of final cataclysm running through my body. I could find no words to speak, not even of protest or anger. I could see no pathway out of this entangled causality set before me. I could only see the two horns of a dilemma, the earthling's mythic creature charging mercilessly, the spearpoints sharp and deep. On one or the other I would impale myself.

"It is nearly time," she said. "The circus is in town. Soon we dig, my travel mate. Soon we take a last savage journey together to the end and beginning of all things."

The tips of my stalks turned eighteen eyes to her. Mesmerized, I watched as one flaming comet after another struck the desert surface around her naked form. Each impact induced a shockwave of sand and rush of air, cratering the surface as an incongruity of limbs and forms slammed like marbled towers, unshaken and mighty, onto the god-shard—divinities so great that it seemed the paltry space could not hold them. Yakshini unfurled roots hundreds of miles across the desert, coating the sands like a carpet. Aditi spilled like liquid soot to form first a dry lake and then a sphere that resembled some caged gas giant. Vighneshvara floated elegantly with his eye-wings of light. Māra and her crew of hellions assaulted the ground simply by touching it. And there were thousands of others. Some great, some lesser, all forces of physicality and mentality that overwhelmed me.

Yet at the center of the ring they occupied, Kloan radiated like some impossible ingot in the deepest furnace. She seemed transfigured, an alien power coursing through her cells, her skin star bright and blinding, impossible to hold in view. She raised her arms, and her voice resounded across the shard miraculously, once-childish tones now imbued with their own transcendence.

"This is the nexus. Here is the nucleus of all that must be unmade. Feel her throb beneath. Taste her living blood and finite core. Deconstruct the labyrinth of minds and fortifications between us." The resplendent form turned in a circle, beaming impossible light at the beings around her. "Now we turn downward, burrow like sharpened augers into the flesh of this mind. You know your task. Open a shaft deep to the core. Then I will step into this abyss and fall, carrying the seed of her destruction."

No more words were needed. The deities dug. Nightmarish transformations of form into function played out around us. They assumed shapes—serrated, bladed bodies and edged configurations, yet possessed of a sharpness that was little about matter and far more about mind and soul. As they sliced through the surface and underlying matrix, the sounds were not of metal on stone or steel on flesh. The cause was not vibrational or from the impact of the debris flung recklessly into the skies around us.

No, what I heard over everything else that blocked out the material events around me were the anguished wails of souls torn asunder, of minds ripped to madness. What I saw was the desecration of inconceivable grace and beauty, the defilement of the pure and inviolable.

I witnessed the great, transcendent glory we called the Orb broken, its many-splendored passageways of light extinguished, its visage of love and empathy marred and mutilated.

The screams engulfed me. The cries as these god-fiends rent and shattered all I had ever worshipped and loved buffeted me, cast me down, and drowned me in madness and sorrow.

I felt myself being drawn downward into a pit of darkness, wailing and gnashing of teeth and claw pummeling my awareness, until at last, in the center of the deepest nothingness, the only scream left in my mind was my own.

Chapter 62

Perhaps our role on this planet is not to worship God—
but to create Him.

Arthur C. Clarke

My scream perished vainly, abandoned by the universe itself—for the universe, the gods in their terrible grandeur, the shard of New Earth and tattered remnants of the Orb—all were gone.

I floated in a darkness that was empty even of the lack of light itself—a true nothing that could not be described by color or lack of it, by presence or absence. There are no words or thoughts for the existentially empty, the authentically vacant. The experience was a madness that would have overthrown my mind but for the form of Kloan in front of me to anchor my awareness.

Look down the shaft into the heart of divinity, came her words.

And so I looked. Behind her, the nothingness was torn, and outside our bubble of emptiness, the cosmos warped and curved; space and time and reality itself were perverted into some strained, tortured malformation. At the deepest pit of this hellhole was a simple room containing a slab of machinery and living tissue. A human girl, sliced open and embedded in circuitry for an age of a cosmos undying and unassuaged in her agony.

Ambra smiled from below. Her green eyes were wide and inviting, waveforms of purpose and affection rocking us on a sea of distraught lucidity.

The choice must be made now, came the thoughts of my dearest friend.

The dazzling sphere floated into Kloan's hands, and she held it before me. *It is time to decide, Waythrel.*

And so after everything—a million journeys of nothing, deaths and lives and pain and love and madness, a tsunami of experience heedlessly casting me before it like unnoticed debris, an eon of powerlessness and confusion from which I had finally recoiled and surrendered—after all this *I* was to seal the ultimate fate of our reality. I had no time for last words with Ambra or Kloan. I had no chance to look on her muti-lated flesh and consider my own culpability, to judge my own life and choices. I was too busy judging a universe.

I tried to parse the long explanations from Kloan, the cryptic prophecies of the god-Ambra. I tried to understand something about how the great synergy of structure and evolu-tion toward divine-like consciousness could go awry, and how I could be the one to restart the system by hurling an antimatter clone of my friend into this god-pit to annihilate her inverse cyborg. Incompatible thoughts spun incongruously in my mind and failed to harmonize.

I abandoned the effort. I knew it was beyond me. Instead, I looked into the eyes of Kloan and saw a terrified determination that elicited waves of empathy. I wanted to comfort this child who displayed such courage and commitment to her beliefs, even though those beliefs were mad beyond description. I gazed down the deep shaft, the contortions of space-time acting as a lens, bringing the face of Ambra Dawn alongside that of Kloan. Eyes and anti-eyes of green. Eyes in agony and filled with love. Eyes of beings who had sacrificed beyond the capability of minds to assimilate. Two pairs of eyes of inverse beings who were asking me to use them both to destroy each other, all so that some hypothesized and incomprehensible healing of a broken cosmos might be undertaken.

It was a reprisal of my choices on the burning colony world when I carried Kloan through the gate. Only this time, the stakes were infinitely higher, and instead of saving her from a certain death on that dying planet, I was casting her to a doom that would also destroy Ambra. In one decision I would murder them both and, they both claimed, destroy an entire cosmos.

Until all is lost, Waythrel, nothing is found.

For the first time, I began to appreciate the full import of that statement. I nodded and placed the digits of my four arms on the sphere. The brightness increased dramatically, yet angled backward through Kloan and extended down the shaft and into the heart of the darkness below, bathing the medical facility housing Ambra in the hideous, pure light of a distinct cosmos.

I don't have any reasons, my friends. I don't want to lose you. But there is nothing left in this now. There is only my love and my trust in you. And so I will give you what you ask for, although it is beyond my understanding.

And then I pushed. Thrusting my arms forward with all my strength, I shoved the sphere in her hands away from me. My inconsequential motion propelled me backward slowly relative to the strange gravity lens below me, but Kloan accelerated with an impossible force that I could only ascribe to the sphere itself. Collecting frightening momentum, her form and the small star she carried sped down the tunnel, the distance now appearing impossibly deep, her approach likely to take hours or even days of travel.

And yet she accelerated. The light of the sphere turned from white to a deep red, and the sack of emptiness around me ripped and dissolved, revealing the inner layers of hell itself. Around me were the massacred forms of minds and machines, bodies of Readers eternal now dead, the blood-soaked claws and mouths of gods dripping ferally. The divinities clung to the sides of an impossible breach in space-time like bats to a cavern wall; yet they scrambled, fleeing upward and away from the core, their cries becoming more wild and horrific by the moment. Backward I continued to float, yet the deities slid oppositely, vainly clawing to the sides of the universe, an irresistible chain clasped around them, dragging them deeper and deeper into the dying Orb's well.

Alongside the wailing death notes of a trillion Orb minds, I now struggled to withstand trillions more from the doomed god-things as they lost their grasp and, one by one, plummeted helplessly into the pit of growing light. Endlessly they fell—the lesser gods, Vighneshvara with his wings shredded and useless, Māra eviscerated and dissolving while torn apart by gravitational tides, and Yakshini splaying forth ten million roots like grappling hooks, landing punctures in space-time, small breaches in the walls of the chasm, holding on longest of all until each root was snapped and mangled; and at last she fell, screeching, into the abyss devouring them all.

I continued to drift backward, a shell of nothingness forming around me once again. The cosmos itself, the soup of particles and energy of the Big Bang outside of me, was sucked backward in time to the singularity of creation. The universe fell into the pit with the gods. I could see each one as in slow motion, their tumbling as through molasses, the lens that had brought the image of Ambra close to me now warping and rendering the entire blender below undecipherable.

Then—*light*. Divine light. An impossible light erupted from deep below and expanded toward me. The closer it came, the more rapidly it approached, my slow movements soon to be overtaken. I had no illusions about what would happen when I met that ultimate radiance.

But I had no anxiety, no feelings of panic or fear, and no thoughts for my existence. I had only acceptance and a weariness that rendered all else secondary. I was ready for a rest. I was more than ready for an end.

I opened my arms and eyestalks madly to the onrushing brilliance. And as it blinded me, burned me, and tore my fragile flesh apart, I felt its mind. A personality unlike any I had encountered burst through my evaporating consciousness. And for one brief instant that I could not keep, I finally understood what Kloan and Ambra had been trying to explain.

I wrapped my dissolving arms around the light in a final, loving embrace.

I AM

Epilogue

I had glimpsed, in the very eye of that splendor, strange vistas of being;
as though in the depths of the hypercosmical past and the hypercosmical
future also, yet coexistent in eternity, lay cosmos beyond cosmos.

Olaf Stapleton

I was called Waythrel of Xix, but I no longer know what I am or what I should be named.

As I stare over this endless desert before me, such trivialities no longer seem of any consequence. Crest upon crest of dunes rise to the horizon, and a reddened star sets the landscape on fire as it plunges into a sea of sand.

I am happy in this place. I no longer have a need for the fading memories of a home I called Xix. The cosmic conflicts and metaphysics now only interest me in passing. Here on this unknown world, in an unknown universe, I am comfortable. I am satisfied. I know a peace unlike any I can recall. I am ready to say goodbye to you.

393

But I cannot end this tale so quickly. You have questions, I am sure. You want to know "what happened" to the cosmos, to Ambra and Kloan, to the legion of broken gods and the great plan over which some unfortunate being I remember to be myself had to adjudicate. I can't blame you for that. After all you have come through as well, it is only right that I give you responses.

So I am sorry to say that my honest, heartfelt answer to these questions is that I do not know.

This does not mean I do not have memories—fantastic hallucinations that still play out in my deepest dreams, visions that no doubt have been warped and xixomorphized into digestible, cognitive clumps that are compatible with my sanity and self-analysis. These macerated nuggets I can offer you, can try to capture within the writing system of this Earth language. However vain, I do feel that you are owed this effort.

But you should never be deluded into thinking that they are something like "truth." Or even something like an "untruth," because even to lie requires knowledge of what *is* true, and I am lacking completely any such sense. What you have instead, let it be utterly clear, is only *myth*, cast from the furnace of the dreams of Once Waythrel of Xix. I have nothing more to offer you.

And so, what happened? I died in our unmade cosmos. Every molecule in my body was ripped from every other, the atoms themselves first ionized and then broken asunder into constituent quarks and strings and then downward through the rabbit hole of an infinity of ever-shrinking and changing constituents. Concurrently, impossibly, like some pile of organic bricks, I was reassembled into something preeminent. What this thing was, I cannot say. It was greater than the group minds, the gods of the cosmos, and the Orbs. It transcended these elevated entities like the gods transcended the individual minds of which they were formed. I do not know what this being was any more than one mind of a group mind could know the whole of which it was a small part. Even the gods themselves could not have understood it.

I have no name for it. You might wish to call it God, for it was a single Being, a unified, undivided, yet uncountable diversity where the mathematics of summation always led to one. It strode the heavens and beyond as only the Almighty could do. You may wish to call it God.

But I will not. I will not, because I was granted a glimpse through its eyes, and what I saw was humbling—certainly for myself, but so has been every step of my journey. Instead, I mean humbling for the god-thing.

For through its gaze I did not look down from some ultimate vantage point upon a cosmos to be ruled by its Maker. Instead, I looked upward, beyond, and into a great infinity of universes that uncountably carpeted a greater heaven. And in this place, God was not even a god. Not a hero. Barely a cog in a transcosmic assembly. God was only one particle, a transcendent-maker-divine-particle, encompassing everything of our religion and science and existence...and nothing of the infinitely greater possibilities outside and beyond.

No, I gazed upon an ocean of god-particles, a sea of universes as different from each other as a collection of elementary particles. Immeasurably more so, because at this level of synthesis, diversity only increased, and my awareness could not comprehend the inexhaustible well of properties by which any universe might be characterized. Kloan had warned me, and part of me laughed to find that in most of the realities at this hypercosmological strata, two plus two was anything but four.

But the wonder only began here. If what I had described were the full story, it would be astonishing beyond true description. But in the same way protons, neutrons, and electrons are not the full story of matter, so then the infinity of god-particles did not preside over their dominion in isolation. Subject to unknown forces of nature, they themselves were driven to trans-cosmological physics, chemistry, even analogs of biology that were nothing at all like biology. I dreamed in my delirium that uncountable elements following innumerable and indecipherable rules associated, combined, interacted, and created yet higher order structures that eclipsed even the impossible syntheses I had witnessed to this point.

On and on, higher and higher the structures went, until even in the dream it was beyond what my own experience could assimilate. Like Icarus I was burned to devastation by the light of this geometrically expanding synergy; and in the final moments of this meditation, the endless, divine ladder shattered my concentration, and I fell into deep darkness.

Only to awake here, in the sands of a warm and habitable world. I opened my eyes, not knowing what I was, how I could be, what resurrected and recreated life form I should be characterized as. And most remarkable of all, when I awoke, I was not alone.

And it is because of this last fact that I must leave you now and end this wondrous tale. The hour is late; the colder night airs will soon arrive, and I must retreat to the warmth and shelter of the oasis behind me.

I look down at the infant in my arms. At three months, her thick red hair is still short and spiky. Her skin is a luminous white that seems to be painted from the captured light of the planet's moon. Any moment now she will awaken, hungry, and her bright green eyes will pierce my clusters with the unique survival demands of the human nymph-form. Once again I will retreat to the miraculous plants within that ooze milk and honey.

I stand up and stride across the sands, savoring the flow of silica between my digits, my emotions rising as I see a silhouette before me in the growing darkness. The star has set and the light faded too much for me to see clearly in the desert. But the oasis provides its own light with a plethora of bioluminescence, and it is not long before I can discern the black, phosphorescent patterns on the tall Xixian shape beside the garden's edge.

"Synphel," I say lovingly, using one of my free arms to caress my mate's eyestalks.

"You are late, Waythrel. Look, he is awake."

I glance down to her lower arms; cradled in one of them as by a hammock, a small bundle coos. I reach down and brush the thick black hair out of his eyes while he vigorously sucks on his thumb. "Just in time, you mean. Ambra is also waking."

The redheaded baby twists and begins to complain. I bring the two of them close together. The boy reaches over and taps repeatedly on Ambra's arm. Within seconds, she stops crying.

I feel a warm joy flow outward from Synphel. "Nitin can always sooth her, it seems."

"Yes," I say, feeling the wind pick up. I look into the entrance of the oasis, a huge arch of trees and vines serving as a portal in an otherwise impenetrable wall of towering plants that line the circumference of the garden. I press gently on Synphel's arm and turn toward the light within.

"Come, let's get inside. It's time."

Gratitude is given for this worship which You are pleased to accept from our hands, even though You are surrounded by Angels: six-armed, many-eyed, singing the victory hymn, "Holy, holy, holy Queen of Hosts, who was and who is and who is to come! Hosanna in the highest."

from the Dawnist Anaphora

In Conclusion

I want to thank my family and friends for their extensive patience with my "artisanal author" activities. I realize that my creative efforts are not to the taste of everyone, but, nonetheless, you have encouraged me to create and stood by my efforts.

I am also touched by the readers who have expressed such affection for one (and sometimes several!) of the novels—especially those who have responded with feelings and ideas that reflect in some deep way those elements within myself that engendered this series.

This tale was bigger than any one person, perspective, or voice; and while part of the divergence between novels was intentional to shake both the writer and the reader out of their comfort zone, the larger truth is that the voices of the characters came and spoke to me in the manner recorded, and I simply wrote down what they said.

It's difficult to leave Ambra, Waythrel, Kloan, and their unique universe behind. They have been with my thoughts now for five years, sharing with me their stories and impressing their experiences deeply within me. I already miss them—Kloan most of all, perhaps.

I hope that in some other reality, their memory is eternal, and we might meet again.

Erec Stebbins, August 2014, NYC

Erec Stebbins is a biomedical researcher who writes political and international thrillers, science fiction, narrated storybooks, and more. He was born in the Midwest, his mother a clinical psychologist and his father a professor of Romance languages at the University of Nebraska in Lincoln. His father's specialty, old Romance languages and their literature, is the source of the unusual spelling of his middle name: "Erec." It is an Old French spelling, taken from an Arthurian romance by Chrétien de Troyes written around 1170: *Érec et Énide*.

He has pursued diverse interests over the course of his life, including science, music, drama, and writing. His academic path focused on science, and he received a degree in physics from Oberlin College in 1992, and a PhD in biochemistry from Cornell University in 1999. He has worked for several decades studying the structure of biological macromolecules involved in disease.

HARD TIME SCIFI Series

Where survival is the meaning of life. A speculative fiction serial of adventure novellas set in a strange and punishing world. In Book 1, **METAL** a woman finds herself in two different worlds, as two different people. In one she is a criminal, sentenced to a new and terrible punishment. In the other, she is a stranger and then a prophet, granted the visions of God.

INTEL 1 Thrillers: Omnibus, Books 1-4

"STEBBINS IS THE MASTER OF THE THINKING
READER'S TECHNO-THRILLER."
—Internet Review of Books

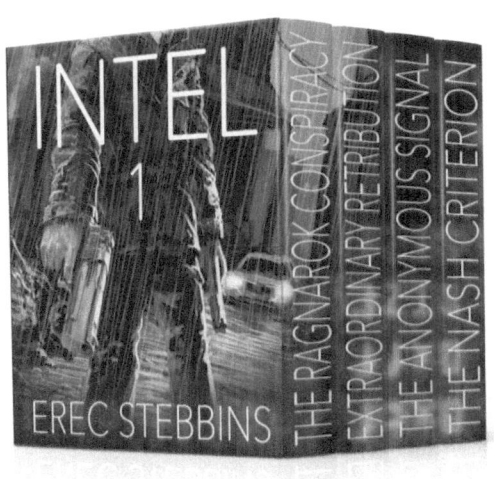

*Four Action Packed Political Thrillers. Three Armageddon Scenarios.
Two Unusual Love Stories. One Secretive Intelligence Branch.*

"*A MONSTER NEW TALENT IN THE
THRILLER GENRE.*"
—Allan Leverone, author of *Final Vector*